Since he didn't have a natural thirst for blood, still being human and all, he didn't slurp greedily at the wound as a hungry vampire would. Instead, I felt the warm touch of his mouth, tentative at first, as he tasted me.

After a minute he looked up at me with surprise. "I think it's working. The pain is lessening." He smiled and lowered his mouth to my arm again.

I felt something stir deep inside of me from the sensation of his tongue sliding hungrily against my skin. It disturbed me a million times more than anything else that night.

He's evil. No matter what he tries to make you believe, it doesn't change anything. It's only words.

He made a strange sound, like a sigh of relief. "It's the first time since the accident that the pain is completely gone."

He rose to his feet in front of me with renewed strength. His hands moved to the small of my back and he pulled me up against him. I braced my hand against his chest.

"I think the bar is closed," I said.

"Then I should probably settle my tab."

And then, suddenly, he was kissing me.

Gideon Chase was *kissing me*.

This was *so* not good.

Even less good was the fact that I was kissing him back.

Please turn this page for praise for Michelle Rowen . . .

Praise for Michelle Rowen
STAKES & STILETTOS

"4 Stars! Über-talented Rowen is back and once again combining the weird and wacky as only she can. There's plenty of humor and a touch of danger; truly a biting good time!"

—Romantic Times BOOKreviews Magazine

"5 Stars! Rowen's books never fail to thrill. *Stakes & Stilettos* is delightfully charming and keeps the wonderful mixture of tongue-in-cheek humor and well-fleshed-out plot that made her earlier books so entertaining. The story keeps you guessing, always twisting in unexpected ways . . . An exceptional tale told by a master storyteller."

—BittenbyBooks.com

"A glorious, amusing, and suspenseful story . . . This is excellent!"

—RomanceReviewsMag.com

"5 Stars! Truly funny . . . outbreaks of spontaneous laughter are likely. There is no shortage of excitement for the characters of *Stakes & Stilettos*, or for the readers. Hugely good fun!"

—LoveVampires.com

"With a generous dose of suspense, Ms. Rowen leads readers on a journey of hateful revenge, the quest for immortality, and the amazing power of love. Readers will be eager to see where this talented author will take them next."

—DarqueReviews.com

"5 Stars! A series that just keeps getting funnier and funnier . . . A rollicking good time . . . I can't remember the last time I giggled so much at a book. I can't wait to read more about Sarah Dearly and her misadventures!"
—FallenAngelReviews.com

"Rowen never disappoints, her stories are wonderfully funny, quirky, and full of laugh-out-loud moments, but there's also a great, clever plot. *Stakes & Stilettos* is an original, super funny story and I can't wait to read the next book in the series."
—NightOwlRomance.com

LADY & THE VAMP

"4 Stars! Fans will appreciate the light tone, the smooth and swift narration . . . and the comedy throughout the third book of Rowen's Immortality Bites series."
—*Romantic Times BOOKreviews Magazine*

"Michelle Rowen has again successfully written a funny and highly entertaining vampire story . . . I was delighted."
—ArmchairInterviews.com

"The best of Rowen's series thus far . . . promises a few hours of light, entertaining paranormal fun."
—BookLoons.com

"If you like your romances filled with humor, unique and entertaining characters, and above all else, a little bite, you're gonna love *Lady & the Vamp*."
—RomRevToday.com

more . . .

"A cute little romp through the world of the fanged! Rowen's cheeky humor is sure to please those readers looking for a light paranormal read."

—TheRomanceReadersConnection.com

"Enjoy *Lady & the Vamp* when you want to escape into a fantasy world for a while."

—JandysBooks.com

FANGED & FABULOUS

"You can't put this book down!"

—CHARLAINE HARRIS

"4 Stars! Rowen once again presents an exciting, action-packed, and . . . humorous tale."

—*Romantic Times BOOKreviews Magazine*

"A hoot . . . Rowen's character list is awesome, the humor is hilarious . . . [a] delightful book."

—MyShelf.com

"*Fanged & Fabulous* is a hugely fun, lighthearted vampire chick-lit romance and yet it is a surprisingly satisfying read, too. Sharp wit and classic romance . . . perfect reading for the summer."

—LoveVampires.com

"A funny and witty tale . . . I laughed out loud all through the book. The dialogue by this bestselling author is sarcastic and hilarious and the characters will leave you waiting impatiently for the next installment."

—ArmchairInterviews.com

ANGEL WITH ATTITUDE

"4 Stars! Rowen does a delightful job mixing things up with her sassy and sexy characters. She has her own unique spin on life and the afterlife and good and evil, which makes for downright fun reading."
—*Romantic Times BOOKreviews Magazine*

"Divinely funny . . . A subtly provocative paranormal romance that shines a new light on angels and demons and witches, oh my!"
—*Heartstrings Reviews*

"You have to read this book! It is quirky, funny, and sweet. If you love original and hilarious, you have to pick up *Angel with Attitude*."
—*FallenAngelReviews.com*

BITTEN & SMITTEN

"A terrific vampiric chick-lit tale filled with biting humor."
—*Midwest Book Review*

"4 Stars! Fun and clever . . . this novel is bound to appeal to those who like their romance a little offbeat and definitely humorous."
—*Romantic Times BOOKreviews Magazine*

"A study of contrasts: frothy chick-lit wrapped around a grittier reality and a flip side featuring a modern heroine paired with a Brontean hero. Let us welcome this fresh voice to the genre."
—*Booklist*

Tall, Dark
&
Fangsome

Michelle Rowen

FOREVER

NEW YORK   BOSTON

Copyright © 2009 by Michelle Rouillard
All rights reserved. Except as permitted under the U.S. Copyright Act of 1976, no part of this publication may be reproduced, distributed, or transmitted in any form or by any means, or stored in a database or retrieval system, without the prior written permission of the publisher.

Book design by Giorgetta Bell McRee
Cover design by Diane Luger
Cover photograph by Herman Estevez
Handlettering by Ron Zinn

Forever
Hachette Book Group
237 Park Avenue
New York, NY 10017
Visit our website at www.HachetteBookGroup.com.

Forever is an imprint of Grand Central Publishing.
The Forever name and logo is a trademark of Hachette Book Group, Inc.

Printed in the United States of America

First Printing: September 2009

10 9 8 7 6 5 4 3 2

ATTENTION CORPORATIONS AND ORGANIZATIONS:
Most HACHETTE BOOK GROUP books are available at quantity discounts with bulk purchase for educational, business, or sales promotional use. For information, please call or write:

Special Markets Department, Hachette Book Group
237 Park Avenue, New York, NY 10017
Telephone: 1-800-222-6747 Fax: 1-800-477-5925

Acknowledgments

Writing the Immortality Bites series has been a pleasure from beginning to end. I am so grateful to have had the opportunity to spend five books with these crazy characters, who have become so real to me I expect them to show up at my door any day now. I have the restraining order ready to go. Sarah Dearly, I'm looking at you.

Thank you so much to my editor Karen Kosztolnyik, who has an uncanny and enviable talent for cutting through the surface of a story and seeing what needs fixing in order to make it better. I love working with you and respect your fabulous editorial skills more than you know.

Thanks also to my wonderful agent Jim McCarthy. If it wasn't for you, my vampires would still be wandering around in my head instead of lurking about in bookstores.

A big shout-out to Laurie Rauch who betaread this book for me, the Toronto Romance Writers and the Write-Ons, as well as everybody on the Michelle Rowen chat loop, Twitter friends, Facebook friends, MySpace friends (wait, I'm almost done), and commenters on my blog! (Whew!) You're all seriously fangtastic. A parallel shout-out to my family and friends with a big thanks for keeping me (relatively) sane as I try to do this writing thing full-time. Okay, not sane at all. But thanks for trying anyhow.

Last, but definitely not least, thank you to my wonderful, smart, good-looking readers! If it weren't for you, this would have been only one book—not five! If I've managed to convey a fraction of the love that I feel for my characters to you when you read about them, then my job is done. You know, for now.

Tall, Dark
&
Fangsome

The Basics

My name is Sarah Dearly.

I am a vampire.

But don't be afraid. I don't bite.

Actually, scratch that. Recently I do bite, but not because I want to.

Three months ago I was turned into a vampire by an amorous and misguided—not to mention *creepy*—blind date. Shortly after he tried to bury me (don't ask), some vampire hunters came by and staked him dead. They wanted to stake me as well, but I ran away and straight into the arms of a super-hot, suicidal six-hundred-year-old vampire named Thierry de Bennicoeur. French name. No accent, though. Did I mention hot?

Angsty though he was, I fell for him. Hard.

Bad things happened. Good things happened.

Mostly bad things, though.

I learned that hunters were everywhere and focused on killing vampires—even though we're not evil. Or dead. Or undead. We're exactly like humans except for the drinking-blood-to-exist thing, which, unfortunately, is true. And a couple other things like not being able to eat solid food. We have increased strength and senses. We don't have reflections in mirrors, which, to say the least, is inconvenient. Alcohol no longer has any effect on us, alas. But we have beating hearts and can go out during the day, even though the sun tends to get a bit bright without dark sunglasses.

Oh, the immortality thing is true, too. That is, if somebody doesn't stake us.

So, even though we're relatively normal, hunters want us dead. *They're* the bad guys.

One of those hunters tried to kill me and I shot him in self-defense. Yes, *shot* him with a gun. No fangs involved. The incident succeeded in giving me the false reputation of slaughtering a whole bunch of hunters and the catchy title of "Slayer of Slayers." Some people are scared of me, some impressed, and others find it a big fat challenge to sink a stake through my heart.

One of those hunters is Gideon Chase. He's the leader of all the vampire hunters, and a billionaire who was considered quite a ladies' man before he slayed a demon and was burned by hellfire. The hellfire scarred him horribly and is slowly and painfully dragging him, body and soul, to hell.

Now he wants my help.

Because, thanks to a couple life-or-death situations, I've had to drink the blood of two master vampires— Thierry being one of them—I now have some sort of supercharged blood. This allegedly means that any vampires I sire will be very strong. Gideon is under the impression this means that I can heal him if I turn him into a vamp and keep him from his one-way ticket to hell, but it has to be done along with a ritual under the next full moon.

And if I don't do what he says, he'll murder everybody I love.

Obviously, I agreed to help him out.

He made me end my budding relationship with Thierry because Gideon's afraid that I'll reveal his nefarious plans to him in a private moment. But my attempted break-up didn't work. We're still together, only now we have to keep it a secret from everyone, even my closest friends. If Gideon finds out that I didn't do what he demanded . . . well, he simply *can't* find out.

The guy is evil. Literally.

Last, but certainly not least, I'm dealing with a curse that turns me into a nightwalker—a vicious, neck-biting, sun-fearing, sultry vixen of a vampire (in other words: *so* not me)—unless I'm wearing an ugly but effective magic-infused gold chain.

I'm trying to stay positive that everything will work out in the end, but it currently sucks to be me.

The pun is fully intended.

Chapter 1

O kay, Sarah, try not to freak out," Amy said.

That's not really a good opener—not when you're already close to the edge like I was.

My two best fanged and fabulous friends, Amy and George, had taken me out for drinks at a place called Darkside, the only secret vampire nightclub in Toronto currently open for business.

I'd known Amy for years, since we were both nonvampiric personal assistants—a day job she still held. I met George three months ago after I was sired into my new life as a vampire. They were trying to help me mend my broken heart and shattered self-esteem after my big, nasty break-up with my master vampire boyfriend, Thierry, a week and a half ago.

Unfortunately, since alcohol didn't affect vampires other than remaining a tasty treat, I was on my third Tequila Sunrise and not feeling any differently about life, the universe, and, well . . . *everything*.

"Perky" was no longer my middle name. Not that it ever was.

I eyed Amy cautiously. "What are you talking about?"

She didn't reply. Amy's red-lipsticked mouth was frozen in a slightly scared-looking smile. She wore her short, platinum-blond hair like a *Papa-Don't-Preach*-era Madonna to contrast her low-cut, black sequined top and tight black skirt.

When I glanced at George, he shrugged. He looked like a male model with shoulder-length, sandy-colored hair he currently had back in a low ponytail. He had chiseled features, a square jaw, and under his tight white shirt and black leather pants I knew he had a body worth crying over. Crying, mostly because he batted for the other team. Not that I'd ever harbored any unrequited fantasies about George. Not a chance. I had enough trouble with men without adding him to the list.

But he was mighty pretty.

"She's definitely going to freak," he confirmed.

Before I could ask for any more details about this predicted freak-out, a man approached the bar at which we were belly-up on rather uncomfortable stools. He was tall, built, attractive, and wore a dark blue button-down shirt exactly the same color as his eyes. His gaze was entirely fixed on yours truly.

I tensed at the unexpected attention.

"You're Sarah, right?" he asked.

"Uh . . ."

"I'm Jeremy." He smiled wide enough to show off his shiny white fangs. "Amy's told me all about you, but your reputation precedes you, of course."

I flicked a confused glance at Amy, and then back at Jeremy. "Um . . ."

His grin widened. "Maybe we can get a private table so we can get to know each other a bit better."

I shot Amy a horrified look as it all started to click in. Was this a . . . a *blind date*?

Oh, hell no.

Amy cleared her throat nervously at my expression. "Jeremy works at the office in the HR department. When I realized he's a vampire, too, I knew you two would be absolutely adorable together. So I kind of asked him to join us here tonight. You know, without telling you first."

The last blind date Amy had set up for me resulted in a hickey I'd remember forever since the guy had bitten me and turned me into a vampire. Needless to say, I wasn't a big fan of impromptu setups with strangers. Especially ones orchestrated by Amy.

"Great to meet you . . . uh, Jeremy, was it?" I plastered a smile on my face while my eyes tracked back to my Cupid-playing blond friend. "Can I talk to you for a minute, Amy? In private?"

She nodded tightly. "Mmm hmm."

"We'll be back in just a sec. Talk amongst yourselves." I slid off the leather-covered barstool and sidestepped Jeremy and George as I threaded my way through the crowd of thirsty, club-going vampires toward the hallway leading to the washrooms. Amy trailed silently behind me.

"Really?" I said after we were out of earshot and away from the loud music. "You're kidding me, right?"

"But he's so nice. You haven't even given him a chance."

"I'm sure he's the nicest vampire bachelor in the city. This has nothing to do with him."

"I wanted to cheer you up. So sue me." She pouted at her failed attempt to love-match me. "Ever since you and jerk-face broke up you've been no fun at all."

Jerk-face was her pet name for Thierry. I had a similar term of endearment for her vampire husband, Barry, so I guess it all equaled out.

I cleared my throat. "That doesn't mean I want to start dating again. At least, not this soon."

"Jeremy would be perfect for you." She paused. "Although, he'd also be perfect for George, if you know what I mean. Don't you love a man who's flexible about certain things?"

Sounded like an episode of Jerry Springer in the making, actually.

"I appreciate the thought, but I need some time on my own right now."

She nodded sadly and patted my arm. "Your heart is broken in a million pieces. Sometimes the best thing to do is to get back on that horse and gallop right out of town into the sunset with a new, perfect man." She cocked her head to the side as she thought about it. "Or having a one-night stand with a super-hot guy would probably work wonders, too."

"Wallowing in solitude is also a great use of time after a breakup. No one-night stands need apply."

She sighed. "You're not thinking there's a chance you and Thierry are going to get back together, are you?"

I chewed my bottom lip and shook my head. "It's over. Him and me were completely wrong for each other from the very start. This is all for the best."

It sounded perfectly rehearsed because it was.

Amy nodded. "Well, you're right about that. He was a pompous jerk who didn't deserve you. I knew from the beginning that he was a complete waste of your valuable time."

I blinked. "Yeah, except for that dirty little crush you had on him, you mean."

She blanched at the reminder. "I thought we were going to forget about that."

"The image of the goo-goo eyes you used to make behind his back is still burned into my brain cells."

Her cheeks reddened. "Please stop."

I repressed a smile. "Listen, don't worry about me. Seriously. Every day is a little easier. I hardly ever think about Thierry anymore."

Also rehearsed. Every morning when I woke up in my bed all alone I said it to the stucco ceiling—which rarely had any critiques of my acting ability.

"Have you heard from Veronique lately?" Amy asked. "I wonder if she's planning on swooping down and grabbing him now that you're out of the picture."

"Haven't seen her lately, so I have no idea what she's up to."

Veronique was Thierry's wife. Yes, the man I'd been involved with had been married for hundreds of years to a woman who was the epitome of perfection—beautiful, charming, rich, and powerful.

Their marriage was in name only. They'd been separated for more than a century before I even met Thierry. Veronique unapologetically and frequently dated men a fraction of her age and enjoyed her own life, which she lived mostly in Europe with occasional visits to North

America. There was no love there anymore between them.

Thierry had recently attempted to get an annulment from vampire contacts at the Vatican itself—apparently the only way to get out of a marriage the length of theirs—but she refused to sign the papers. She wasn't evil, she was simply self-centered. Ending their marriage didn't benefit her in any way so she didn't see any logical reason to sign.

Her lightly French-accented explanation still buzzed in my ears like a swarm of Gucci-wearing bees.

"Love has very little to do with a successful marriage, my dear."

The memory still made my blood boil with equal parts frustration and annoyance.

Amy and I returned to the bar, and I let Jeremy down as gently as possible. He took it like a champ.

"If you ever want to hook up, give me a call." He handed me a business card, then turned to George. "Great talking to you."

"Yeah, you, too," George agreed as Jeremy walked away. Then he gave me a dirty look. "Big mistake, Sarah. He was H-O-T. He actually made working in Human Resources sound like fun. Which I cannot imagine it actually is."

"Sounds like you liked him."

"Well . . . I *was* getting a vibe."

I handed him the business card. "He's all yours."

"Thanks!" He smiled at me. "Now I totally forgive you for spilling your nasty dollar-store shampoo on my carpet yesterday."

I frowned and absently itched my scalp. I couldn't help

it if I was on a strict budget as the remainder of my meager savings trickled away like cheap shower gel down the drain. Hair doesn't clean itself, after all.

Thankfully, the drinks tonight were on Amy's tab. I couldn't eat solid food without yakking, but for some reason mixed drinks didn't bother me at all. Along with not having a reflection—definitely one of my least favorite parts of my new life—I racked that up to unexplainable phenomena.

Over the last couple of weeks, I'd been on a crash course to learn as much about vampires as I could. Counting on other people to guide me was unreliable at best, dangerous at worst. I'd learned that the hard way. The Internet, however, was a vast resource. As soon as I broke through the crusty covering of popular myths, everything I needed to know about real vampire culture was right there at my fingertips.

I might be getting carpal tunnel syndrome and becoming a fanged computer geek, but at least I was getting educated. Better late than never.

I sucked the remainder of my drink clean right down to the naked ice cubes.

Another Tequila Sunrise immediately landed in front of me.

I glanced up at the bartender. "You must be psychic."

He shook his head. "This is compliments of the gentleman in the corner."

I swiveled around on the stool to look where he indicated. Other than two slutty-looking vamps shaking their groove thing on the dance floor, nobody was there.

"Who did you say sent this?" I asked the bartender.

"He must have left. Tall guy. Good-looking in a dark and miserable sort of way."

"Sounds exactly like Sarah's type," George observed, then poked me in the shoulder. "I need to dance. Let's go dance. I love this song."

"Not in the mood."

"I'll go." Amy slipped off the stool and teetered precariously on her four-inch platform heels. She gave me a pointed look. "After all, *somebody* should have some fun tonight."

Well, that was a bit rude. *Accurate*, but rude.

I watched the two of them depart to shimmy to Madonna and Justin singing about saving the world in four minutes. I absently twisted the gold chain I wore until it began to cut off the circulation to my index finger.

The chain was ugly. It looked cheap and heavy and didn't go with any of my wardrobe. I'd never wear it if I had any say in the matter.

I didn't have any say.

Thanks to my nightwalker curse, the chain was the only thing keeping me from biting necks and killing people for kicks. Nightwalkers had existed a few hundred years ago, their vicious nature caused by a rare strain of the virus that turned humans into vamps. They were the reason for all the untrue myths about vampires being totally evil. They were the reason that hunters exist in the first place.

Nightwalkers were wiped off the face of the planet by those hunters to protect unassuming humans—*and* other vampires.

Which meant that, currently, I was the only vamp in the world with nightwalker tendencies—an uncontrollable dark thirst that spread over me, a need to feed on humans or other vamps as if they were an all-Sarah-can-eat buffet. I also couldn't go out during the day or the sunlight would fry me. There was no sunscreen on earth that could keep me from turning into a crispy critter if I wasn't wearing the chain.

The witch who'd cursed me was dead now. No chance to get her to reverse the curse.

Which meant I had to find the answer on my own. If I ever lost my chain—the only thing keeping me from truly becoming a creature of darkness—then I was seriously screwed. And so was anyone who crossed my path and looked remotely appetizing.

I shuddered at the thought and willed myself to concentrate on something, *anything*, else.

I stirred the cocktail in front of me with a swizzle stick and stared down into its orangey depths. I pushed the cherry down, holding it under the surface as if trying to drown it. After a moment, I let it bob back up to the surface.

Dark and miserable.

Just my type.

I pushed the drink away. With my luck, Mr. Dark-and-Miserable had poisoned it.

"Hey, can I get a shot of B-Positive?" I asked the bartender.

A couple of seconds later he slid a shot glass filled with familiar red liquid in front of me.

Don't get grossed out. It's really not that bad.

Blood is sent to places like Darkside by professional blood delivery services. They get their blood from willing donors who are paid well for their contributions. It was all very civilized. The rarer the blood type, the more expensive the shot.

I stuck with B-Positive. It was my fave. Because of the name, I could fool myself into believing it would cheer me up.

I tossed the shot back and waited for the euphoria to hit me.

A couple of minutes later I was still waiting.

The complimentary drink rested on a Darkside coaster. Other than the logo for the club, I noticed something else on the thick, round piece of cardboard. Handwriting. In blue ink.

Sarah—

I took in a shaky breath and glanced around the club again, paying particular attention to the corner the man who sent me the drink had allegedly been in. Still empty.

My palm was sweating as I picked up the coaster and turned it over to see there was more writing on the other side.

Meet me out back. I must see you.

I casually slipped the coaster into my handbag. Without saying anything to Amy and George, still dancing their little hearts out, I slid into the shadows of the club on the other side of the dance floor, moved past the bouncer at the door, and emerged into the cold night air outside. With a quick check over my shoulder to make sure no one was following me, I swiftly walked around the building to the back where it was dark and silent. The nearly full moon cast a pale glow on the deserted alley.

"Hello?" I whispered, barely loud enough for even myself to hear. "Where are you?"

Other than the expected Dumpsters and snowdrifts,

there seemed to be no one there. With my sensitive vampire ears, I could hear the bass thump of the dance music from inside very weakly. I hugged my arms tightly around myself. The temperature didn't bother me much anymore, but it did seem particularly cold that night.

I took a few more steps into the darkness. "Don't worry, we're alone."

I was answered only by more silence so I moved over to the other side of the building and peered around the corner. I didn't have very long before my friends wondered where I'd gone. Although, considering how many drinks I'd downed, they'd probably assume I was in the washroom.

I froze when I heard footsteps behind me. The very next moment, strong arms came around me and my back was pressed up against the cold brick wall. A hand came over my mouth, since my first instinct was to scream my lungs out.

Luckily, it was the person I'd been expecting.

Thierry removed his hand, leaned over, and crushed his mouth against mine in a kiss that took my breath away. I gasped against his lips, but then kissed him back deeply, wrapping my arms around his neck before sliding my hands up into his dark hair. His body warmed me in the cold night.

It wasn't the first time we'd secretly met after everyone thought we'd broken up, but I hadn't expected it tonight. Everyone else thought he'd only just returned from a trip to France, but he'd never left the city. Since it was vital that nobody saw us together, it had been difficult finding a time and place to meet. I'd missed him a lot.

When the kiss broke off and my heartbeat came back

to a normal pace, I looked up at him, raising an eyebrow. "A message on a coaster? Is that seriously the best you could do?"

"I wasn't sure you'd be able to get away. Calling or messaging you on your phone could be traced."

"And being spotted in a nightclub buying me drinks is much less risky?"

"I'm very discreet."

I managed to smile. "By the way, your handwriting is nearly illegible."

His mouth quirked. "Yet you figured out what it said."

"Barely." I grabbed hold of his black shirt and kissed him again quickly. We were shielded by the very romantic trash holders on either side of us but I still felt nervous that somebody might see us together. "What are you doing here?"

"I had to see you." His silver-eyed gaze moved down the length of me and back up to my face.

Just as the bartender had described my drink sender, Thierry de Bennicoeur was tall and knee-weakeningly delicious—my words, not his. Dark hair, broad shoulders, full lips, straight nose, stern black eyebrows over gray eyes that sometimes appeared to be silver. You'd never expect that he was pushing seven hundred years old, a vampire sired during the Black Death plague in Europe in the 1400s.

Not even my closest friends could find out we were still together. Amy and George were total blabbermouths. Since I wasn't the best secret-keeper in the universe it had been sheer torture to keep my mouth shut.

I had to keep my mouth shut about a lot of things.

I even kept a few things from Thierry.

For example, if he knew that over the last week and a half I'd become Gideon Chase's personal assistant and general errand girl, he wouldn't be very happy about that.

And that was an understatement.

He considered Gideon the most dangerous man in the world—and somebody he wanted me to stay far away from for my own safety. But when the burned-by-hellfire leader of the vampire hunters wanted something, he could be extremely . . . well, *insistent* was a good word.

Gideon couldn't find out that Thierry and I were still together, and Thierry couldn't find out I was currently at Gideon's beck and call.

Gideon usually checked in with me daily. In fact, he'd sent me to pick up a package for him earlier that day on the other side of the city. I got the impression he knew where I was and who I was with at all times. Just being in the alley with Thierry for a few stolen moments made me extremely nervous and more paranoid than usual. Which was saying something.

"Any luck finding Gideon's hired guns?" I asked.

His expression was tight. "No. That's one of the reasons I needed to see you this evening."

"To tell me to be careful?"

"Of course." He hissed out a long sigh. "I hate standing back and seeing you in harm's way like this. It has to stop."

"It will."

"Not if we can't discover his secrets. He has too much power at the moment, even if it's only lent itself to verbal threats. If he harms you—"

"He hasn't." I stroked Thierry's tense face. "Gideon isn't going to hurt me."

"Not until he gets what he wants."

"Exactly." I frowned. Wait. That didn't make me feel much better.

"I will kill him," he said darkly. "If he harms you in any way, the pain from the hellfire will be a pleasant memory for him."

"I appreciate the offer of mayhem and torture, really. But it's best if we stay calm and collected about this."

"You seem calm and collected enough for the both of us."

"I'm trying to stay Zen. I do yoga now, you know."

He raised an eyebrow. "You do?"

"Well, I have an instructional DVD on yoga. Haven't had a chance to watch it with all the drama going on lately, but I'm looking forward to it."

"We must find a solution in three days. You *cannot* sire him."

Thierry had a black-and-white attitude about pretty much everything. He drew his lines in the sand in permanent ink—and how he felt about Gideon was one of those lines. To him, Gideon was 100 percent evil incarnate. Couldn't say I blamed him much for that impression. After all, Gideon was the leader of the hunters. They didn't exactly make our lives a Technicolor musical production number. And Gideon, from everything I'd heard about him, had no problem getting his hands dirty when it came to slaying. He was exactly like Buffy—that is, if she was a six-foot-five billionaire playboy with hellfire scars from slaying a demon. And a tendency to kill things that weren't actually evil.

So, really, not like Buffy at all.

"I need to get back inside," I said, "and try to act like everything's normal—"

Another kiss managed to easily push my words and thoughts away. Thierry could kiss. Six hundred years of practice would make someone an expert, after all. I'd prefer not to give a lot of thought to how many women may have come before me. We both had our romantic histories. His was simply a little longer than mine, that's all.

By about 650 years.

My heart felt heavy when we parted. This whole situation seriously sucked. Just when I found a man I could be completely crazy about—despite our many differences—and one who loved me in return, we couldn't be together except for stolen moments like this.

"You shouldn't try to see me again till this is all over." I tried to ignore the lump in my throat. "I'm afraid he's going to find out."

"Perhaps you should have taken Amy up on the blind date she arranged for you."

I eyed him. "So Gideon's not the only one spying on me?"

He smiled. "If you had someone new in your life, or I in mine, Gideon would have no suspicions about us, would he?"

"Good point. But are you trying to say you want to see other people? Because I'm in the mood to kick some ass tonight and it might be yours."

Amusement slid behind his gaze. "I'm talking about appearances, nothing more. In fact, I think it's a very good idea."

"You want me to start dating somebody else?"

"Desperate times call for drastic measures. And speaking of that—" He was quiet for a moment. "You need to know something important."

That sounded ominous. "What?"

"I contacted the Red Devil. He's in the city right now. I thought we could use his help."

My eyes widened. "Really?"

He nodded gravely.

The Red Devil in a nutshell was this: a vampire vigilante who had been around for a thousand years, give or take a century or two. He saved innocent vamps from slaughter at the hands of hunters. He wore a mask so nobody knew who he was, and, in fact, most thought he was only a legend. Legend or not, he'd disappeared a hundred years ago and hadn't been seen since.

Gideon Chase, wearing a scarf over his scarred face to hide his true identity, had convinced me he was the Red Devil—in fact, he'd saved my life when I'd been staked so he could gain my confidence. But the *real* Red Devil was now in Toronto? Stop the presses.

"Who is he?" I asked.

"His identity is secret."

"So you don't know who he is? How did you contact him?"

"We have a mutual connection."

"Who?"

"I can't say."

"You can trust me."

"I know," he said. But he didn't go into any further detail.

I pushed my frustration at his vague answers away. Or tried to, anyhow. "What's he doing here? Or is that a secret as well?"

"I wanted him to assess the situation with Gideon. I thought it also important for him to keep an eye on you and he has agreed to this."

I felt stunned. "Are you trying to tell me that the Red Devil is my shiny new bodyguard?"

"He promises to be very discreet. You won't even know he's around."

I leaned back against the cold wall behind me and tried to process this info. The legendary, reclusive Red Devil was *my* bodyguard? And Thierry was acting as if this was a completely normal decision?

"You trust this guy?" I asked.

"Implicitly."

He sounded pretty certain about it. But how could he trust somebody who'd been off the map for a century? Somebody who'd just pop up thanks to a well-timed phone call?

"Where is he right now?"

"Close. It's best you know as little as possible, Sarah. It's safer that way."

"For him or for me?"

"Definitely both." He hooked a finger under my gold chain. He knew what it was and what it did. When I didn't have it and was acting all murderous and deadly and seductive, he'd done everything in his power to find a solution. Although truthfully, I think he kind of liked the *seductive* part.

"If I learn anything new I will contact you as soon as I can," he said.

"Same here." The fresh guilt at not telling him about my strange new job as Gideon's assistant ate at me. It was on the tip of my tongue but I didn't want to worry him more than he already was. "I love you, Thierry."

He touched my face softly and slid his thumb over my bottom lip. "I love you, too."

And, with a last kiss, he was gone.

Well, he didn't just disappear, but he could walk really fast. I watched his dark form move away into the shadows.

Then I slowly trudged back around the side of the building until I'd nearly reached the front doors. A woman was being unceremoniously kicked out of the club by the big, brawny bouncer.

"Go home and don't come back," he advised her harshly. "We don't want you here."

She hurled a couple of choice expletives at him and turned her back, stomping away down the dark street in a short red minidress and silver stilettos.

"Nice girl," I said.

"Fledgling vamp caught her sire cheating on her," the bouncer explained. "She'd only been turned a few nights ago. She made a scene and nearly bit the chick the guy was with tonight." He swept his gaze over me. "You're the Slayer of Slayers, aren't you?"

Oh, brother. Just what I needed. A fanboy.

I shook my head. "You know, I actually get that all the time. We're both brunettes and there *is* a fleeting resemblance. I saw her once, but she's kind of ugly. Probably from all that slayer slaying."

"If you say so." The bouncer shrugged. "You coming back in, or what?"

"Yeah." I glanced over in the direction of the jilted fledgling and I noticed two men a block up step out from a dark alley and begin to silently trail after the oblivious vampiress. "Hey, check that out. Do you think those are hunters?"

He followed my line of sight. "Could be."

I looked at him. "Don't you want to do something about it? She's a helpless fledgling out on her own. They'll kill her."

"What do you suggest I do?"

"Go save her?"

He laughed. "Not going to happen. I don't think they saw where she came from, and I'm not getting a stake through my chest tonight for trying to save some worthless bitch."

"Oh, that's really charming."

He smiled thinly at me. "For fifteen bucks an hour I don't have to be charming. Why don't *you* go save her?"

I narrowed my gaze at him. "Maybe I will."

"Good luck with that." He turned around and slipped back inside the club. The door closed heavily behind him leaving me out in the cold night alone.

I scanned the street again. No one was around. It wasn't that long ago that *I* was the hapless fledgling who wandered dark and lonely places I shouldn't go.

Since then, I'd aged. I'd matured. I would eternally look twenty-eight years old, but I'd been through enough stress in the past three months to give me gray hair. Metaphorically speaking, that is. Thankfully, I had no gray hair, and if I did I'd totally dye it back to normal.

But that was neither here nor there.

I began following the girl and her stalkers. Maybe it was just my overworked imagination that she was in danger. They were probably just heading in the same direction, was all. Nothing to be concerned with. Paranoia was one of my closest pals lately, although normally I had it about myself, not somebody I didn't even know.

It was a gut thing. I had to know. Something felt terribly off.

I'd check it out, make sure the girl was safe and sound,

and then I'd go back to the club and pretend to have a good time.

And then I heard a shriek: female. And a laugh: male. *Shit*.

I picked up my pace and my breathing increased. Damn that bouncer for not helping out. I was right. The girl was in trouble, and now what?

Save the fledgling, save the world. Did I look like a superhero?

As much as I'd like to think I was tough and able to bravely face off against those who'd harm others, I knew I didn't have a chance in hell against the hunters. They were two big, muscular guys, and I was . . . well, *me*. And I'd be willing to bet each of them had done this many times before.

Unfortunately, there was no time for me to go back to the club and get reinforcements, and from the terrified whimpering I now heard just around the corner in the alleyway where the hunters had cornered the fledgling, I had only seconds to decide what to do next.

Maybe I should have turned my back and run away. There'd been plenty of vamps who'd found themselves on the sharp end of a stake since I'd been sired. But this . . . this was different. It was here, it was now, and I couldn't simply walk away and pretend it never happened.

The girl let out another frightened scream and the decision was made. There was one way I knew how to be a bit tougher than I naturally was. It wouldn't hurt if I did it just once, would it?

I sure hoped not.

Cursing under my breath, I reached back and undid the

clasp of my gold chain with shaking fingers. It slipped off my throat. I slid it into my purse for safekeeping.

It was a bit like Diana Prince spinning around three times to become Wonder Woman, only I wasn't suddenly wearing a shiny red, white, and blue leotard with a magical golden lasso and tiara. My change was a little more subtle than that.

I'd tested taking off the gold chain a couple of times since I got it. In the beginning, my nightwalker symptoms took a while to completely manifest in all their nasty glory. But now they came on me almost immediately. It was dangerous—mostly for other people—so I didn't play around with it much.

It started with my vision closing in on either side so I could keep my prey in sight. No distractions. Clear, predatory focus. My heartbeat came to a slow stop. Or *almost* a stop. A vampire's heart beats slower than a human's, but now my heart, without the chain, would beat approximately four times an hour. Nightwalkers weren't living beings like regular vampires. Nightwalkers were the reason regular vamps had the reputation of being undead. Barely a heartbeat and no real need to breathe.

Only a desire to feed.

Horror movie: table for one.

Being a nightwalker was scary as hell, but that was the rational Sarah talking. Without the chain I wasn't all that rational. But I was still in control.

At least, for short periods of time.

Hopefully this wouldn't take very long.

Chapter 2

One of the hunters leered at the terrified fledgling. "You have a nice body for a bloodsucker."

"Leave me alone!" Tears streamed down her cheeks.

"She is mighty pretty," the other hunter agreed. "Fresh, too. I'd say the evil thing is less than a week old. She doesn't even have her fangs yet."

"Vampires aren't evil! Please, you have to believe me."

"Sure, we believe you." The hunters exchanged a droll look. "She's not even denying being a vamp. That makes it way simpler. No unfortunate mistakes."

"Please, don't hurt me," she begged.

"Do you want to see my stake, honey? I'll bet it's the biggest you've ever seen."

"I highly doubt that," I said dryly from behind them.

They turned to look at me.

It was dark in the alley, but I could see them as clear as day. Nightwalker eyesight was better than night-vision goggles. One had a bald head and a precisely shaved goatee and the other had long shaggy hair that touched his shoulders and an angry-looking scar on his right cheek-bone. They held no fear in their eyes as they looked me up and down.

"One for me and one for you," Baldy said to his friend. "This is going to be a fun night."

"Wouldn't count on that." My attention drifted from his ugly face to the subtle throb at the side of his throat. I sensed the blood racing through his veins just below the surface. My senses were way more acute in nightwalker mode. It was as helpful as it was distracting.

"Check out her eyes," the second hunter hissed, and I could finally detect a trace of fear in his voice. "They're black. She must be really hungry. That's not good."

"Don't be such a wimp," Baldy scoffed. He pulled his allegedly monstrous-sized stake out of a holder on his belt—as expected, not all that impressive—and confidently approached me.

"See this?" He indicated the stake. "Do you know how many bloodsuckers I've killed with this thing? It's my lucky stake. I whittled it myself."

I rolled my pitch-black eyes. "You're a regular Martha Stewart. Do you keep a scrapbook, too?"

"Shut up, bitch."

"Please help me!" The fledgling's voice shook, her attention now fully focused on her potential rescuer, aka: me.

"Just a minute." I felt bad for her—this small, pale, shivering thing with really bad hair and supremely tacky shoes. A couple of months ago that was me. Except for the bad hair and shoes, of course.

The bald hunter laughed. "You're going to help her? Is

that why you're here? To rescue one of your own kind? How sweet."

"Why do hunters talk so much?" I asked. "All talk, no action. Yawn."

"Dude," the shaggier of the two said. "Didn't you hear me? Her eyes are *black*. She's dangerous. Don't provoke her. Maybe we should take off. I don't feel good about this."

"Your friend is way smarter than he looks." I couldn't stop studying Baldy's deliciously exposed throat above the line of his leather jacket. "Why don't I give you a chance? Leave now with the promise to never kill another vampire and we won't have a problem."

Baldy laughed louder at that. "Who the hell do you think you are, *bitch*?"

"I'm the Slayer of Slayers, *asshole*. Ever heard of me?"

That stopped him for a moment as he recognized my well-known nickname. His eyes widened a fraction and he took a step back so he could study me from my low-heeled, knee-high black boots—fashionable yet easy to run in; an important combo for any female vamp—past my casual yet sparkly outfit of a short black skirt and silver lamé tank top, to my shoulder-length brown hair, currently tucked firmly behind my ears. Since the cold was only a minor annoyance for me now, I'd left my coat inside the club.

A slow, confident smile spread across his features. "I heard that rep of yours was only a rumor. So if you're trying to scare me you've failed. The only question is, when I slay you, are you still young enough to leave a body behind for me to prove I was the one to do it, or are you more ancient than you look?"

Vampires die in one of two ways. Those over a hundred years old turn to goo. Those under a hundred leave a corpse behind. According to my recent research it seemed to have something to do with human lifetimes. If vamps lived beyond what would naturally have been their allotted years, then their bodies disintegrated when they were killed. The stains were nearly impossible to remove from carpeting or clothing. Believe me, I'd tried.

"Oh, it *was* a rumor," I agreed. "But I've had a few changes in my life recently that have altered a few things. I'm not quite as helpless as I might look."

"All I see is a disgusting black-eyed monster who needs to die."

"Sticks and stones, *cue ball*."

"I'm going to kill you." He raised the stake.

"Drop it," I said very firmly, holding eye contact with him.

He dropped the weapon and then looked down at it with confusion. "What the hell?"

One of my abilities as a nightwalker was mind control over weak-minded humans. Amy called it my "thrall." I could tell with a glance that this guy might have lots of muscles on the surface, but cotton balls between his temples. The thrall didn't work on everybody, but it was a neat trick when it did.

"Why are you taunting her?" Shaggy whimpered. "We gotta get out of here, man. Now!"

Instead of taking his friend's wise advice, Baldy lunged at me. I easily grabbed him by his throat and he gasped for breath as I dug my fingernails in on either side of his Adam's apple.

My vision narrowed and some more of my nightwalker's darkness bled through into my conscious mind.

Kill him, it suggested in a helpful manner.

"Give me one reason why I shouldn't kill you," I said evenly.

The hunter replied with a gurgle. His face was turning purple.

It would be so easy to squash this pathetic excuse for a human as if he were no more than an annoying insect.

The unexpectedly dark, murderous thought made me falter a bit and loosen my hold on him. I wasn't a killer. I hadn't planned on doing anything but scaring the crap out of these two—although, I hoped, not literally—before I sent them scurrying away.

"Let him go!" Shaggy pleaded, obviously convinced I was about to tear his friend's throat out with a flick of my wrist. "Don't kill him. Please!"

"Why not?" I grappled for control of myself and knew it was my nightwalker's fault. She really wanted to kill this guy. After all, hunters didn't care who they killed. Would it really be that big a loss?

Shaggy was crying openly now. "Because . . . because *I love him*! I love you, Mark! I'm sorry I never told you. I've been waiting for the right moment, but it never happened. I can't lose you. Not now. Not like this!"

There was complete silence in the alley for a long moment.

And then, "I love . . . you . . . too, Cal."

I raised an eyebrow. Wasn't expecting that. I loosened my grip on Baldy's throat a little more.

Vampire hunters in love. Terrific.

"You . . . you love me?" Cal sounded surprised. "Since when?"

"Since we . . . first met . . . at Clancy's." He gasped for breath. "Remember the eighteen beers . . . we drank . . . that night? The game of pool? Comparing our . . . kill counts?"

Cal's expression turned wistful. "Like it was only yesterday." He looked pleadingly at me. "Please, let him go. We'll leave this city forever. We promise, don't we, Mark?"

Mark struggled to nod. "Yeah, we promise."

I eyed him skeptically. "Seriously?"

He nodded. "Maybe we could go to Los Angeles, or something. Open a little Oceanside bar. It's always been a dream of mine."

Their eyes met. "That sounds really nice," Cal agreed.

After another moment, I released Mark. The red imprint of my hand on his throat was oddly satisfying.

"Fine," my voice was shaky. "Go. I won't try to stop you. But I swear, if I see you in town after tonight, then all bets are off."

The two hunters embraced and then ran out of the alley together.

What the hell was this? I thought. *A freaking romance novel?*

I felt a warm hand on my arm. It was the fledgling.

"Thank you! That was so amazing. You're so strong and brave."

I cleared my throat. "It's a work in progress, but thanks." I opened my purse and reached inside to retrieve my chain with trembling fingers, knowing I had to get it

back on ASAP. Every moment it was off my neck was a
risk—as evidenced by my nearly killing the hunter.

And he would have totally deserved it, my inner nightwalker reminded me.

Exactly.

I frowned at the thought.

I paused to look at the fledgling. "You need to be more
careful out here all alone, you know. It's dangerous."

"My sire—" Her voice hitched and she covered her
face with her hands and began to sob. "He . . . he doesn't
want me anymore. I wanted to be with him forever but
now I'm all alone."

"It'll get better."

She shook her head. "Maybe the hunters should have
killed me. They almost did." She reached up to her forehead, which had a small gash on it, and pulled her hand
away to inspect the blood. "They whacked me pretty
hard."

A sensation of warmth and wooziness moved through me.

"Well . . ." I braced my shoulder against the wall to
steady myself. "You need to be more careful. It's too bad
your sire was a jerk, but it happens. Find some new friends
to help you out—"

"Like you?" she asked hopefully.

My head felt very cloudy. "Like me, or there
are . . . there are lots of other helpful vamps in the city." I
swallowed hard. "It's really warm out tonight, isn't it?"

"It's February."

"Hot for February."

The fledgling looked at me strangely. "Are you feeling
all right?"

My purse dropped to the ground as the warmth continued to course through me. "I'm just fine."

She squinted at me. "Your black eyes *are* a bit freaky."

The slight cloudiness in my mind turned to thick fog.

"Black eyes are a warning sign. Even the nicest vampires are dangerous when their eyes turn black. Consider that your first lesson in survival."

Something in the tone of my voice made her take a quick step away from me. She was trembling again.

"Uh . . ." She gulped. "So I think I'm going to, like, leave now."

She gave me a look that could only be described as fearful and then nervously began to walk around me. I reached out and grabbed her by the throat much as I'd done before with the hunter. She made a scared, strangled sound.

The blood flowed from her forehead like honey. So warm, so alive . . . so tempting. My vision narrowed more than it already had.

"P-please . . ." she stuttered. "Please d-don't hurt me."

Why did she think I was going to hurt her?

Because you are *going to hurt her*, the nightwalker inside me said.

It was as if I could see myself, but from miles away. The rational me was far away now and I was yelling and frantically waving my arms, scared for the girl, scared for myself. My chain had been off for too long. My nightwalker had taken control now—and she was very hungry.

I pushed the fledgling up against the wall, focused only on one thing—the gentle pulse at the side of her throat. I felt my fangs elongate. Normally a vampire's fangs were small and barely noticeable—sharper than a human's canines, but nothing that would raise any alarms if you didn't know what you were looking at.

But a hungry vampire . . . well, that was a different story. Whether at her core she was a good vamp or a bad vamp, the hunger that raced through her body turned her fangs into the perfect weapon meant to sink into soft, warm skin to get what she desired most. Human blood was necessary for survival, but vampire blood was addictive and decadent—like dessert, like alcohol, like a drug.

And no matter how much the normal me screamed or fought, the nightwalker's need to feed would win out. It was clear, focused, and so very natural. And there was no way to predict if the fledgling would survive when it was all said and done. Not tonight. Not with the way I currently felt.

My lips peeled back from sharp fangs as I pushed the fledgling's head to the side, swept back evidence of her bad dye job, and grazed the surface of her skin.

The very next moment something yanked me away from her and I staggered across the alley. I turned with a hiss. There was a dark figure standing in the shadows.

He wore a red mask that covered most of his face.

The man glanced at the fledgling. "Leave now."

Without needing to be told twice, my potentially delicious bleached blond meal ran out of the alley. I couldn't see straight. I was so hungry. It blinded me to everything else. My thoughts were cloudy and my darkened gaze now locked on the stranger's throat.

"Don't even think about it," he said, his voice low.

But I *was* thinking about it—in my foggy kind of way. The anger at being interrupted filled me and I clenched my fists at my sides. I moved toward him, my focus never leaving the side of his neck. "Let me guess. You're the Red Devil? The real one?"

He took a step further into shadow so all I could see was his outline. "I am."

"So that means you're my bodyguard now."

"Correct."

"I don't need a bodyguard." My eyes narrowed. "As you can see."

"All I see is a stupid woman who should be wearing the gold chain that dampens behavior like this. You could have killed that fledgling."

Stupid? A flash of anger cut through me. Did a pathetic excuse for a vampire vigilante just call me stupid?

I really didn't like it when people called me stupid.

"You need to mind your own business," I hissed through clenched teeth.

"This *is* my business."

Normally—since Thierry hadn't exactly been very forthcoming with the details—I would have been curious to know more about who this guy was and where he came from, but I'd had enough talking. I walked directly toward him. He glared down at me through his mask. I registered nothing except his heartbeat and the knowledge that warm blood coursed just beneath his skin. Everything else was background noise. I slid my hands up his firm chest and he didn't resist or try to pull away.

I went up on tiptoes to whisper into his ear. "I bet you taste very good."

The moment before my fangs would have sunk into his throat, his hands came around my upper arms like iron vises. He pushed me away, turned me around, and before

I could do anything about it, he slammed me up against the cold hard wall.

I tried to fight him, but I was in an awkward position. He crouched for a moment and then got back to his feet. Something cold and thin pressed against my throat.

My eyes widened. Was he going to strangle me? Maybe try to decapitate me? According to my research, that was one of the most effective methods to kill a vampire if you didn't mind the wet work.

But nothing painful happened. The very next moment he let me go. I felt at my throat to find the gold chain he must have retrieved from my open purse on the ground and put back on me. The hunger and darkness left in a near-painful whoosh and my knees buckled. I had to fight to remain standing.

The Red Devil's back was now toward me.

"Don't let this happen again," he growled.

When he left, I sank to the ground, one hand on my chain and the other over my mouth to cover my shock.

Shit. That was close. That was too damned close. I'd been mad about what the Red Devil had said before, calling me stupid. But he was absolutely right.

I could have killed that girl. And if he hadn't stopped me I think I would have.

So much for coming to her rescue.

Chapter 3

Sarah!" George exclaimed when I returned to the club. "We've been worried about you."

I glanced at Amy, who was still on the dance floor, attempting an awkward, high-heeled version of the Running Man. "Yeah, it looks like it."

"Amy hides her concern really well. Where have you been?"

Secretly meeting with Thierry. Trying to save an innocent, but badly dressed fledgling. Going homicidal and nearly making the fledgling more than just a fashion victim. Getting reamed out by the Red Devil.

All of the above.

"I was in the washroom," I told him instead.

"For twenty minutes?"

I put a hand over my stomach. "You do *not* want to know the details. Trust me."

He made a sour face. "Forget I asked."

I would never take my chain off again. Ever. Stamped it,

no erasies. I twisted my finger around the very necessary piece of jewelry.

George gave me a thorough look. "Now that you mention it, you don't look so good."

"Really?" I said dryly. "Because I feel like a million bucks."

He crossed his arms. "Then the inflation rate is not in your favor. Do you want to leave? Had enough with the partying for one night?"

I let out a long, shuddery breath. "To put it mildly."

I felt sick and ashamed by what had happened. And sweaty. And miserable. And horrifically embarrassed. And scared. And . . . well, that basically covered it.

That was a whole smorgasbord of emotions to deal with at one time so I knew the stress showing through on my face was impossible to hide.

Amy pranced off the dance floor and made a beeline over to us. "Hey! You're back. Want to dance?"

I looked at her wearily. "Not a chance."

"You're such a poet!" She grinned and pulled a cell phone out of her small, beaded bag. "I borrowed this from you earlier. Mine was dead and I had to call Barry. You have a text message waiting there. Somebody with the initial G?" She could barely control her curiosity. "Who's G, Sarah? Hmm? Someone hot?"

I snatched the phone away from her. I hadn't even realized it was missing. I glanced at the screen and my stomach took a deeper nosedive. "G is for God, if you must know. I've recently become incredibly religious. It must be my Bible quote of the day."

Yeah, like she was buying that one.

"Grant?" she guessed. "Maybe Gary? Geoffrey? Gerard? Greg? Gaston? Stop me if I'm getting close."

Gideon.

My knuckles whitened as I clutched the small pink phone.

"I didn't mean to read it," she said innocently. "But he wants to see you immediately and apparently you know what he wants."

I gave her a tight smile. "Super. Thanks for letting me know."

"Well? What does he want? A midnight rendezvous? A little boom-shaka-laka?" Her smile was blindingly white. "Sarah, I'm so impressed. You had me convinced you were still pining over stupid Thierry. You could have told me, you know, instead of being all secretive about this new piece of yummy. Then I wouldn't have bothered setting you up with Jeremy."

"I am obviously an enigma," I sighed wearily, "when it comes to the yummy."

"Details! I want details!"

George raised his eyebrows. "That makes two of us. I live with you and even I didn't know about this. Keeping secrets from your bestest friends, Sarah?"

If only they knew.

I slipped the phone into my bag. "Right. Well, I think I'm going to call it a night."

Amy and George exchanged a glance.

"Fine," she said, pouting. "Be that way. But I'll figure out who your new mystery man is. Just give me time."

I pasted a frozen smile on my face. "You're immortal now. Take all the time you need."

Then I grabbed my coat and left the club, attempting

to ignore her dirty look and George's curious one. Neither attempted to follow me, which, based on my dour mood and where I was headed, was a very good thing.

"You got my message?"

Gideon's deep voice greeted me from the shadows of his fourth-floor suite at the Madison Manor. If I could find a bright point in this otherwise dark scenario, the boutique hotel at Spadina and Bloor—in the part of Toronto called the Annex—was only a few blocks away from Darkside. His room in the restored Victorian mansion even had a fireplace, which currently wasn't lit despite the cool temperature of the room. As far as I knew, he didn't go out. Why should he when I was only a text message away to do all of his chores?

The ensuite bathroom light was on. Otherwise the main room was dark, the blinds drawn. To my left, double French doors led to a snow-covered balcony overlooking Madison Avenue.

"Obviously I got your message," I said tightly. "I'm here, aren't I?"

"You are."

"Can I turn on a light?" I felt at the wall for the switch.

"I'd rather you didn't."

But it was too late as I flicked on the overhead light. Gideon glared at me from the chair in the corner. He immediately raised his hand weakly in an unconscious attempt to cover the scars on his face, but then gripped the armrest instead.

I'd seen enough pictures of Gideon in his prime, before the accident, to know that he used to be extremely attractive. Those days were over, at least for half of him. One side of his face was covered in ugly scar tissue, but the other side was still flawlessly handsome.

When I first met him, before I even knew who he really was, he wore a scarf over his face to hide his identity and disfigurement as well as pretending to be the Red Devil. Now I didn't think he left his room at all. Along with the scars came a whole lot of pain as the hellfire continued to burn through him. He was not a happy camper to say the least.

"How are you feeling?" I asked.

"As well as I look."

"That bad, huh?"

He raised an eyebrow. "Possibly worse."

"Serves you right. You ever heard of karma? Maybe this is your punishment for killing so many vampires."

"Maybe." He drew in a breath and let it out slowly. "Did you bring it?"

"Yup." I knew what he was talking about. I reached into my purse and pulled out the small package. I didn't know what it was, only where to go to get it. The man behind the desk at the New Age store had handed it over to me earlier today as if he knew exactly who I was and what I wanted, no questions asked.

"Bring it to me."

When I approached, he turned his face so I couldn't easily see the scars. I wanted to roll my eyes. Gideon was very vain. He hated how he looked now and he didn't want anyone to see him. Couldn't say I blamed him for that. He looked like hell. *Literally.*

The scars seemed to be spreading and getting worse, causing him even more pain than before. Despite myself, my stomach twisted at that thought. He'd threatened the people I loved in order to blackmail me into siring him. He'd shot me with a tranquilizing garlic dart—*twice*. He'd forced me to break up with the man I loved.

Gideon Chase was evil, no question about it.

But being face to face with him reminded me how much I hated seeing anyone in constant, agonizing pain, no matter who they were or what they'd done.

I was such a wimp.

"Is that concern I see on your face?" he asked, as if he'd read my mind, a small smile in his green eyes.

"Concern? For you? Not likely. I hate you. And in three days when this is all over, I never want to see you again."

He shook his scarred head. "I don't think you hate me half as much as you'd like to."

After everything he'd threatened, with everything he represented, it would be completely crazy and illogical for me to feel anything for him *except* hate.

Right?

Of course it would.

"No, trust me," I assured him. "I despise you."

His lips curled, except on one side they didn't move at all because the scar tissue was too thick. "Quite honestly, I think you should be thanking me for helping you to end things with the master vampire."

I crossed my arms. "I'm not discussing Thierry with you."

"You don't have to." He placed the package I'd delivered on the small table next to him and leaned back in his chair. "I'm just saying that he didn't appreciate you as much as he should have."

"Can I go now?" I eyed the door.

"In a minute. I think you have me all wrong, Sarah. You've convinced yourself that I'm the bad guy—"

"You *are* the bad guy," I reminded him.

"If I was the bad guy, would I have saved you from being staked that night? You'd be dead right now if it wasn't for me. I also gave you that very special gold chain you wear around your neck right now."

I touched the jewelry in question. "That was all to get me to do what you want."

He sighed. "I don't see why this has to be unpleasant between us. We can be friends."

"*Friends*?" I repeated. "You're a hunter and I'm a vampire."

"And your point?" He looked amused with me.

"I'm going now. I brought your . . . whatever it is. Party on." I turned to leave.

"Don't you want to stay to see what it is?"

I actually did. I was extremely curious, so sue me. I'd decided not to open the package when I received it, but curiosity killed the cat and all that. This kitty had had plenty of brushes with death lately, so I wasn't going to take any more chances.

There was a crinkling sound as he unwrapped the brown paper packaging. I swiveled around on my heels as he removed a black box from inside, which he opened to reveal—

"A wristwatch?" I said, feeling less than impressed. "That's what you had me pick up for you? That's very underwhelming, I have to say."

"This is a very special watch. It's not as special as your chain, but it's pretty close." He traced the tip of his index finger over the face of the very ordinary-looking timepiece. Then he stroked the scars on his face. "It's actually a glamour spell cast into a wearable object. I had it specially made. You wouldn't believe what something like this costs. Luckily money is no problem for me—I set aside a great deal of cash in case I ever needed to go into hiding."

I knew that a "glamour" magically helped someone appear beautiful or different. If somebody had a large nose and he or she had a glamour it could look like a small nose. Real-life airbrushing. Didn't change what was underneath, but sometimes appearances were enough.

Without another word, he slipped the watch on his wrist and fastened it. The very next moment a thin band of light moved over him. Wherever the light touched, Gideon's scars disappeared completely.

My eyes widened in shock.

"How do I look?" he asked, reaching up to touch his now scar-free face.

I swallowed hard. "You look . . . different."

Actually, different wasn't really accurate. He looked the same as the pictures I'd seen of him. Hair almost as dark as Thierry's, a disconcertingly warm intelligence behind piercing green eyes, a movie-star-perfect face. He still wore the simple clothes he had on before, of course—black, loose-fitting pants and a baggy blue T-shirt—but now the scars on his muscled left bicep and forearm had smoothed out completely.

He flashed a grin at me. "Different is good."

I felt stunned. "So what does this mean? You're cured, just like that?"

His grin faded. "No. This is only a glamour. It

changes nothing. In three nights the ritual will go on as scheduled."

"When I sink my fangs in your neck and suck the life out of you? I'm actually looking forward to it."

His smile reappeared at my false bravado. "Sure you are."

"I am. I mean, how many vampires can say they were able to chomp on Gideon Chase with his full permission? I should have promotional postcards made up, or something."

He pressed his lips together for a moment. "I do have some concerns."

"The fact that I have to keep my fangs in your neck for a few minutes before I can properly vampify you? Is there a little fear creeping in at the sides, Gideon?"

"No. It's actually the fact that you've only consumed the blood of two master vampires. My research leads me to believe that might not be enough to gain enough power to fully heal me."

I nodded. "Well, in that case, you can feel free to find someone else for the job."

"I'm sure it'll be fine, but I do feel some anxiety."

"Gideon Chase, anxious? Wherever is my camera?"

He rose from his chair to pull the blinds away from the window. He was quite an imposing man, even without taking his reputation into account. Beautiful women from around the world had allegedly flocked for the chance to spend time with him in the past, and it hadn't only been because he was a billionaire.

Flocked.

He turned and moved toward me.

I took a step backward.

"I have something for you," he said.

I took another step back until I bumped up against the door.

He held up a hand. "Don't panic. It's something non-threatening, I promise."

"Why do I find that hard to believe?"

He moved toward the table next to his king-sized bed to grab a small fabric bag, which he brought over to me. "A gift for you."

I hesitated, then took it from him. I opened it up to find a pair of earrings inside. *Diamond* earrings. *Big* diamond earrings.

"What is this?"

He raised an eyebrow. "They're diamond earrings."

"I can see that. But why are you giving them to me?"

"As a show of appreciation for everything you've endured so far. I know it hasn't been easy for you. I can be a bit of a—"

"Insanely evil villain?" I finished.

"I was going for 'pain in the ass,' but you can finish the sentence any way you like." A smile that I was quite sure had melted the panties off many a socialite in the past spread across his handsome features.

"I can't accept them." With a twinge of regret—I mean, come on, diamond earrings!—I gave them back to him.

He nodded. "Then I'll have to find something else you can't turn down so easily, won't I?"

There was a buzzing sound and Gideon fished into the pocket of his pants to draw out a BlackBerry. He glanced at the screen and then put it away again.

My focus had narrowed on the device. I wondered if the names and phone numbers of his contacts were in it. That would be very helpful.

"So, Sarah, did you have a good time at the nightclub tonight with George and Amy?" Gideon asked.

A shiver went down my spine. Had a spy just reported in regarding my whereabouts for the evening? And if so, what else had been observed? My stomach churned thinking that Thierry and I had been spotted together. Gideon was being all gift-giving and amiable right now, but I knew better than to push him.

"I had a great time," I replied. "Amy set me up on a blind date. But don't go getting all jealous. He's in human resources. And it's very possible he prefers men."

"How is the Red Devil?" he asked evenly. "He stopped you from giving in to your nightwalker instincts, right?"

I spy with my little eye . . . somebody that is screwed.

"He's just peachy." I touched my chain. "Obviously when trying to keep her dark side at bay, a lady should never leave home without her accessories, should she?"

"Why is he here?"

"He's not much of a talker."

"What does he look like?"

I chewed my bottom lip. "He was wearing a mask. Plus, I was dealing with a little case of bloodlust at the time, so my vision was a tad fuzzy. He's tall, that's all I know."

"You need to be very careful around him."

That surprised me. "Around *him*? This advice coming from the man who bankrolls the wooden stake carriers of America?"

"If this is the true Red Devil, then he is very dangerous. Very unpredictable. I know a great deal about him, enough to know he's a threat to anyone who crosses his path."

"So am I when I'm not wearing my chain."

"It's different. The Red Devil, whoever he really is,

has killed many over his long lifetime—both hunters and vampires. It would have been safer for everyone if he'd stayed away." He shook his head at my skeptical look. "I know you see hunters, including me, as evil, but I think you know very well that it's not always the case. There are many hunters who only want to keep the world safe from evil predators."

"The Red Devil is not an evil predator," I said firmly.

"Are you sure about that?" He walked to the other side of the room to look out at the view past the balcony. His newly perfected reflection showed up in the glass door.

I shifted my feet but didn't answer him. I really didn't know the Red Devil from Adam, as the saying went. All I knew was that Thierry trusted him.

Thierry. If he knew I was having a friendly convo with Gideon in his hotel room, all alone, he'd probably have a conniption.

"I do have something else for you," Gideon said. "I wasn't going to mention it yet, but since you didn't like my earrings . . ."

"I won't like anything else you got off the Shopping Network, either. Just an FYI."

He shrugged. "Maybe you're right. It's nothing really. Only the grimoire of the witch who cursed you. The book in which she recorded all of her spells, including the one she used on you."

All the breath left me in a rush. That was the last thing I had expected him to say. "The witch you killed, you mean."

"She was evil," he said firmly.

"And it's great that you've appointed yourself judge, jury, and executioner."

"You're entitled to your opinion. But it doesn't change

the fact that I have her magic book. And in it is the incantation to remove that pesky little curse of yours."

My heartbeat quickened. "You're kidding me."

He shook his head. "Not kidding."

"Where is it?" I scanned the room.

"Somewhere safe. And you can have it for giving me something in return."

I eyed him with equal parts skepticism and hope. "What do you want?"

"The Red Devil."

My stomach did a backflip worthy of an Olympic gymnast. "What do you want with him?"

"You're not that naïve, Sarah."

I raised my eyebrows. "You obviously overestimate me."

"I want to slay him. I want to stop him from doing any harm to others now that he's chosen to return to the public eye."

"So the only way you'll give me the grimoire is if I help you kill the Red Devil?" I wanted to make sure I understood him properly.

"That's right."

My small piece of shiny hope flittered away. "Don't you have more important things to be thinking about right now?"

He let out a long, shaky sigh. "Actually, I could use the distraction. I need a new challenge to concentrate on. To defeat the Red Devil—a vampire whose reputation others have raised to mythic proportions—would be my greatest accomplishment." He blinked. "Other than that demon in Vegas, of course. As you can probably imagine, it's not exactly a memory I currently cherish."

The grimoire. The answer to all of my nightwalker problems. "I don't know, Gideon—"

"Damn." He groaned, then staggered back a few feet and clutched at his face. "Why did I have to mention it?"

Before I could say anything else, he cried out and fell to his knees on the plush carpet of the suite. It was the hellfire. Gideon convulsed in pain as he fought against the flames that couldn't be seen, only felt.

I stood, frozen in place, feeling sick as I watched him suffer. I pressed up against the door, wanting to leave, but finding it difficult to move.

"What should I do?" I asked.

"Nothing." His voice caught as a shudder went through him. His teeth were gritted. I was willing to bet my bottom dollar that nobody had ever seen Gideon like this before. So weak and needy and pathetic. The thought didn't make me feel the least bit better.

"Maybe I can call a doctor—" I offered lamely.

He looked up at me with glassy eyes. "I don't want you to see me like this." When I didn't budge, he raised his voice. "Leave me! Now!"

"Fine with me." I turned around, opened the door, and left Gideon alone to his suffering and solitude.

I didn't care if he was in pain. This was the man who held my life in his hands and was forcing me to do what he wanted.

I hated him.

And, even more than that, I hated the small part of me that *didn't* hate him. It was very inconvenient.

Chapter 4

Maybe I should have taken the diamond earrings after all.

No. I pushed the thought away. In fact, I tried very hard to push away all my thoughts about Gideon, his pain, his plans, and his new scar-free but still evil face. My thoughts, however, had other plans as they continued to churn through my tired cranium.

I left the hotel and walked quickly down the sidewalk, my arms crossed tightly over my chest. I wanted to call Thierry and go see him, but I couldn't. Which sucked. Besides, I really didn't want him to find out that I was seeing Gideon on a regular basis behind his back.

I'd fully planned on tonight being the last time I came to his hotel like an obedient Girl Scout, but now he'd presented me with something I couldn't simply forget even if I wanted to.

The grimoire. Did he really have it or was he just messing with me?

Was the Red Devil really as bad as Gideon suggested?

I mean, I had figured he didn't go around giving people fashion advice or handing out gift certificates. He was an immortal vigilante, after all. It was possible that he'd done some super-nasty things in his life to achieve his reputation—things that I might even consider *evil*.

But was that enough proof to stick an apple in his mouth and offer up his head on a platter just so I could get what I wanted?

I felt sick at the thought. I wished I could be a little more heartless. Just a smidge. Nice girls don't get the corner office, after all. They get trampled on. And, well, *cursed*.

Speaking of heads-on-platters, I sensed something then. It was strange. I didn't actually hear any footsteps and I didn't see anyone, but on a deeper kind of vampire-sense level I felt that someone was following me. The sensation of ants doing a conga line down my arms was a tipoff.

And I had a funny feeling I knew who it was.

"I figured you'd be better at the stalking thing," I said a little shakily to the silence as I approached the nearest bus stop. There was no one else around. "But you're definitely no ninja, are you?"

"I guess I'm a bit rusty." The Red Devil's voice sounded strange, as if he was trying to make it sound lower and raspier than it really was. Maybe he had a cold.

Did vampires get colds? I made a mental note to Google that later.

I didn't turn to look at him. I was too busy feeling a tug-of-war of emotions. On one side I was wary of him after what Gideon said. On the other side I was still embarrassed about what had happened earlier with the fledgling.

Bottom line, the night had only reminded me how terrible my curse was and how desperately I wanted it to be ancient history.

If the Red Devil hadn't stopped me earlier—

A shudder ran through me at the thought.

"Who did you just visit?" he asked.

Uh oh. I'd forgotten about my new bodyguard when I'd casually sauntered into the lair of the vampire hunter.

"My aunt," I said quickly. "She's in town for a few days."

"You're lying. Tell me who you saw."

The jury was out on whether this guy was bad news or not, but he wasn't making a great second impression on me. "None of your business."

"Your safety is my business."

"Thierry must be paying you very well."

He didn't say anything for a moment. "Is *Gideon* staying here?"

Busted. The Red Devil was bossy, but insightful. I made a mental note.

I licked my dry lips nervously. I still didn't want to turn my head and meet his masked face. "Look, I know I shouldn't be here. I know it's dangerous and whatever. But it's not as bad as you think. He wanted me to pick something up for him and I did. That's all."

"You've done this before tonight as well?"

"A couple of times." I hesitated. "But there's no reason you need to tell Thierry about this. Or about what happened in the alley earlier. I don't want him to be worried."

"You keep a lot of secrets from him, do you?" His voice was cold.

I swallowed. "Unfortunately, I have to."

"I see."

"No, you don't. You don't know him. He'd take this totally the wrong way."

There was no reply.

I chanced a look over my shoulder. There was no one there anymore.

Leaving right in the middle of an awkward, unfriendly conversation? That was rather rude.

Who was that masked vamp, anyhow? I wondered as I waited at the bus stop. I planned to catch a ride back home to the small house George and I shared, even though I had yet to give him any rent money.

I wondered where the Red Devil had been hiding out for a hundred years. What made him stop helping people? What made him return? Thierry wouldn't tell me anything, but I was burning with curiosity.

Would he tell Thierry that he'd seen me leaving Gideon's hotel? I sure hoped not. I'd tell Thierry the next time I saw him. Get it out in the open and deal with his reaction then.

I'd also tell him about Gideon's bargain—the Red Devil for the grimoire. I'd originally wanted to wait until my issues with Gideon had been resolved before I dealt with the curse, but now I saw that there was no time to waste. I had to de-curse myself or somebody was going to get hurt. It was only a matter of time.

But was his nausea-inducing deal the only way to save myself? Had I completely painted myself into a corner when it came to dealing with my thirsty nightwalker?

My life had become one big sensible-footwear-owning question mark.

George wasn't home when I arrived, but someone else was.

"Twice in one night?" I said. "I'm a lucky girl."

Thierry was waiting for me inside the little house. Silently. In the dark. You know, like a regular, everyday boyfriend.

I moved toward him for a kiss, but stopped in my tracks when the look on his face registered with me. He rarely showed any emotion. I'd trained myself to read him pretty well, but even I ran into difficulties when he got all expressionless.

He wasn't expressionless at the moment. He looked angry.

"Why didn't you tell me?" he asked.

Oh, *damn*. The Red Devil was a total gossip ghoul.

Maybe he had a blog and a Facebook page, too.

"About what?" I decided to play coy even though I knew it was pointless.

"You've been seeing Gideon, but haven't mentioned it to me. I was under the impression you hadn't seen him since that first night. That you didn't have to see him again until the full moon."

I threw my purse and coat onto the sofa, trying to seem at ease when I felt anything but. "I have to see him. If I don't do what he says then he might go all homicidal and kill everyone like he threatened to, remember?"

"So he's forcing you to come to his hotel against your will?"

"No, he's not exactly *forcing* me." Damn, this was

complicated. And it was all my fault. "He actually asks politely. It's not a big deal."

"If it wasn't a big deal you would have told me about it."

"In the three or four minutes we have together these days?"

"The reason we can't be together at the moment is his threats. Or do you forget that small detail?"

"I don't forget it for a moment."

He shook his head. "Gideon is well known for his ability to charm others. Don't let him make you believe he is anything other than a killer."

"I haven't forgotten that."

"You haven't?" His brow furrowed and his hard expression finally softened. "I know you have a great capacity for compassion, Sarah. Don't let that get in the way of your better judgment."

"It's not. I wish the Red Devil hadn't told you."

"I'm glad he did." He drew closer to me and stroked his cool hand against my flushed cheek. "He told me about what happened with the fledgling as well."

I cringed. "That I went insane and almost tore her throat out?"

He shook his head. "That you tried to help her."

"And *then* I tried to tear her throat out." I hugged him tightly and inhaled the light, spicy scent of his familiar cologne.

"But you didn't."

"Only thanks to Red. Whoever he is." I looked up at him. "Are you going to tell me more about him?"

"Perhaps he will remain as much a secret as your meetings with Gideon Chase have been." There was a strange edge to his words.

I raised my eyebrows. "Don't tell me for one moment that that's jealousy I hear."

He leveled his gray gaze with my own. "I know all too well that you have a soft spot for hunters you feel you might be able to redeem."

I tensed in his arms. "Gideon isn't redeemable."

"And you mustn't ever forget that." He brushed his mouth against mine in a kiss that helped me stop thinking about all of my problems for a moment.

"Can you stay tonight?" I whispered against Thierry's lips.

"Do you want me to?"

I slid my hand under his shirt to feel his warm skin. "Very much."

A smile twitched on his lips. "Then—"

There was the sound of a key in the door and his gaze flicked to it.

"—unfortunately it will have to wait for another time." Thierry's smile faded. "Please be careful, Sarah. And please don't see Gideon again alone. It's too dangerous."

The next moment he was gone from my arms and the room.

George entered the house and looked at me standing in the dark all by myself. "Oh, hey. Feeling better?"

I sighed. "Until I was interrupted."

"Did you have fun with the mysterious *Mr. G*?" he asked and waggled his eyebrows.

I forced a smile. "So much fun they should lock me up and throw away the key."

"Well, I'd love to hear the details, but I'm exhausted. As Scarlett says, tomorrow is another day."

It was. And I wasn't entirely convinced that was a good thing.

The next morning, I felt something poke me in the shoulder and it yanked me out of a perfect, dreamless sleep. I liked perfect, dreamless sleeps. They were my favorites and very rare these days in my usual sea of nightmares. I pulled the covers off my face and glared at my intruder.

George smiled down at me. "Morning, sunshine."

"What is it?"

He had the cordless phone in his hand. "It's your friend Claire. She says it's urgent."

That jolted me the rest of the way awake. I grabbed the phone. "Claire? What's going on?"

"Sarah, I have good news. I found someone who can help you."

Claire was an old high-school friend of mine who had been present at the reunion when I'd been cursed. Since she was also a witch, she'd done her best to help, but it hadn't worked out. She left to go home to Niagara Falls with the promise she'd keep trying.

"You have no idea how happy I am to hear that." My heart was already doing a Rockette kick of joy at the thought I might not be dependent on Gideon to break my curse.

"He's a wizard and he can see you today. He's moving somewhere in Europe really soon, so you need to get your butt over to Mississauga while he's still in this country."

I jotted down the info she gave me, a phone number and directions to the place, which was twenty minutes west of Toronto. "This is fantastic. How did you find him?"

"Honestly? On Craigslist. But he's completely reputable. He specializes in breaking curses and his track record is amazing. Or so he says. The best part is he'll only charge you two thousand bucks."

My eyes widened. "That's a lot of money."

"Trust me, these kinds of things normally cost way more."

"You wouldn't happen to have two thousand dollars I can borrow, do you?"

She laughed at that. "Sorry, no. Why don't you ask your dreamboat of a boyfriend for the money? He looked like he was loaded."

I cleared my throat. "We broke up."

She actually gasped. "But you seemed perfect for each other."

"You are the only person I know of who thinks that." I glanced at George, who stood nearby with a curious expression. "We're not together anymore. I'm moving on. Know any rich master vampires you want to set me up with?"

"Don't forget *dark* and *miserable*," George added.

"Can't say that I do," Claire replied. "But maybe this wizard is single. He sounds nice enough in the e-mails we've exchanged."

"Thank you so much for this, Claire. I'll let you know how it all turns out." When I clicked off the phone I looked up at George. "Doing anything today?"

He raised his eyebrows. "Am I possibly chauffeuring your non-car-owning self somewhere?"

I nodded. "But you don't have to if you don't want to. It's only the difference between my future happiness and utter, complete misery."

He looked torn. "I have a job interview later."

"The strip club?"

"It's a nightclub with male entertainment. 'Strip club' makes it sound so tawdry."

"I've been there. It is tawdry."

"I know, isn't it great? Unfortunately I'm just interviewing to be a waiter, not the talent. I apparently have no rhythm." He sighed. "But one can dream."

I glanced at my digital clock. It was 9:00 A.M. "We'll be back by noon. At the latest."

"Promise?"

"Cross my broken, cursed heart."

"Okay, get dressed. We'll leave in ten minutes."

I felt a jolt of something. I think it was happiness. I wouldn't know. It had been a long time since I'd felt that particular emotion in such a pure and undiluted sense. I kind of liked it.

"First we have to stop by Amy's," I told him. "I need to ask her for something."

"What?"

"A loan of two thousand bucks. Unless you want to spot me the cash."

"Amy's it is," he replied quickly.

A half hour later we pulled up at the curb across from my friend's house. I tried not to get too excited at the prospect of breaking my curse but had a difficult time staying relaxed. This could be it. A substantial loan of money away from being relatively normal again.

Without wasting any time, I bounded up to her front door and rang the doorbell. George decided to wait in the car.

A few moments later the door slowly opened inward. I

gazed at the interior of Amy's small townhome and then looked down.

Barry Jordan glared up at me.

All you need to know about Barry is that he became Amy's husband after they fell in love and he sired her on their first date. He was short. *Short*, short. He had a tendency to wear small tuxedos and angry expressions, although at the moment he wore a royal-blue bathrobe and an angry expression.

He was also Thierry's . . . I guess *manservant* was as good a term as any. They'd known each other for three hundred years, since Thierry had rescued Barry from being displayed and abused in a traveling fair. This act had won Barry's fierce loyalty from that moment forward.

Oh, and Barry hated my guts with a fiery passion.

From nearly the first moment we met he thought I was trouble, an opportunist, and a gold digger. Not necessarily in that order.

I wondered if he'd be willing to loan me some cash.

"*You*," he said ominously.

"Well, hello there," I replied, deciding it was best not to provoke him in any way. Too much rode on everything going swimmingly today. "Might I speak with your lovely wife for a moment?"

"She's not here. She's getting her nails done." He glared at me with distaste. "Go away."

He was giving me the evil eye so intensely it burned a bit. It was really too bad that the moment he started to believe I was genuinely in love with Thierry I'd had to "break up" with him, thereby confirming Barry's original opinion of me.

Oh, well. Can't win 'em all.

"Who's there, Barry?" a familiar voice said, and Thierry stepped into the front foyer. Our eyes met and held.

As far as Barry knew, this was the first time we'd seen each other since we officially ended our relationship. Even Barry, who I knew wouldn't betray Thierry for any price, couldn't be trusted with this info. There was too much at risk.

I really wanted to run to Thierry and throw my arms around him and finish what we had only barely started last night. I wanted to tell him about the grimoire and the appointment with the wizard today. But I couldn't say anything out loud.

Too bad, really. He was a total ringer for the money.

I wasn't a gold digger, seriously I wasn't. But come on. The man I loved wore a different black, tailored Hugo Boss suit every single day. That had to count for something, didn't it? Other than a high-end, yet oddly monochromatic taste in clothing.

"It's nobody, master," Barry said pointedly. "And *nobody* was just leaving."

Oh, that was subtle.

I tore my eyes away from Thierry as someone else came into view. Someone wearing a red dress, with long raven-colored hair, perfectly applied makeup and flawless ivory skin.

"Sarah, my dear." A smile spread across Veronique's perfect face. She glanced at Thierry. "Is this an awkward moment?"

Why, yes it is, thank you for asking.

Thierry didn't move his gaze from mine. "Not at all. Sarah and I have chosen to go our separate ways. There is nothing to be awkward about."

"And she's leaving," Barry said again. I resisted the urge to kick him sharply and make him cry.

"I have been very curious," Veronique began. "Whose idea was it for your relationship, short as it was, to end?"

"Mine," Thierry and I said in unison. He raised a dark eyebrow at me.

"It was a mutual decision," I clarified quickly.

Veronique's impeccably arched brows drew together. "It's very strange to me. One moment you," she nodded at Thierry, "are asking me for an annulment, and you," she glanced at me, "are proclaiming your deep and earnest love for my *husband*—"

I always cringed when she used that word.

"—and the very same night your love affair ends." She tilted her head to the side. "Very strange, wouldn't you say?"

Great. All we needed was Veronique doubting our story. Talk about the beginning of the end. If there was one person I didn't trust to keep it quiet, it would be her. "Strange but true. What can I say? Can't stand him now. I'm flaky like that."

There was silence for a long, torturous moment as she inspected me as if I was a slimy but curious specimen under a microscope.

"Is it true that you've met with the Red Devil recently?" she asked.

My cheeks warmed. I guess there was no way to keep what happened a secret. It only brought back my shame at not being able to control myself. It was the reason today *had* to work out. I needed this curse gone. Even now with the gold chain firmly in place around my neck, I felt it there, lurking in the shadows of my mind, like a thick black poison waiting patiently for the perfect opportunity to take over again.

I cleared my throat. "I met with him just for a moment. It was no big deal."

"Are you certain of that?" Thierry asked.

"Yup. He's in town again and wanted to say hello."

And stop me from murdering people. And be my bodyguard. Etcetera.

I raised my eyes to look at Thierry again. He hadn't taken his focus off me. His neutral gaze betrayed a sliver of concern.

Would Veronique and Barry notice if I went directly over to him and kissed him? Wrapped my arms around him and told him how much I missed him and how I couldn't wait until this was all over?

Yeah, they'd probably notice. They were all observant like that.

"So what's going on here this morning?" I asked, wanting desperately to change the subject. "A vampire version of *The Breakfast Club*?"

"It's none of your business what we're doing," Barry replied sharply. "Like I told you earlier, Amy isn't here. Therefore there's no reason for you to be, either."

Again, I resisted the urge to kick him. "You're right."

No Amy. No money. No curse breaking.

"It is time for me to leave as well." Veronique air kissed Thierry on both cheeks and then did the same to Barry.

"Good-bye, Sarah," Thierry said evenly.

After he gave me one last deep, searching look, so deep that I actually felt it as if it were the brush of his lips against mine—I had a very good imagination—I turned and left.

The door clicked shut behind me and Veronique the moment we stepped outside, and I heard the lock turn. Barry wasn't taking any chances of me sneaking back in.

Veronique studied me intently. "One of my many talents is the ability to read people. I read you as being in love with my husband. Even now I see such longing and regret in your eyes."

At least she wasn't treating me like a complete smelly piece of garbage, as Barry had. Her demeanor toward me seemed the same as always—dismissive, but vaguely curious.

I forced a shrug. "What can I say? The man is easy on the eyes. But it doesn't change anything." I hesitated. "Besides, I'm sure there have been tons of women who've fallen for Thierry in the past, right?"

I regretted asking it as soon as the words left my mouth, feeling a stab of jealousy at the thought of other women in Thierry's life. Knowing he was married was enough of a cross to bear.

"Of course," Veronique said simply.

I swallowed. "Oh."

"However," she continued, "this annulment nonsense has never been mentioned before. I still wonder what exactly got into him to even broach that subject after so long. If I didn't know better, I would have assumed he meant for you to have a future together." She looked at me for a moment. "Are you all right, my dear? You've become rather pale suddenly."

Any mention of my future with Thierry tended to make me feel a bit woozy around the edges. That's what I wanted. Despite our multitude of problems, I wanted to be with him, and everything currently happening seemed tailor-made to keep us apart. It's like I was fighting fate itself. I never really believed in the concept before, but I'd lately come to learn that fate was one hell of a mean beeyotch.

"I'm fine. I'm just a bit distracted today." I glanced over at George's car. He'd hunched down in the seat a bit so he was mostly out of view, except for the top of his sandy-blond head and sunglass-covered eyes peering over the edge of the driver's-side window like "Kilroy Was Here." Veronique intimidated him, so avoidance was his preferred course of action.

"Distracted because of . . . your little curse, perhaps?" she asked.

Everyone knew about my problems. I guess when your problem was turning black-eyed and scary as hell, that was a given.

I nodded. "It actually has everything to do with my curse. But there's more than that on my mind, as well."

"Like the Red Devil? You truly saw him?"

"In the flesh." I nodded. "And mask."

Another glance at the car showed George was beckoning for me to wrap things up with Veronique. Time was money, after all. Money I didn't currently have. Would the wizard only see me today? When exactly was he moving out of the country? Why was nothing ever easy?

Veronique's expression lit up. "The Red Devil is magnificent, isn't he? I wonder if he's exactly the same as when he saved my life so long ago—so strong and brave and handsome."

"And dangerous?" I asked, thinking of Gideon's assessment. "And deadly?"

"All of those things." She let out a strange little sigh of

contentment. "I would assume he's a magnificent lover as well, wouldn't you agree?"

Oh, boy. I glanced at my naked wrist. "Wow, look at the time. I really need to get going."

"So many years have passed," she continued, undeterred, "I wonder if he'd still remember me? Well, of *course* he would. Perhaps we could begin again where we left off."

"I don't see why not." I took a few determined steps toward the car. Veronique was difficult to get away from once she'd started chatting about her favorite subject—herself. "In non-Red-Devil-related news, I've found somebody who might be able to remove my curse."

She reached forward and squeezed my hand. "That's wonderful, my dear. Such an unpleasant thing, curses are. I really don't recommend them."

"I totally agree."

She frowned at me. "For such good news you seem rather distraught. Is there a problem?"

I chewed my bottom lip. "Actually, there is. There's a cost associated with the curse removal. If I can't pay for it, the wizard is moving soon and I'll be out of luck. Being that I'm *el broko*, I don't really know what to do."

"How much is it?"

"Two thousand bucks."

"That sounds reasonable." She reached into her Prada bag. "Will hundred-dollar bills be acceptable?"

My eyes widened and I was about to say something to protest, but my hand jutted out as if it had a mind of its own. She counted out twenty one-hundred-dollar bills into it from the *Banque de Veronique*.

"I . . . I can't take your money," I stuttered.

She closed my hand over the wad of cash. "Of course you can. And you will. And you will rid yourself of this horrible burden once and for all."

I felt tears welling inside me. Scratch every bad thing I'd ever said or thought about Veronique, she was incredibly warm, selfless, caring, generous—

"And you will thank me by setting up a meeting between myself and the Red Devil," she said, "so we can become lovers."

—and rather *horny*, apparently.

I looked from her to the cash, and back again. Then I shoved the bills into my purse. "I'm sure you'll make a lovely couple."

"You must also find a new lover. A vampire's life can be very long and very lonely." She pressed her full red lips together for a wistful moment. "It is best to share it with someone special if you can."

"I totally agree." I looked back at Barry's house, picturing Thierry inside. So near and yet so far. "Unfortunately, love can sometimes be a bit complicated."

I noticed that Barry stood at the front window. He gave me the finger.

A half hour later I rang the doorbell at the address Claire had given me.

"This is great," George said when I glanced nervously at him. "I can finally get rid of the stun gun I carry around at all times to protect myself from your dark side."

"Very funny."

"Actually . . . I'm not joking."

I touched my gold chain. I wasn't close to relaxing about this. Not until it was done. But at least I had the money. I'd play matchmaker between Veronique and the Red Devil even though I wasn't totally sure I trusted him. It was so worth it if this worked out.

A moment later, the door opened and a young kid, probably around fourteen years old, looked out at us. He had long, stringy dark hair, and a morose expression. He wore a black T-shirt with a picture of a morose-looking, stringy-haired rock band on it.

"What?" he asked, succeeding in making the single word sound as unfriendly as possible.

I frowned and looked down at the address I'd scrawled on a yellow sticky note. "I'm looking for a Steven Kendall."

"For what?"

My jaw clenched, but I forced a smile. "A business matter. Is that your father? Can you get him for me? It's kind of urgent."

He studied me through narrowed eyes. "Are you the vampire?"

I glanced at George, then back at the kid. "Vampire?"

He rolled his eyes. "Well, are you or aren't you?"

I swallowed. "I am. But I'm a nice one, I promise."

"Depends on the day, really," George said from next to me. I elbowed him in the ribs.

The kid opened the door wider. "Come in, but we're going to have to make this quick. My mom's at the grocery store and she'll be back soon."

"And your father?"

"Last time I checked, he was dead," the kid said without any emotion. "And if he knows what's good for him, he'll stay that way."

"Okay." I blinked slowly. "So, that leads me to believe that *you're* Steven."

"I don't go by that name. You need to call me The Darkness."

"*The Darkness*," I repeated.

"That's right."

"Maybe I'll just wait in the car," George said, but I hooked my arm in his and dragged him into the bungalow. I wasn't facing "The Darkness" without him.

The wizard Claire had found was a teenager. An obviously hate-filled, Goth-boy Harry Potter.

I could deal. It would be fine. After all, it's not as though I had much of a choice in the matter. This had to work. If it didn't, my only option to break my curse was to hand the Red Devil over to Gideon and get the grimoire. But since I'd already agreed to hand him over to Veronique, his schedule was already very full.

"You have the money?" the kid asked.

I nodded.

"Then follow me." He led us down a flight of creaky stairs to a basement with wood paneling and a deer head mounted on the wall. An orange vinyl couch lined the opposite wall and a chipped imitation wood coffee table sat blandly on top of a white, retro shag throw rug. There were piles of packing boxes everywhere, a sign of The Darkness's upcoming move. Other than that, a hundred candles flickered—a fire hazard that I chose not to comment on—strategically placed leading toward a desk holding a computer tower and monitor.

"Money first," The Darkness said, holding out his hand.

I clung onto George's arm. "I'm going to be really up

front with you. I was expecting somebody older. I don't want to get scammed here."

"You have a curse." He sat down in front of the computer and tapped away on the keyboard for a moment. "I can eradicate it for you. Wipe it away completely."

I glanced at George, who shifted his feet uncomfortably, then returned my attention to the teenager, who looked over his shoulder at us. "So it's some kind of a reversal spell?"

"Not exactly."

My stomach dropped. "Then what are we doing here?"

He rolled his eyes again. "Reversal spells are unstable magic and they're not my thing. When dealing with another witch's spells or curses, I have to go deeper with my own magic."

"What exactly does that mean?" George asked.

The kid leaned back in the chair, swiveled around, and studied me, starting at my feet, up my jeans to my purple blouse. He stopped and blatantly stared at my breasts for about ten full seconds. I crossed my arms over my chest.

"Hello?" I prompted. "Earth to The Darkness."

"I get half the money now," he said. "Half when it's done. But you'll have to give the money to your friend so I can make sure I'll get it."

"What do you mean, 'make sure you'll get it'? If the spell works, then I'll pay you. Believe me, you will have earned every penny as far as I'm concerned."

He shook his head and forked his fingers through his greasy hair. "I already told you, this isn't a spell, it's an *eradication*. I have to use dark magic for this, that's why it's not cheap."

"Why is an eradication different from a spell?" George asked.

The kid glanced at his computer screen again. Even the website he had his browser set to looked creepy—skulls, caskets, black background, purple text. A laser eye surgery waiting to happen.

"I've never done one on a vampire before. I'm pretty excited about it." Excited or not, his expression didn't change from sullen. "An eradication is taking a handful of black magic, shoving it into the subject's very soul, and scooping out the curse."

I shuddered. "Sounds like a macabre trip to Baskin-Robbins."

"There will be side effects, of course."

Claire hadn't mentioned anything like that. "What kind of side effects?"

"Sit down."

"I'm not so sure about—"

"You want this curse gone, or what?" He looked annoyed with all my questions now. "Like I said, my mother is going to be back any minute, and if she catches me doing another eradication then I'm going to be grounded." He touched his rock band T-shirt. "And if I miss seeing Death Suck in concert this week I'm going to kill myself."

I sat down on the vinyl couch and it squeaked in protest. Then I handed George the money, which he folded and slid into his pocket.

"If anything goes wrong," he said. "I promise to spend this on a fabulous flower arrangement for your funeral."

"Very funny."

"Again . . . not really joking. But let's hope for the best, shall we?"

The Darkness brought a black candle over to me and he waved it slowly in front of my face, so close for a moment that I felt my eyelashes singe. I jerked back from him. Then he dragged a chair over so he was facing me.

"I need to concentrate," he announced.

"Are you going to tell me what the side effects are, or what?"

"I will," he snapped. "God, be patient, would you? Old people are so annoying."

I gritted my teeth. I would be patient with this little Emo-with-Attitude. I would. If I could get rid of my curse, I could be the most patient person in the universe. However, I felt the stress welling up inside me and ready to burst out of my chest. It took all my concentration to stay calm.

Could he do it? Could he "eradicate" my curse? A line of perspiration slipped down my spine like a waterslide at an unamusement park.

Relax, I commanded myself. *Try to stay calm and think positive thoughts.*

I strained my mind and focused on an image of Thierry in a tuxedo. And me in a big, white, expensive gown. Getting married in a big, fancy church. It was one of my favorite calming fantasies.

Ommm.

"Half the money." He stretched out a hand to George, who counted off a thousand dollars and gave it to the kid.

"Okay." The Darkness closed his eyes and then breathed out through his mouth. The scent of SpaghettiOs hit the air. "I need to concentrate. I need to allow the dark magic to fill me."

For a long, disappointing moment, I doubted this kid was anything other than a teenage scam artist. It was worth a try, but I felt that nothing would come of this. It was too easy. I appreciated Claire for trying, but this was too good to be true. I was about to stand up, grab Veronique's money back, and walk out of the house instead of wasting any more of my time.

Besides, what would Thierry say about this little situation I'd gotten myself into? It was best he never found out about this, either. Unless it worked. In which case I might throw a small party to celebrate.

The candle's flame flickered and turned blue. I inhaled sharply as the temperature in the room cooled about twenty degrees in five seconds.

The Darkness nodded slowly. "I see the price beyond money that you must pay. Performing this eradication will remove half a year of life."

A chill went through me. "Which means what?"

"The results are specific to the subject; in this case, *you*. Six months will be gone and with it everything that happened during that time. Any injuries, any illness, all of it will leave your body forever. It will still be today, but you'll be like you were then."

I looked at George as my heart slammed inside my chest. My eyes were so wide I could feel them quickly drying out. "Does that mean what I think it does?"

His eyes were just as wide. "I don't know."

I reached forward and poked The Darkness in the chest. "A lot has happened to me over the last few months."

He nodded without opening his eyes. "I can feel it. The

curse is not the only thing that will be removed. There is also the fresh vampire virus inside you."

Was this kid saying that when he eradicated the curse, I wouldn't be a vampire anymore?

The light from the candle flickered against his face. "When I eradicate the curse, you won't be a vampire anymore."

Okay. I guess that's exactly what he was saying.

Chapter 5

$\mathcal{M}$y cure. This was it.

Holy crap.

In the beginning, adjusting to vampire life was so traumatic for me that I'd latched on to the rumor that there was a cure. The journey had led me to a whole heap of trouble, but didn't result in anything but disappointment when I learned there was no real cure for vampirism. Once you were infected, that's just the way it was.

Forever fanged.

But this wasn't a cure. It was an *eradication*. A completely clean slate, an erasing of everything that had happened to me. Along with getting rid of my curse, I would become human again.

No more worrying about getting staked by an overzealous hunter. No more pointy teeth. No more drinking blood to survive.

I'd get my reflection back. I could eat solid food. I'd have the chance to live a normal life and not need to fret about finding a vampires-only club to hang out at that served my favorite blood type.

"This is great, Sarah," George said. "I know it's what you've wanted all along."

Of course it was.

This was seriously too good to be true. Which meant only one thing.

"What's the catch?" I asked.

The Darkness's eyes were still closed. "The catch?"

"I go through with this and it removes my curse and my inner vamp."

"And six months of your life."

Then it dawned on me. "My memories will be gone, won't they? Everything that's happened to me in the past six months."

"That's right."

My heart sank down to my toes. It was one thing to come here looking for the solution for my nightwalker curse. The cure for vampirism was a gift with purchase. But losing my memories of everything that had happened to me as well?

Including everyone I'd met. Everything I'd experienced. Everything that had changed me, for better or worse, into the person I was today?

And aside from that fact, if Gideon found out that I'd played deal or no deal with Goth-boy to get rid of the part of me that he was counting on to cure his own problems—*and* I no longer even remembered who he was in the first place . . .

He probably wouldn't take that news very well. Call it a hunch.

He wouldn't be trying to give me jewelry then. He'd

be following through with his threats—whether or not I remembered who he was or why he was doing it.

Rock and a hard place. My new sucktastic address.

"Listen . . . Darkness—"

"It's *The* Darkness."

"Whatever. Can we adjust this? Any way we can just lose the curse, and maybe come back later for the other stuff if I happen to have a change of heart?"

His eyes snapped open. I drew in a breath and grabbed George's hand when I saw that his eyes, even the whites, were fully dark red. I guess he really was a wizard after all. Normal eyes didn't do that. Obviously.

"You're joking, right?" he snapped.

"Uh . . . no. I'm not."

"Look, lady, this is a one-shot deal. You pay me, I do the eradication. You leave. Besides, this sort of black magic doesn't usually work in a browse-now-pay-later way. It's already assessed you. If you don't do it now, you're tainted."

"Tainted?"

"Yeah. Which means if I try this again, there's a good chance the demonic power I'm channeling might mess me up. Badly. We're talking a lobotomy and a whole lot of drooling. Even if you weren't tainted, my mom and me are moving to Germany and we're not coming back. I'm just lucky she's letting me stay to see the Death Suck concert. After that, it's all over."

"Maybe you should go for it, Sarah," George said. "What's the difference of a few memories for something this major?"

"Speak up soon." The Darkness's voice was even less

friendly than it had been before. "Because the moment this candle goes out, the deal is off."

George squeezed my hand. "You can get rid of your curse. Poof. Gone. That alone is worth it, don't you think? Don't you want to forget all this and be normal again?"

He didn't know the reason I was stalling. He thought the idea of losing my memories was my only reason for hesitating.

Every possible scenario raced through my mind like a bat out of hell. My head ached. I really wished I could think of another solution, but there wasn't one. Not today. Not tomorrow. Possibly, not ever again.

"I guess normal—" My voice sounded as strained as I felt "—doesn't live here anymore."

I blew out the candle.

The Darkness, otherwise known as the Germany-bound Death Suck fanboy Steven Kendall, pitched a hissy fit when I asked for the thousand-dollar retainer back. We left without it. George pulled his car away from the curb just as the wizard's mother drove up to the house.

That wasn't very much fun. To say the least.

I was disappointed. It was as if a piece of chocolate cake—cake that could solve all of my problems—had been dangled deliciously in front of my face a moment before I was reminded I was one of the vampires who couldn't eat solid food.

Wiping away six months of my memories was a much heavier price than two thousand dollars. At least money could be paid back.

Forget about six months. It was the last three months

that had contained some of the worst moments of my life. But they'd also had some of the best.

If I hadn't become a vampire, I wouldn't have met Thierry.

Or George.

Or Barry.

Well, at least there was one bright spot.

My cell phone vibrated, and I grabbed it out of my purse to look at the screen.

G CALLING.

The day was not looking up.

I considered letting it go to voicemail, but then with a glance at George, whose attention was firmly fixed on the Gardiner Expressway, I pressed the talk button.

"Yes?" I began.

"Did your appointment with the young wizard go well?" Gideon asked.

The hair on my arms raised. He seemed to know almost every move I made as if he had supernatural powers instead of spies. It was so unnerving. "It didn't."

"You're still cursed?"

"Afraid so."

"Who is it?" George asked, reaching over to lower the volume on the radio. "Is it Amy?"

"Nope," I told him. "Definitely not Amy."

"Amy's having a facial right now after receiving a French manicure," Gideon informed me. "At a quaint little spa slash hair salon called Studio V. She tips exactly 15 percent, in case you were wondering."

A vampires-only business probably wouldn't be thrilled to learn that somebody like Gideon had discovered it. Easily, too. Any sense of security from hunters I'd ever felt vanished. We thought our vampire clubs were remotely safe from harm?

"I can't talk," I said.

"Wouldn't want George to know about our little partnership."

"I'd hardly call it that." I swallowed as I thought about how I had left him last night in his hotel room. "So, are you feeling better today?"

"See, I *knew* you cared about me."

I gritted my teeth. "Hardly. But you were in pretty bad shape."

"I thought I was looking pretty good now, all things considered." He was quiet for a moment. "But you're right. I'm not well. If I can hold on for two more days everything will be better."

"What do you want? Or did you just call to remind me about that? Can't you leave me alone until I absolutely have to see you again?"

"If I leave you alone, you go running out of town to try to change things. Maybe if you could try behaving yourself for a few more days, then I might be inclined to give you more space." Some of the charm had left his deep voice. This was my warning. My slap on the wrist. Did he know how close I'd come to screwing up his plans?

"I *am* behaving myself."

"I know you saw Thierry this morning. I'm fairly certain we agreed that wouldn't happen."

I felt fingers of panic reach toward my heart and squeeze. "It was nothing, just a coincidence he was there. I didn't mean to see him."

"I believe you." But there was something in his voice

that made me think he *didn't* believe me. I'd made him doubt me. "Please don't let it happen again."

"Well, since you said please."

"I have to see you later. I need something from you."

"What? Witty repartee? You dialed the wrong number."

"Something else. Come to my hotel room at eight o'clock. I'll be waiting."

He hung up. I clutched the phone so tightly that my fingers were numb.

I cleared my throat. "Okay, Mom. Great to hear from you. Hope to come visit you and Dad again real soon. Bye now."

I flipped the phone closed and looked at George, who stared back at me with confusion. "That was your mom? I only heard one side, but that seemed like a strange conversation."

"You obviously don't know my mother very well."

I thought I knew what Gideon wanted. Now that he knew my search for a curse solution had fallen through, he figured I was desperate enough to give him the Red Devil in exchange for that grimoire.

He was right about that.

I didn't know the guy. Maybe he *was* evil. Maybe he did deserve to end up on the wrong side of Gideon's stake.

Then again, maybe he didn't.

That teeter-totter style of thinking wasn't going to get me de-cursed. I twisted my fingers through my chain. I needed more time to figure everything out. I'd have to put him off a bit longer. As long as I could.

*   *   *

I tried to have a nap after George dropped me at home and then went to his job interview. I couldn't sleep. No big surprise. The events of the day repeated over and over in my brain like bad Mexican food.

So I paced. And I watched TV. And I researched stuff on the Internet.

Vampires didn't get common colds. It was very good to know.

Then I tried to find out as much as I could about Gideon Chase. There was lots of information and some very flattering pictures with him and a variety of arm candy at movie premieres and fancy restaurants. He gave money to charity. He bankrolled wings of children's hospitals.

He was a freaking hero. At least, on the surface.

I had to dig a little deeper to find any references to his even being associated with the vampire-hunter organization. Most regular web surfers wouldn't pay any attention to that at all, considering 99 percent of the world was ignorant or in denial of vampires existing outside Hollywood. They might think it was just a rumor—much like my nickname of Slayer of Slayers. Or that vampires were completely fictitious. To them, Gideon Chase was simply a billionaire—a rich, handsome dude who liked to travel and have fun.

Now he was—as far as everyone in the rest of the world believed—*dead*.

And about to be resurrected as a vampire in two days, courtesy of me.

I could totally sell the film rights if I lived long enough.

Amy obviously got the message that I'd been looking for her earlier because she called me late in the afternoon wanting to meet me for coffee. Since I didn't have any plans aside from my eight o'clock meeting with Gideon, I decided to stop obsessing about my problems and meet up with her.

I dragged my butt to a place called Bodacious Bean, a local Starbucks rip-off that had a mighty fine Colombian hazelnut blend. Amy was already there, sitting at a table in the corner of the café. She had a moccaccino and a piece of banana bread in front of her.

Another vampire fact: Some vamps could eat solid food without wanting to immediately vomit out all of their internal organs. Other vamps, like me, didn't have that luxury.

Amy could eat anything she wanted. And she usually forgot that anyone might be different from her.

"Banana bread?" she offered.

I waved a hand. "No thanks."

I sat down across from her and slid my sunglasses up to the top of my head. The always busy Yonge Street was the view from the window, and it looked like your average bustling, chilly Sunday in late February.

She seemed as if she was attempting a smile, but failed. Her mouth seemed to be stuck in Downward Dog. "How are you, Sarah?"

"You sound a bit melancholy. Your manicure didn't go very well?"

"It was fine." She looked down at her airbrushed French manicure with her ring finger sporting both a ring with a tiny diamond—courtesy of Barry—and a tiny airbrushed bat on the nail itself. "Barry said you stopped by."

"I'm surprised he'd even mention it considering how much he hates my guts."

She shrugged. "I don't know why he's so cranky lately."

"Lately?"

"He said that Thierry was there when you were there and you looked extremely unhappy about that."

"He said that?" I took an awkward slurp of my coffee.

She nodded gravely and I frowned at her. What was up? She was far from her bubbly blond self today.

There was silence for a long time.

Amy let out a long, shaky sigh. "I'm worried about you."

My eyebrows raised. *"Moi?"*

She nodded. "I know you're trying to convince everybody that you're okay, but I can see that you're not. Sarah, we're friends. You can't lie to me."

This wasn't starting off very well. "I don't know what you mean. Everything's fine and dandy. Wonderful, really."

"I know that you said you were the one to break things off with Thierry, but that's not true, is it?"

I felt sick. Was I so bad a liar that I couldn't even convince Amy? I loved her to death, but she wasn't the brightest star in the sky. She normally accepted news as it was presented to her, with no questions asked. I'd told her that I'd finished things with Thierry and she'd believed it. Been happy for my break from "that miserable jerk." Those were her exact words, actually.

"Of course it's true. I broke it off."

"Then why were you over at my house earlier wanting to talk to him?"

I took a moment to visually scan our general surroundings. Since Gideon seemed to know what I was doing all the time, I was sure he had somebody spying on me right now. But who? The convincingly distracted-looking group of teenagers? The old woman with the double espresso over by the rack of overpriced, hand-painted ceramic coffee mugs? The guy with the seeing-eye dog and the chai latte? He looked shifty. For that matter, so did the dog.

"I went there to see *you*, not him," I explained. "The fact Thierry was there was coincidence only. I can't help it if your husband happens to be my ex's slave boy."

"I really don't like that term. I prefer *valet*."

"Right. Well, whatever he is, I didn't stay very long. Didn't want to intrude on whatever he, Thierry, and Veronique were meeting about."

"It had something to do with the Ring," she said. "They contacted Thierry recently."

The Ring? Very interesting and enough to near-painfully pique my interest. The Ring was the vampire council, based in California, that had representatives spread across the entire world. They'd been interested in me when my Slayer of Slayers reputation came into being.

I frowned. "I wonder what they want now?"

"It's your curse," she said matter-of-factly. "They heard about it and they wanted to know if you're a threat to life, liberty, and the vampire way."

My eyes widened. "And?"

"I know Thierry defended you. He said that the curse is a temporary condition and doesn't reflect on you overall."

My hero. "That was sweet of him."

"Although he did tell them you're extremely unpredictable at the moment."

Bad hero. "He said that?"

She shrugged. "That's what I heard."

I'd only met one member of the Ring's elders before. He'd tried to kill me. Even though he was crazy, it didn't leave me with a favorable impression of the organization.

"So that's why you wanted me to meet you here?" I asked. "I appreciate your concern, but I'm not going to freak. Thierry can handle the Ring, and as long as I have my gold chain I'm not a threat to anybody."

Yeah, as long as I keep it around my neck. Forever. A flash of the fledgling's scared, pale face came to my mind. And the tasty pulse at her throat. I dug my fingernails into the side of the table until my knuckles whitened. Then I forced myself to take a shaky sip of my coffee.

"You're still in love with him, aren't you?" she asked pointedly.

I shook my head. "Amy—"

"And he's the one who dumped *you*, isn't he? Not the other way around?"

Oh, it was pointless to try to convince her otherwise once she'd made up her mind. She might not be a Rhodes Scholar, but she was relentless. "You got me. Thierry's the one who broke things off. I was just trying to save face when I said it was me."

She looked distraught by my false admission. "I knew it."

"I'm doing what I can. It's over. It hurts like hell but I'm trying very hard to accept it."

I had lied so much lately that I was honestly surprised my pants weren't literally made of fire.

"Barry did say he couldn't believe you would be the one to walk away."

"I just bet he did." I refrained from rolling my eyes. "So,

just relax. It's no big deal, okay? I'm fine. I'm accepting the way things are slowly but surely."

"He left you just when things were really difficult . . . with your curse." Her expression tensed. "I always knew he was a selfish jerk. First, cheating on his wife with you—"

I cringed at that. "I wouldn't exactly call it cheating when Veronique knew and was fine with everything."

"Still." Tears were actually welling in her eyes. "Oh, Sarah, I don't want to tell you this, but I have to."

I leaned over the table and grabbed her hand. "Oh, my God. Amy, what is it? What's wrong?"

"I . . . I saw Thierry an hour ago in a restaurant down the street. In fact, he might even still be there. That's why I called you."

"Well, that is shocking considering that he doesn't eat anything."

She shook her head. "He was having drinks with somebody. When I saw who it was—I was so shocked. I never would have guessed it for a million dollars. Sarah—" She let out a shuddery sigh. "I think Thierry may have been having an affair on you while he was having an affair on his wife. He's a two-timing two-timer!"

My eye began to twitch. "What are you talking about?"

"I wasn't going to tell you but it's important that you know this. It just proves that he's a supreme creep and not good enough for you."

"You're saying that you saw him having drinks with another woman?"

She nodded gravely.

"And it wasn't Veronique."

She shook her head gravely.

I cleared my throat. "And it seemed as though they were *together* together. Not just having drinks, but romantically."

Another grave nod.

"What exactly led you to that conclusion?" I asked stiffly.

She reached into her bag and pulled out her cell phone. "I have proof."

"You took pictures of him?"

"I'm thinking about getting my private investigator license." She brightened slightly. "I think I might be good at catching good-for-nothing men in the act of adultery. And I hear there's some great money to be made in that field."

I wasn't sure why I found it hard to believe. She regularly sent me pics from clothing store change rooms to get my opinion on new outfits. Why would this be any different?

"You don't have to look if you don't want to. I mean, you have gone your separate ways. I just wanted to show you that he's a cad. An absolute *cad*, considering who he's taken up with. And if you're still upset about your breakup, you shouldn't be."

I didn't believe a word. Especially when that word was as outdated as "cad." Thierry wouldn't do this, would he? No. Of course not. We might not agree on absolutely everything—to say the least—but he loved me. We'd been through too much together for him to casually start a new relationship in the midst of this mega crisis in our lives. I trusted him with every fiber in my being.

Sarah + Thierry.

True love forever.

But, still. It wouldn't hurt to have a quick look.

"Show me," I said tightly.

She scrolled through the menu and then handed me the phone. I stared down at the first picture, then went to the next. Then the next. And the next.

Thierry was having drinks inside an upscale restaurant, right near the window, which was why Amy got some good shots.

There was a picture of Thierry laughing.

Uh. *Laughing?* That was *so* unlike him.

Another of him reaching across the table to take his companion's hand.

Another of him . . . *kissing* . . . her . . . hand.

My jaw clenched.

Another had him actually leaning across the table . . . and . . . *kissing* . . . *her* . . . *on* . . . *the* . . . *mouth.*

My vision went a bit red at that one and my heart slammed against my rib cage.

The woman was smiling widely, obviously enjoying herself. One photo showed a clear shot of her face as she glanced out the window.

"Can you believe it?" Amy said breathlessly. "I thought she was engaged to be married. That skank! That sneaky blond skank ho!"

I recognized her immediately. There was absolutely no doubt who Thierry appeared to be blatantly romancing in the pictures.

"It's Janie Parker," Amy said with obvious disgust and outrage. "Can you effing believe it?"

I couldn't. I really effing couldn't.

Janie had recently been my bodyguard, hired to protect

me from hunters due to my unfortunate and false reputation. In the end, I learned she'd been lying about who she was, and that she was actually a freelance mercenary who wanted revenge on me for killing her crazy hunter brother in self-defense—which is where my Slayer of Slayers rep had originated.

She'd redeemed herself by saving my butt in the end, but we definitely weren't BFFs. The last I'd heard, she was engaged to another friend of mine, Quinn, after a superfast romance that took even me by surprise.

Quinn used to be a vampire hunter, but he'd been turned into a vampire and had had a very difficult time dealing with that transition. To put it extremely mildly. I considered him a very good friend, although he'd originally wanted more from me than friendship. I tell you, if I hadn't fallen hard for Thierry, Quinn would have *gotten* more. Even though as a hunter he'd tried to kill me a couple of times, he was a good guy. And damn hot, too.

He'd left town. Janie had left town. And I heard that they'd hooked up, which surprised me on many levels. The last I'd heard, they were going to come back here to get married.

By the look of Janie macking on my man, I'd say those plans were canceled.

I was going to kill her. And him. Not necessarily in that order.

But, no. *No.* There had to be more to this.

Thierry had suggested "seeing other people for appearance's sake" last night, hadn't he? How it would help to convince Gideon that there was nothing between us anymore and that I'd definitely followed through with his explicit order for us to break up.

If there was one thing I didn't have the time or patience for at the moment, it was being part of some lame vampire soap opera in the making. But I had started thinking that dating others might throw Gideon off our scent, so to speak.

I wondered if the pictures of him and Janie had anything to do with making everyone think we were definitely seeing other people. But if Janie was with Thierry right now, then I wondered where—

"Hey, Sarah," a male voice over my left shoulder said. "I've been looking everywhere for you."

I recognized that voice. And so did Amy. She looked past me with a shocked expression, which slowly turned into a wide and bright smile before her gaze moved to me again.

"You sneaky little devil," she exclaimed. "Of course! This all makes sense now. Why didn't you tell me you were back together? This is so wonderful!"

A man slid into the seat next to me. "Sarah likes to keep her secrets, doesn't she? But yeah, Amy, we're together and never been happier. Make sure you tell absolutely everybody you know, okay?"

She was already keying in a text message on her cell phone. "Way ahead of you. George is going to go ballistic when he hears about this. *Ballistic!*"

I slowly turned to look at Quinn. The shock at seeing him again out of the blue like this was enough to knock me completely speechless.

Chapter 6

Quinn looked exactly the same as the last time I saw him, which, since it was only a month ago, wasn't surprising. He had dark blond hair, vivid blue eyes, and a very attractive boyish charm about him even though I knew he was now forever thirty. He dressed casually in faded blue jeans and under a black leather winter jacket he wore a green T-shirt that fit his muscular frame perfectly.

I was used to seeing him rather unhappy and angsty, but today he had a smile on his face wide enough to partially reveal his fangs.

"You look gorgeous, Sarah," he said, and then before I could say a word in reply or greeting, he leaned forward to kiss me.

My eyes widened and I heard a clicking sound as Amy took our picture.

He looked at her. "Good to see you, too, Amy."

"Ditto." She was beaming. "You have no idea how happy I am right now. I always thought you and Sarah were perfect together. I was totally on Team Quinn. It's good to see she finally clued in to who her real Mr. Right is."

"You're obviously very savvy when it comes to love," he told her. "That's definitely what I like most about you."

"When I heard that you were getting married to Janie—"

He waved a hand. "Rumors."

Her forehead creased. "But you told me yourself. When you called a couple weeks ago, remember?"

"Oh, right." He coughed. "Uh . . . let's just say that Janie and I had a change of heart. It happens. No hard feelings on either of our parts."

"Awesome." She slid the phone back into her bag. "Well, somebody's feeling like a third wheel. I'm going to take off and leave you two lovebirds to it."

"Um . . ." I began awkwardly. "Wait a minute, Amy—"

Quinn reached down to take my hand in his and he squeezed it. "We'll see you later, Amy. Thanks for taking care of my angel while I've been gone."

She grinned. "No problem!"

She left with a few more excited glances over her shoulder at the two of us.

"She's sweet," Quinn said after she'd left the café completely. "A natural blond, right? You should probably keep an eye on her in the future. Wouldn't want her to hurt herself."

"Quinn—"

"Come on." He stood up. "Let's go for a romantic walk outside, shall we?"

"But, Quinn—"

He squeezed my hand again and this time it actually hurt.

Okay, I got it. *Shut up, Sarah.*

We left the coffee shop and walked slowly down the street, hand in hand. I eyed him from the corner of my dark sunglasses. "Okay, what's going on?"

"Not here," he whispered, then picked up his pace. "Somebody might be following us. All you need to know is that we've started seeing each other again and all is well with the world."

"Who contacted you?"

"Who do you think?"

Thierry, of course. Instead of being impressed by his planning skills, the thought that he'd done something like this without even giving me a heads-up kind of pissed me off. That man kept too many secrets from me—about the Red Devil and now this with Quinn and Janie that Amy had to tell me about like a fanged Nancy-Drew-in-training.

"I never knew how much I adored you until I left," he said loud enough for anyone we passed on the sidewalk to hear. "I've traveled all over. Arizona, Las Vegas, Florida. I was in New York before I came back here. But you are the ray of sunshine in my dark, dark life that led me back to you."

"Spreading it on a bit thick, aren't you?" I couldn't help but smile a little despite my current annoyance at Thierry. I really did like Quinn a whole lot. When he'd left I thought that he hated me, even though he said he didn't, and that I'd never see him again. We'd been through a lot together with the whole vampire-fledglings-united thing. He'd be another aspect of my vampire life I would have forgotten if The Darkness had performed that curse eradication.

We turned a corner and his cheery smile faded at the edges as he glanced over his shoulder. "Okay, I think we're clear. Thierry contacted me."

"I find that hard to believe, but go on."

He snorted. "Yeah, I know. We're not exactly poker buddies, are we? Anyhow, he explained the situation. Shit, Sarah. I feel like I'm to blame here. I'm the one who told you all that Gideon was dead."

"He's not."

"Obviously. He's like a cockroach; he can survive anything. The man is dangerous. Even more now that he's desperate."

My cheeks felt tense as I tried to smile. "And now you're supposed to pretend to be dating me. What a great way to deal with a desperate killer like Gideon."

He shrugged. "You don't know Gideon like I do. We were friends ten years ago until I realized he was a complete sociopath. Don't underestimate him for a moment."

"I don't." I frowned hard. "So you don't think there's any part of Gideon that can be reasoned with? Some part of him that still has a chance of being redeemed?"

"He kills vampires."

"So did you and you turned out okay in the end."

He grimaced. "I never took pleasure in it like he does."

I'd helped Quinn. In fact, I'd helped him when I probably shouldn't have, back when he thought I wasn't any better than a mosquito that needed to be squashed. It had taken him a while to realize he didn't feel any different as a vampire than he did when he was human. He saw what he'd done in the past was wrong. He was a hunter who wasn't truly evil.

Now Gideon was going to become a vampire—if all went according to his master plan. Would he see the light? Was it possible that he wasn't completely evil? That there was a kernel of goodness somewhere inside him?

Hey, you never know.

"Thierry also told me about your curse," he said in a near whisper and glanced at me sideways. We began to walk again. A few average, harmless pedestrians—at least that's what they looked like—moved past us going in the opposite direction. "And he thinks it's a good idea for me to be around just in case."

My stomach lurched at that. "Just in case what?"

"Just in case the Ring sends somebody to investigate you. And by investigate, I mean *eliminate*. Consider me a layer of added protection at the moment."

I swallowed hard. One more thing to obsess about.

"What about Janie?" I asked quietly.

"She's willing to help out, as well."

I raised an eyebrow. "I saw a picture of her kissing Thierry."

His jaw clenched and his expression darkened. "Maybe I'll kill Thierry just for old times' sake. I'm sure I still have a sharp stake lying around somewhere."

"So it's true? You and her are together?"

He was silent for a moment. "Unless she decides she prefers ancient humorless vampires with zero personality, like some women I know." He glanced at me and gave me a slight grin. "Yeah, we're together."

"You have strange taste in women."

"You have strange taste in men."

"Touché."

He laughed at that. "I know it might seem crazy, but I love her. Completely. And I want to spend the rest of my life with her."

"But she's human. Won't that be kind of awkward when she's eighty and you look exactly the same as you do today?"

"She's . . . well, she's not exactly human anymore. She's a vampire, too." He took a deep breath and let it out slowly. "Long story, okay? Life or death situations call for rash decisions."

I tried to keep the shock off my face. Everybody seemed to want to become a vampire lately. Were vampires the new black? The old black? We were in fashion? Maybe being a vampire was cool and desirable.

Sure, I believed it. If I was still as naïve as Amy. I kind of wished I was.

I let out a long breath. "I'm sure Janie probably wasn't too thrilled with the idea of you pretending to be with me."

"She said something about slicing you open and eating your heart if you touch even one square inch of my body."

My eyebrows shot up.

"She was kidding, of course. Well, *mostly*." Then his eyes narrowed as he looked farther up the block. "Speak of the devil."

We'd turned a corner that brought us back onto Yonge Street. We'd walked around the block during our rushed and half-mumbled conversation. Up ahead I saw two very familiar vampires leaving the upscale restaurant they'd allegedly spent a good chunk of the afternoon at—the site of Amy's earlier stakeout. Quinn slid his arm around my waist as we approached.

Thierry narrowed his gaze at Quinn, and then at me. "What a coincidence. Sarah, a pleasure as always."

His words were warm, but his expression was not. In fact, it was subzero.

For that matter, so was mine. Half of me was happy to see him. The other half wanted to give him the cold shoulder for not being forthcoming with the info. *Any* info.

So annoying.

And yet I was supposed to just go along with everything and keep a smile on my face.

"Thierry," I said, not trying to sound the least bit pleasant. "I see you have a new friend."

"Old friend." He took Janie's hand in his and kissed it.

I felt my cheeks heat up and forced myself to relax and play along. *For now.*

Janie's gaze fell on me like a death ray. "Great to see you again, Sarah."

"Likewise," I said tightly.

"What an ugly necklace," she said. "But I guess you don't have much of a choice in accessories these days, do you?"

I touched my gold chain. "Bite me." I glared at Thierry. "You, too."

His dark eyebrows went up at that. "Is that an invitation or are you trying to be rude?"

"Let's try door number two," I said.

I could tell that amused him. Super. I should charge admission for my afternoon comedy show.

Janie smiled thinly. "Geez, I was just kidding. Somebody's not as lighthearted about life as they used to be."

"Somebody's roots are darker than they used to be."

She touched her hair. "Take that back."

I tried to control my inner bitch. It was like my night-walker was poking around in her cage, growling, and trying to find a way out while I still wore the gold chain.

"You know, Janie, I never would have thought Thierry was your type," I said. A couple emerged from the restaurant and crossed between us to get into a cab. When they pulled away from the curb, I continued. "I mean, the last time I saw you two together you had him handcuffed and were going to stake him."

She leaned against his tall, solid form. "No more stakes in our relationship. But the handcuffs are always fun to have around."

I dug my fingernails deeply into Quinn's side.

Quinn cringed and cleared his throat. "We should probably get going."

Janie's expression softened when they looked at each other and I felt like they shared an unspoken moment. "Wouldn't want to keep you and your new girlfriend from . . . whatever it is that Sarah does with her unemployed free time."

"Tons of sex," I said. "And maybe a movie later if Quinn's not too tired. You know, from *all the sex*."

"Right. Well, likewise," she said curtly, hanging tighter to Thierry's arm.

Well, this was uncomfortable.

"Bye now," I said, as we brushed past them. Thierry reached out and grabbed my hand in his. His touch made my heart thump wildly.

"It was very nice to see you again, Sarah," he said. I could have sworn I saw some regret slide behind his silver-colored eyes. Did he know why I was peeved? It must have been written all over my face. Luckily it just would have looked as if I didn't want to be anywhere near him—a believable reaction to being faced with one's ex.

Our fingers brushed against each other as he let go of me.

I blinked and nodded, fighting the sudden lump in my throat.

I finally managed to tear my gaze away from his. Thierry briefly eyed Quinn and, despite the fact he was the one to ask the ex-hunter to help out, there wasn't an ounce of friendliness in the look.

Quinn and I started to walk away down the street.

"That wasn't a lot of fun," Quinn said. "And now I even have to turn down the tons-of-sex suggestion since I'm a one-woman kind of guy."

"Then it's good that I was kidding." I turned back to see Thierry and Janie moving in the opposite direction. Thierry glanced briefly over his shoulder at us, his expression still tight.

I was glad that seeing me with Quinn seemed to still bother him. Call me petty.

Quinn smiled. "Honestly, Sarah, back when I was all fixated on you I didn't think there would be another woman for me. But Janie slammed head-first into my life at the completely wrong time. I couldn't have been less interested in starting a new relationship, but it's like fate intervened to let me know she was the one."

"Yeah, she seems like a real sweet girl." Sarcasm at no extra charge.

"She actually is. But she can hide it when she wants

to." He was quiet for a moment. "Thierry told me the Red Devil's back and he's keeping an eye on you as well."

I sighed. "So many people are watching me I feel like I'm starring in a reality TV show."

"It won't be long before everything's back to normal."

"Except for my nightwalker curse and the fact that I've sired Gideon to become a super vamp."

"Except for that, yeah." He actually laughed. "You're a magnet for trouble. Anybody ever tell you that?"

"It's a gift." It *was* a bit funny, actually. If I turned my head to the side and squinted—*and* if this was all happening to someone else—I guessed I could see the humor. "So is there an actual plan you and Thierry discussed that I should be aware of or is everyone just planning to run around the city all helter-skelter?"

Quinn pulled me off the main sidewalk and away from the growing crowd so we could speak in virtual privacy. "Gideon has to die. After we're sure who his assassins are and that everyone is safe."

I don't know why that surprised me. "And who's planning to pull the trigger? You?"

He shook his head. "Thierry's given that job to the Red Devil, or whoever the guy actually is. He loves you, Sarah. I know I doubted that in the past. Hell, I didn't think there was actually a living, breathing person behind that miserable prick exterior—" he grinned "—no offense."

"We can agree to disagree about each other's significant other."

"It's a deal."

"Do you think the Red Devil is trustworthy?" I asked. "Don't you think he's dangerous? I mean, where's he been for a hundred years?"

"No idea. But Thierry seems confident in his abilities. That has to count for something, doesn't it?"

"I guess."

It seemed fair, actually. Gideon wanted to kill the Red Devil. Now the Red Devil was going to kill Gideon.

Then why did it feel so wrong?

Did I think this story was going to have a happy ending for everyone involved? Not very likely, was it?

I crossed my arms. "So you condone killing Gideon in cold blood?"

Quinn cast a wary glance at our surroundings and pulled me closer to him as if we actually were going out and he couldn't keep his hands off me. His voice dropped even lower in volume so I had to strain to hear him. "What is this, Sarah?"

"What do you mean?"

"The man is a murderer. You're not going soft on him, are you? Because that would be a huge mistake."

"Of course I'm not."

"Thierry says you've seen him a few times at his hotel."

"Thierry seems a lot chattier with you than he has been with me lately." I crossed my arms. "But it's true. What am I supposed to do? Say no? In fact, I'm seeing him again tonight."

"Why?"

"Maybe he can't get pizza delivery where he is. I don't know. Are you going to stop me from going?"

"No." Any humor left his expression. "But I know it's in your nature to see the good in people. It's an asset, but it can also get you in serious trouble. Like now."

"I saw the good in you, didn't I?"

"That was different." His expression was tense. "I don't know what he's said to you or how he might act, but he is a vicious killer. Remember that."

"I can handle Gideon."

"Gideon thinks vampires are a lesser form of life that needs killing. I don't give a shit if he's proclaimed his desire to become one to everyone he knows or if he likes to flash that billion-dollar smile at you. He's dangerous. And because you're a vampire he thinks you're disposable. Don't ever forget that."

I flashed back to a cold, dark warehouse. Pictures of my friends and family laid out on a table to show me he knew where everyone lived. His cold, desperate warning in my ear.

"I will kill them all."

Since that night, I hadn't seen that particular side of Gideon again. He'd either been amiable and happy to see me when I came to his hotel room or he'd been wracked with pain and suffering.

But I couldn't forget what he really was. What he could do.

I swallowed. "I won't forget."

He leaned forward and kissed me on the cheek. "Just be careful. And also be careful if you see the Red Devil again. Not sure I trust him as far as I can throw him, either."

"Me neither. You don't have any idea who he really is, do you?"

He shook his head. "All I know is I wouldn't want to be Gideon right now."

I chewed my bottom lip. "If Gideon dies, he'll go to hell. The hellfire will drag him there."

"Gideon was bound for hell anyhow after everything he's done in life. Don't lose any sleep over him, Sarah."

"I won't."

And I wouldn't. I hated Gideon. He deserved to die.

If that was the case, then why did the idea of leading him to that fate make me feel a bit sick inside?

Quinn was right. I *was* a softy. Like a wimpy marsh-mallow.

I wouldn't think of Gideon as anything more than an unrepentant serial killer. He wasn't Quinn, who'd changed his ways, and he wasn't Thierry, who'd had his own share of darkness to deal with in his long, immortal life.

I had to remember that. There was way too much at risk if I forgot.

Chapter 7

I was as tense and jittery by the time I arrived at Gideon's hotel room as if I'd been mainlining double espressos all day. Thierry would be upset if he knew I was there again. I also knew he would likely find out due to my potential tattletale tag team of Quinn and the Red Devil.

But there I was.

I'd deal with the aftermath in due course.

Gideon sat, waiting for me, in the same chair he'd been in last night. His glamour held up well—I still couldn't see any scars marring that undeniably handsome face of his. The scars were still there, of course, but now they were hidden by magic. He wasn't dressed for company, however. He wore only the bottoms of loose pajamas, and his toned chest was bare.

On the table next to him I couldn't help noticing a dagger with a curved blade.

He hadn't said anything since I'd entered his room. He simply stared at me from where he was seated.

It made me more uncomfortable than I was to start with. Which was saying something.

"Is it nice out?" he asked after a long moment went by.

"Nice?" I repeated. "What do you mean?"

"I noticed it was sunny earlier. I didn't go outside today."

Small talk about weather with the deadliest man I'd ever known. Sure. Why not? "It was fine. Not too cold."

"The sun doesn't bother you at all as a vampire?"

I shook my head. "Not really. It's a bit glary, like if you forget your sunglasses and you're driving into the sun, and prolonged exposure makes me feel like taking a long nap, but it's not too bad."

"And when you're a nightwalker?"

I swallowed. "Then I do my impression of the Wicked Witch of the West and melt into a puddle of death."

"That doesn't sound pleasant."

No, it didn't. And that's why I needed the witch's grimoire he mentioned. Badly. The teenaged wizard didn't give me the impression he was likely to attempt the eradication again, even if I agreed to give up a half year's worth of memories. I think he mentioned something about needing a lobotomy if he tried. But how was I supposed to get the grimoire without selling out my current enigmatic bodyguard? Whether he deserved my loyalty was up for debate, but there had to be a way for me to get the grimoire and yet also avoid being an accessory to murder.

Although that particular decision was subject to change without notice. The threat of turning into a death puddle was a strong motivating force.

I took a good look at the leader of the vampire hunters.

"I hope you don't mind me saying, Gideon, but even with the glamour spell, you look like hell."

He held on to the chair arms so tightly that his muscles flexed. His skin was sickly white and there was a fine sheen of sweat on his forehead. "That's a very appropriate word to use for the way I'm feeling."

"Are you in pain right now?"

"Ever since I was touched by the hellfire I'm constantly in varying degrees of pain. Today it's worse than ever before."

I couldn't help but cringe at Gideon's obvious distress. As Quinn had reminded me earlier, I was basically a vampire-shaped Peep.

Suck it up, marshmallow girl, I told myself. *This is the man who threatened to kill everyone you love if you say or do the wrong thing. Never forget that.*

I *wouldn't* forget.

"I need something from you," he said through clenched teeth.

"What?"

"Come here."

My eyes flicked again to the dagger next to him as I tentatively approached. "What's that for? Whittling stakes? I met a hunter who said that was a hobby of his."

"I need some of your blood. Now. It can't wait."

That surprised me. "But the ritual—"

He drew in a shaky breath and raised his green eyes to meet mine. "The ritual will go on as scheduled. This . . . this is different. The research I've done on your unique blood makes me think it may help to ease my pain. If I can have some of it now—it may help me to think straight. The pain . . . it's destroying me. Please, Sarah . . . *help me*."

So what flowed in my veins was a magical elixir that healed all ailments? I'd been looking for a new job. Now I knew what it was. I'd charge people big bucks to suck my blood.

Gideon wanted me to ease his pain. He was relying on me. I could work with that.

"I'll help you," I said. "But first I need you to promise that everybody I know will be safe. No assassins, no spies. I want all of them called off."

"No."

My eyes narrowed. "Just no? Not even a negotiation?"

"Ask for something else. Anything else."

"The grimoire."

He shook his head. "The grimoire is payment for information leading me to the Red Devil. Ask me for money, gifts—furs, diamonds, anything. I can give you whatever you want."

"I don't want gifts." I stood firm. "Lose the assassins or give me the grimoire and I'll help you out."

His strained expression flinched. "Then what assurance do I have that you'll go through with the ritual?"

"You'll have my word."

He glared at me for a moment. "I can't do that."

"Don't you trust me?"

"No, I don't."

"That stings, Gideon. Really. I thought we were friends."

He managed to laugh a little. "Sure you did."

I crossed my arms. "Okay, I didn't. But you've been trying real hard to convince me you're a nice guy."

"Not buying it?"

"I don't buy anything from the Chase boutique. I don't like the return policy."

His lips twitched a little. "You're the first woman in the world able to resist me."

"Even when you're in agony you're still full of yourself." I rolled my eyes. "No, I'm able to resist you, Gideon, because I know what you are. And I know what I am. Hunters kill vampires, in case you've momentarily forgotten."

"I haven't forgotten anything."

I shook my head. "Why should I help you if you're not willing to do anything for me in return? Doesn't sound like a very fair trade-off."

He raised an eyebrow. "Well, there is that matter of those handy assassins I have only a phone call away. Do you think I won't follow through with my threats?"

My eyes narrowed. "Oh, believe me, I don't underestimate you. I know exactly who you are. I've done my research."

"And who am I?"

"You're a murderer. Why would I ever help somebody like you out of the kindness of my heart? You have to threaten me or you'd never get what you want."

"You're absolutely right," he said quietly.

"I've met a lot of hunters in the past three months and I have to say, a lot of them are dumber than a box of hair. But you're not stupid. I can't imagine that you're convinced that vampires as a whole deserve to die. They're people. They can think, they can cry, make jokes, make love; they have lives and jobs and marriages—and just because they're a little different you feel justified in killing them. You know what you do is wrong and yet you do it anyhow."

When he didn't answer, I paced to the other side of the room and then came back to stand in front of him. "Even with all your women, money, and power, are you *that* dead inside, Gideon? That must be it. Forget the hellfire. You're already dead and killing vampires must be the only thing that makes you feel alive."

Okay, that was a way longer speech than I was planning. I should go into politics, maybe. But it wasn't every day that a mere fledgling like yours truly got to face off against the leader of the hunters and say what's on her mind.

I guess my half a semester of psychology in university had paid off after all. Maybe Gideon was devastatingly handsome and popular with the bimbos at one time; maybe he had a ton of power and hunters across the world looked up to him, and his father, and his grandfather before him. But he was just an empty candy wrapper that happened to look like a man. I felt strangely sorry for him suddenly.

Gideon stared at me, still and silent. The only thing that showed he was still alive was the constant flicker of pain in his eyes.

I waited for a response, afraid that I'd stepped over the line, but pissed off enough that I didn't really care.

"You're not the first female vampire I've spent time with," he said. "A while ago I met another one. She was beautiful and strong and deadly. I was going to kill her but she seduced me instead. The sex was great, some of the best I ever had, but I knew she was only doing it to save her own skin. She was an opportunist. Totally self-absorbed. Willing to do anything it took to ensure her own survival. When I woke up the next morning she was gone."

I licked my very dry lips. "You should write that story up and send it to Letters at *Penthouse*. I'm sure they'd love it."

His gaze remained fixed on me. "For a moment during our tryst I considered her more than a vampire, more than what I'd always thought of as a monster. I thought of her as a woman. If she'd been there when I woke up I don't think I would have killed her. I felt changed inside. Something was different. But her absence made that sensation easy to forget. Ever since, there's always been that kernel there in the back of my mind that agrees wholeheartedly with your assessment of me. That I am the monster. Not her. Not *you*."

"Wow, she must have been really great in the sack." I said it lightly, but my throat felt thick from hearing that he'd come an inch away from changing his evil ways. "However, you did go back to business as usual, didn't you?"

"I did. I can't deny that. And it's true what you said. Hunting made me feel whole. It gave me purpose when otherwise there was none. But—" his brow furrowed. "—now I'm on the brink of becoming a vampire, myself. Of my own free will—"

"Not that you have much of a choice."

"No, but the thought of becoming the thing I've always hunted doesn't fill me with fear or apprehension. It fills me with hope. I don't want to go back to what I was. I want to be different. I want to change. And when I do, maybe I can change other hunters' views on vampires."

A chill went down my arms. I shook my head, not wanting to believe him. "You're lying to me right now, aren't you?"

"I'm not." He blinked. "Help me, Sarah. Please give me some of your blood tonight. It might not even work, but you're the only one who can stop this pain right now."

I couldn't process what he'd said. It was too incredible. Gideon wanted to be different? He wanted to change things?

"Dammit," I said under my breath when I saw him shudder again as a wave of agony swept through him. His chest hitched.

Fine. The Sarah Happy Hour was officially open for business—even though he'd given me nothing in return but words.

I didn't even feel the blade as I slid it over my forearm. Okay, that was a lie. It stung like a son of a bitch, but it did help that I was currently quite numb from hearing Gideon's tales from the dark side.

Then I presented my arm to him. "Cheers."

He studied it for a moment as if surprised I'd actually agreed to be his nightcap. The line of red welled up where I'd made the cut. He finally brought my arm up to his mouth.

Since he didn't have a natural thirst for blood, still being human and all, he didn't slurp greedily at the wound as a hungry vampire would. Instead, I felt the warm touch of his mouth, tentative at first, as he tasted me.

I felt awkward and more than a little bit scared by our proximity as he drank deeper. He didn't let go of me. In fact, his grip became stronger.

After a minute he looked up at me with surprise. "I think it's working. The pain is lessening."

"I'm a walking, talking cure-all for demonic injuries."

"You are." He smiled and lowered his mouth to my arm again.

I felt something stir deep inside me from the sensation of his tongue sliding against my skin. It disturbed me a million times more than anything else that night.

Gideon is not Quinn, I sternly reminded myself. *He's evil. No matter what he tries to make you believe, it doesn't change anything. It's only words.*

And he wasn't Thierry. I loved Thierry. No matter how frustrated I got with his stubborn and secretive nature, it didn't change the fact that I wanted to be with him. That's why I did what Gideon wanted. To make sure everything went smoothly. That everything turned out okay in the end.

Gideon had my arm so tightly in his grip that I had to brace myself against his chair as he continued to drink.

He made a strange sound, like a sigh of relief. "It's the first time since the accident that the pain is completely gone."

He rose to his feet in front of me with renewed strength. His hands moved around to the small of my back and he pulled me up against him. I braced my hand against his chest.

"I think the bar is closed," I said.

"Then I should probably settle my tab."

He moved his mouth down to nuzzle at my neck, his hands moving lower to skim along my waist and hips.

"Gideon, stop—"

And then, suddenly, he was kissing me.

Gideon Chase was *kissing me*.

This was *so* not good.

Even less good was the fact that I was kissing him back.

But only for a second.

I pushed at him using every ounce of my vampire strength. It was more than enough to force him away from me.

I wiped at my mouth with the back of my hand. "That wasn't on the menu."

"I haven't felt so well in some time. I couldn't help myself." He smiled widely at me, showing off his perfect white teeth. "And I *knew* you liked me, despite everything. You can't deny it anymore, can you? I think we could be very good friends if you let yourself."

"Think again."

"I'm going to be a vampire very soon and you'll be my sire. That brings with it a very special bond, doesn't it?"

My cheeks felt like they were on fire. "Not the kind of bondage you're thinking of. I think this little meeting is over. I'm leaving." I turned toward the door.

He easily cut me off and blocked my exit. "Stay with me."

"I don't think so." I reached past him for the doorknob.

He grabbed my wrist. Above it, the wound had already begun to heal. "I know that you and Quinn are involved again. I was informed you were seen with him earlier today."

News did travel fast. It must have been the man with the suspicious-looking seeing-eye dog in the café. I knew it. "So what if I am?"

He shifted his grip to take my hand in his and entwined his fingers with mine. "Forget him." He leaned in to whisper against my lips. "And forget Thierry. Stay with me tonight. I want you."

He kissed me again. But he'd succeeded in putting the thought of Thierry firmly in my head and a wave of guilt swept over me. What was I still doing here?

I pushed at him, but he only deepened the kiss and slid his tongue into my mouth. I bit it. A small nip wasn't enough to transfer any of my trusty vamp virus to him but it did manage to get him to jerk back from me. He held a hand to his mouth.

"Don't try that again," I said darkly.

His eyes narrowed and he grabbed my arm tight enough to hurt. "I usually take what I want when I want it."

"I'll remember that if I have to fill out a police report." I shook my head. "See? I knew the real Gideon was in there somewhere under that nice shiny surface."

He raised an eyebrow. "And yet you can't seem to stay away from me, can you? And you willingly kissed me before. Don't try to deny it."

My stomach sank. "I won't deny it. But listen to me, Gideon. I don't care what you say to me or what you try to make me believe, the only reason I'm doing what you want me to do is that you're forcing me to. You threatened my friends. You're holding the grimoire as ransom to use against me."

"I do regret having to use such extreme measures, but I was very desperate for you to agree to what I need from you. I promise to make it up to you one day. Rethink staying with me tonight. We could explore if we have anything more between us than our many differences." He slid his hand down my back to the small of my spine.

I shook my head. "Goodnight, Gideon. This meeting is over."

His expression darkened and his grip on me tightened for a moment before he let me go. "Until next time."

I opened the door and walked out of his suite without looking back, feeling completely and totally shaken.

I was in deep shit.

Let me repeat that: *Deep. Shit.*

What the hell had just happened? I'd been so in control when I got there. Totally. Then he was dealing with the pain, we talked about what a psychopath he was for a while, his story had made me think he might have a redemptive bone in his body buried down somewhere deep, I'd given him some of my blood . . . and then I'd kissed him.

Or, rather, he'd kissed me.

Semantics. Kissing had occurred.

I hated him. I did.

Or, at least, I tried to convince myself of that.

Was this a version of Stockholm Syndrome? When the kidnapped victim start to empathize with her captor? Did I really believe that he wanted to change his evil ways after all these years?

I had to go see a shrink. Possibly check myself into a rubber room. The sooner the better.

At least I knew without a shadow of a doubt that I couldn't possibly be falling in love with him. After all, I was already in love with Thierry.

What I felt for Gideon was . . . something else. Something darker and much scarier. Only I had no idea what to call it.

I walked down Bloor Street and tried not to think about anything. Thinking hurt. Currently, a lot.

Even without thinking, I could sense that someone was following me. And if I could sense it, that meant it was my trusty, masked bodyguard whom my spidey senses alerted me to whenever he was within twenty paces.

Maybe since he was super old he cast off some über–master vampire vibes. Thierry and I sometimes had a connection like that. I didn't use it very often because keeping tabs on his whereabouts was also known as "crazy girl-friend behavior." But if I really needed to know where he was I could reach out—using a ton of concentration—and pinpoint his location like an internal GPS tracker. At the moment, however, I didn't have a lot of concentration to spare.

I stopped walking, turned around, but couldn't see him. I let out a shuddery breath. I still felt unsteady after seeing Gideon. He hadn't taken very much blood at all, but I still felt a bit weak.

It had nothing to do with the blood.

Lurky McLurkalot was starting to annoy me. The least he could do was make his presence known. Say "hi" or something. I'd settle for a polite nod in my general direction.

"I want to talk to you," I said, loud enough so the Red Devil could hear me. A woman gave me a strange look as she passed by. "Not you. Carry on."

What was I going to say to him? I didn't really know. But I did know I wanted some answers. If Thierry refused to tell me anything about the reclusive vampire vigilante, then maybe the masked man in question would be a little more forthcoming about himself.

I kept walking till I got to the next block. There was an Italian restaurant on the corner with a half-empty parking lot. I walked around to the back of it and waited, leaning heavily against the exterior wall. It didn't take long before a dark shadow loomed and the Red Devil appeared. He didn't move closer to me, instead staying about twelve feet away and out of the light of the security lamp I stood under. His face was shadowed and I could see little more than the mask, dark hair, and a long dark coat.

He studied me silently.

"Who are you?" I asked simply.

"Someone who wants to help." He spoke in a harsh whisper I had to strain to hear.

I eyed him skeptically. "Where have you been for a hundred years?"

"Around."

So incredibly insightful. I was overwhelmed by information. "Great answer. Really."

He was quiet for another moment. "I know you went to see Gideon again. I waited outside the hotel for you."

"Lurking in the shadows."

"It's what I do."

"Quinn told me what you plan to do. Kill Gideon."

His lips thinned. "Do you take issue with that decision?"

My bottom lip quivered. "Maybe I'm just not comfortable with the idea of murder."

"You seem upset."

"Do I?"

"Yes. Did something bad happen?"

"Other than hanging out behind a restaurant with a guy in a mask who won't answer any of my questions?"

"What happened with Gideon?" His voice was tense. "Did he hurt you?"

"You know, it's funny. He's never laid a finger on me. Well, not in the way you might think."

"What does that mean?"

"He wanted some of my blood tonight. Thought it would ease his pain. I gave it to him."

His eyes narrowed. "And did it work?"

"Surprisingly, yes."

"And then what did he do? Threaten you further? Remind you of his power over you right now?"

"Not so much." I shrugged. "Then, if you really want to know, he kissed me."

"He did *what*?"

The sharp, louder reply took me by surprise, and I glanced at the man who stood in the shadows. I had no idea why I was sharing all this with him. Call it cheap therapy. "What can I say? I guess I'm irresistible when I'm bleeding."

He swore under his breath. "Perhaps I'll kill him right now."

I looked at him strangely. "What do you care what happened? He didn't hurt me."

"You . . ." He cut off whatever he was about to say. "It sounds as if you're defending his actions. I thought that you were distraught over what happened, but now I'm sensing that you might not mind such attention."

"You're sensing that, are you?" I said dryly.

"Maybe you enjoyed it."

I glared at him. "Maybe I did. And maybe that's why I'm upset."

"Interesting." The word was very cold.

"Glad you think so."

"I have heard that you like receiving the romantic attentions of handsome vampire hunters."

My face burned at that. "You heard that, did you? Gee, I wonder where?"

"To me, that seems a bit . . . what is the word?"

"Stupid?" I finished for him. "I believe you called me that the other night in the alley. You were right then and you're probably very right now."

His lips curved. "I think I prefer the term 'naïve.'"

"Thank you for your opinion."

His gaze fixed on me so intently that I felt scorched by it. "Do you think Gideon is another hunter you can help redeem?"

"You never know."

He shook his head. "As I said . . . naïve. And entirely self-absorbed. You have a hard time seeing this situation objectively."

I glared at this mask-wearing man, my anxiety from before now nicely replaced by a swell of anger. "For your information, Gideon actually wants to kill you, now that you've popped up again after a century of being who-knows-where. He wants me to lead him to you in return for a grimoire that will help break my curse. But I haven't told him anything about you."

"You don't know anything about me other than the fact I'm here to protect someone who seems to actively shun any potential protection."

I deflated a bit at that. "I'm sorry. I know you're trying to help, really. If it wasn't for you, I would have hurt that fledgling the other night in the alley—maybe even killed her."

"Nothing happened."

"Only thanks to you." I crossed my arms over my chest, feeling exposed by my multitude of weaknesses and mistakes. It was time for me to head back home to George's and chalk this day up as another craptastic one. I touched my gold chain. "I'm worried I'm not going to find a way to get rid of my curse. And one day I'll lose control and end up really hurting someone if there's no one there to stop me. And now Gideon seems to hold my only answer."

He was silent for a moment. "There are ways to find the strength to fight back against the thirst."

I raised my eyebrows. "You sound like you speak from personal experience."

He turned away and I thought that was it, he'd just vanish into the darkness. But he stopped. "I believe there is great strength inside you, Sarah. You simply need to believe that as well."

There was something about the way he said my name—something in the quiet rasp of his voice that suddenly struck an odd sense of familiarity inside of me.

I moved toward him just as he was about to walk away and grabbed his arm. "Hey, wait a minute—"

He turned slightly. For a split second I could see his face up close, aside from the mask. His mouth, his chin and jaw line, and his eyes. I was now close enough to also catch the briefest scent of his spicy and strangely familiar cologne.

"Go home," he said roughly, and then he quickly walked away from me.

I'd been walking around in a fog with blinders on the other two times I'd seen him. Even tonight I'd been too preoccupied by what had happened with Gideon to really register anything specific. He'd tried to stay just out of sight. He'd tried to disguise his voice around me.

I figured that was just part of the mysterious Red Devil deal. But it wasn't. Not completely. He was doing it so I wouldn't figure out who he really was.

But now I knew. The truth of who the Red Devil actually was suddenly hit me in the face like a tidal wave.

It was Thierry.

Chapter 8

*H*oly mother of crap.

Thierry was the Red Devil.

In a daze, I made my way back to George's, let myself in, and shakily fired up the Internet. I had an unreliable old laptop Amy had lent me and I must admit that the wireless connection was borrowed from the neighbors—"stolen" is such an unpleasant term, isn't it?—but it worked and I had to do some research. Every minute I was away from the Red Devil I questioned what I'd seen. Maybe I was wrong. Maybe I'd dropped some LSD and not realized it. Maybe I was tired, or projecting . . . or completely insane. I had been feeling more than my share of loopy after seeing Gideon, after all.

There had to be a more logical explanation, because on what planet did it make sense that he was Thierry? Why wouldn't he have ever said anything to me?

Other than his tendency toward keeping everything in his life a secret, that is.

I mean, this was *major*.

The thing about Thierry that made it hard to believe was that although he was wonderful and sexy and I was crazy about him, he'd never struck me as a vigilante type. At all. He preferred to avoid situations of conflict. In fact, he'd always insisted that it was safer to stay hidden than risk meeting the wrong end of a wooden stake. Everyone who knew him, or knew of him, was aware that this was his preferred method of dealing with intense situations. However, he would fight if he had to, and I knew that he could kick some major ass. I'd seen him throw a man right across a room in a fight. Actually, that man had been Quinn, but that was another story.

But this?

This was unbelievable. And yet, down deep, I felt there was a part of me that had always known the truth.

Okay, that was a big fat lie. I had absolutely no damn idea.

I launched my web browser and searched the term "red devil," which brought up links to rock bands and vacuum cleaners. Not very helpful, obviously. I added "vampire" and "vigilante" to the equation. That brought up a few obscure references. Nothing solid. I searched for a whole hour until I found one small sketch of him. It wasn't a good one and it may have been done by someone who never even saw him in the flesh. But the mask was right and the mouth was similar. It wasn't proof, but it was something.

There wasn't much information on him at all, actually, and what I did find only confirmed what I already knew. He saved vampires from hunters and he'd disappeared completely a hundred years ago—coincidentally around the same time Thierry began a century of staying out of the vampire social scene.

Until he met me, that is.

Veronique was interested in the Red Devil. She wanted to have an affair with him and had said as much to me. I knew that he'd saved her life a long time ago so they'd obviously met face to face. She'd given me zero indication that she had any idea it was Thierry. How the hell couldn't she know who he was? I mean, she'd known Thierry for six centuries, hadn't she? I'd known him for only three months and I recognized him immediately.

Well, *almost* immediately. Close enough.

The next morning, after tossing and turning all night in bed, I called Veronique's room at the Windsor Arms hotel and she agreed to meet me for coffee.

"Good morning, my dear," she began when we met at ten o'clock. "Am I to assume that you are now curse-free and wanted to celebrate with a close friend?"

She, of course, meant herself. I truly wish I had even a fraction of her self-esteem.

I pulled out the thousand dollars that remained of what she'd given me and explained to her what happened with the teenaged wizard and the eradication that didn't happen.

"I'll pay the rest back as soon as I can." I pushed the money across the table toward her. "I'm sure I'll be able to save that much in the next . . . um . . . well, I'll write you an IOU in the meantime."

She frowned. "So you're not cured."

"Afraid not."

"That is terrible news."

"Tell me about it." I sighed. "If you happen to speak

with anyone from the Ring, could you let them know that I'm working on it and for them to pretty please not kill me just yet."

"I will certainly do that."

She continued to look disturbed by my news, and that made me very nervous. Veronique never looked this disturbed.

"Is there something wrong?" I asked tentatively.

"Would you consider having this eradication in the future? Even if it meant losing your memories of being a vampire?"

I clenched the mug of coffee in front of me. "I don't know."

"Are there any other ways to get rid of this curse?"

Other than handing over the Red Devil, aka Thierry, on a silver platter and possibly playing evil tonsil hockey with Gideon?

"I'm still researching some options." I touched my ugly necklace. "But at least I have the gold chain. I don't plan on removing it even if it turns my neck green."

Her eyes lowered to my throat. "Yes, you do have a Carastrand."

I blinked. "A what?"

She leaned back in her chair and nodded at my chain. "A *Carastrand*."

"I didn't know what it was called before. And Thierry didn't tell me."

"Thierry doesn't know everything," she said simply. "I remember clearly when the nightwalkers existed in great numbers. Mostly in London and Paris. This was in the nineteenth century. They looked so very human. In fact, some of them never developed vampire fangs at all, instead needing to tear at their victim's throat in a horrifically violent manner." She shuddered.

I touched my chain. "I researched it but I couldn't find any information on it. I figured it was a secret cure."

"A Carastrand dampens dark magic and dark natures. That is its purpose. The name is from the Spanish for face, 'cara,' which is to mean it is for appearance only. Its strength dissipates quickly, as it takes a great deal of energy to keep nightwalkers in control of their hungers. Unfortunately it's only a temporary solution."

This info came like a sucker punch to my gut. "Temporary?"

"That's right."

"Thierry didn't know this," I said. "Or he didn't mention it."

"Like I said, my husband doesn't know everything, my dear." She reached across the table to touch my hand. "I feel that you still have some time. You've only had the curse for a couple of weeks, yes? The strand should sustain you for a while longer. But you must take care that it isn't broken. I witnessed a nightwalker once who wished to control himself, so he wore a strand as you do now. In a fight it was torn from his throat, the clasp broken, and even when repaired it did not work its magic again."

"What happened to the guy who lost his strand?"

"What happened to all the nightwalkers," Veronique said gravely. "He was eliminated to ensure the safety of others."

I shivered. "So even though he wanted to be good, he couldn't."

She shook her head. "However, he was a nightwalker

from the beginning. Your tendencies come from an artificial source of magic. Perhaps they can be controlled."

"You're just saying that to make me feel better, aren't you?"

"Yes, I am. Does it help?"

My stomach churned. "Not so much."

"So you see that you cannot simply discount this potential eradication out of hand, even though the side effects are undesirable."

"I need to think about this."

All of my memories gone or risk becoming a nightwalker 24/7 whether or not I wanted to be. I had to get rid of this curse. The grimoire Gideon allegedly had now became a beacon of hope for me. I had to get my hands on it.

"Now," Veronique said. "Let's talk of less depressing matters, shall we?"

"What do you want to talk about?" I asked weakly.

"The Red Devil," she said evenly. "Have you seen him again?"

"I . . . I actually have. Yeah."

"And have you mentioned my interest in exploring a relationship with him?"

I stared at her for a long moment. "The subject hasn't come up yet."

Her lips thinned a little. "I understand. You do have other issues to consider. However, if you could tell him that it is I, Veronique—"

I held up a hand. "No offense, but setting up a devilish booty call for you is a bit low on the list at the moment for me, as I'm sure you can understand. But I do want to talk about the Red Devil."

She tilted her head to the side. "I am not interested in a *booty call*, I am interested in a relationship, a romance with the most interesting man I've ever met. I took you to be a romantic, Sarah."

"And I am. Depending on the day." I forced all curse-related thoughts temporarily out of my already crowded brain. "What exactly is it about the Red Devil that appeals to you so much? I mean, you could have any man you want."

"Yes, that is very true. But ever since I met him nearly two hundred years ago, I have kept him in the back of my mind and all men since have paled considerably in comparison to that memory. Our meeting was so momentous, so intense and incredible, that I dream about him to this very day."

"Tall guy, about six feet," I said. "Dark hair, broad shoulders, gray eyes."

"Yes. Handsome with or without the mask, I would imagine."

"So you got a good look at him. You actually saw his face."

"Yes." She closed her eyes and sighed like a fangirl. "I even kissed him to show my gratitude."

Tramp. "So he didn't look familiar to you at all? Is there anyone you've ever met who you think might be the Red Devil after hours?"

She smiled. "Much like a modern-day superhero with a closely guarded secret identity?"

"Sure. Something like that."

Her forehead creased slightly in concentration. I imagined that she was thinking of meeting the Red Devil, being rescued by him, and then never seeing him again despite the "be my lover" vibe-fest she was sending out.

She slowly shook her head. "I have met a great many people, human, hunter, and vampire, in my life, and there is nary a one that I believe could be masquerading as the Red Devil."

Seriously? She *seriously* didn't know?

"Just thought I'd ask," I said.

She leaned over the table. "Why? Do you know who the man is behind the mask?"

"Nope," I lied. "But it is something to think about."

"Indeed it is."

I pushed the small stack of hundred-dollar bills the rest of the way across the table to her. "Here. As I said, I'll pay you back the rest when I get a new job. Maybe they're looking to hire staff at Darkside."

"I've heard Darkside has recently been sold. Vampire real estate is a fluid thing. It is likely the new owners will close up shop to protect themselves and their investment."

"Even with . . . *Gideon Chase* . . . dead and buried?" I said carefully. "Is it still that dangerous?"

"*Especially* now. The hunters' need for violence has become even more indiscriminate than before." She pushed her small cup of espresso away from her. "That's why I want to make every day count. Time is of the essence for me."

"What for?"

"To become a part of the Red Devil's life, of course." She frowned at me. "Honestly, Sarah, you seem very distracted to me today."

No shit, Sherlock.

She pursed her red lips and glanced around at our surroundings. "Did you have a meeting with Barry scheduled after this?"

"Barry?" I repeated. "Barry Jordan? The man who hates me with every small fiber in his tiny being? No. Why?"

"Because he is staring at you rather intently right now." She shrugged her elegant shoulders. "A coincidence, I'm sure."

I looked around the small café but saw no one I recognized. Then I turned to the window facing the sidewalk.

I jumped. Barry Jordan stared straight through the pane of glass at me next to my face. He was the same height standing as I was sitting so when I looked we were face to face.

He didn't look amused. He jabbed his right pointer finger at me and then curled it as if he wanted me to come outside.

I looked past him to see Amy but there was no one else with him.

"I think he's trying to tell you something," Veronique observed.

I held a hand to my ear and looked at Barry again. "What?"

He already looked frustrated with me.

I glanced at Veronique. "Please tell me he's not the vampire the Ring assigned to eliminate me. That would be so embarrassing."

"Of course not. Such an important task would not be given to a mere servant."

"That's kind of derogatory, don't you think?"

She looked confused. "There are those who are

servants and those who are masters. Knowing where you fit into that equation helps one in a very long existence."

"So what am I?"

"You are a servant," she said simply. "Your lack of wealth and status gives you no other choice. But you are a charming and amusing girl whose company I greatly enjoy, so that is something for you to hold on to."

"Thierry was poor when he was a human. I think you called him a peasant once, didn't you? But now he's considered a master vampire."

"He has earned that designation over many centuries, but no, not from birth."

"Is that why you wouldn't sign the annulment? Because you think of me as a servant?"

She sighed. "The subject wearies me, my dear. Besides, it doesn't matter anymore now that you and my husband are no longer together."

"Fine." I tried to push away any extra ill feelings I had toward the woman facing me. "Thanks for the info on the . . . the Carastrand. Obviously it's a very good thing to know." I stood up from the table.

She eyed me. "And what of the Red Devil?"

"Honestly, Veronique? I don't think you're his type. I'll mention you to him, but I figure if he wanted to hook up, he would have done it already. Two hundred years is a long time not to call somebody back after a first date. Maybe he's just not that into you."

A microscopic sliver of doubt slid through her gaze. "Are you saying you believe him to be homosexual?"

I blinked. "Is that the only reason a man wouldn't want you?"

"Of course."

"Then that's what he is—he's gay as a handbag full of rainbows." I glanced at the window to see that Barry's face had gone a few shades darker red and the top of his head looked about ready to blow off. "I'll see you later, Veronique."

"Of course." She nodded but still looked disturbed by the possibility of her mystery hunk-o-love being unattainable.

And to think, the man that she wanted, that she thought was the cat's meow—where did that expression come from?—that she was willing to go to great ends to meet . . . she was already married to him and couldn't recognize him to save her own life.

The knowledge that I knew who he actually was bubbled inside me like a teapot ready to whistle loudly. Balanced out, of course, with some major-ass annoyance.

Then again, it was par for the course with Thierry. He had serious trust issues. Did he think I'd go blabbing to everybody in town?

Could I be with somebody who tried to keep nearly every part of his life a secret from me?

Barry was waiting impatiently for me outside the café when I exited.

"Have you seen my wife?" he asked tightly.

I wiped a few flakes of falling snow off my cheeks. The skies above were thick and gray this morning. "I'm doing just fantastic, Barry, thank you for asking. How are you?"

"I don't have any time for your nonsense today. I'm looking for Amy."

"Have you tried her job? She's typically there during Monday work hours, you know."

"I'm not an idiot. Of course I tried there already. They said she went out for an early lunch."

A woman walking a Great Dane passed us and looked at us curiously. I eyed her warily wondering if she was one of Gideon's spies. The dog stopped to do his business and the woman crouched to pick it up in a plastic bag.

Gross.

I returned my attention to Barry. "Then I guess that's where she is. Eating something. Somewhere."

His brow creased further than it already was. "She isn't answering her cell phone."

"Maybe she needs some time away from you. Can't imagine why." I studied him for a moment. "Is that all you wanted?"

He seemed to deflate a little in the anger category. "I wouldn't have bothered you, but I saw you with Veronique and thought I'd ask."

"You've asked. I've answered. Now, if there's nothing else, I need to deal with my daily traumas." I brushed past him, but he grabbed hold of the sleeve of my coat. I turned back to look at him.

"She's happy, isn't she?" he asked.

"Define happy," I said. "I seem to forget what that entails."

"With me." He visibly swallowed. "I mean, she doesn't have any issues that would cause her to find me . . . lacking in any way, does she?"

Oh, brother. Not something I needed today. A miniature vampire with an inferiority complex—who hated my guts.

"Amy is happier than she's ever been," I told him. "She's like a werewolf after a flea bath. Don't ask me why, because I honestly couldn't tell you. I don't think you have anything to worry about."

He nodded. "Good."

A few more potential spy-types walked by us. One even had the audacity to ask me for the time before continuing down the sidewalk. "I'm sure she's off shopping somewhere. Just chill. You two have something special. I guess it was love at first bite. Old joke, but whatever." I turned away from him again before something occurred to me. "Hey, you don't happen to know the Red Devil's real identity, do you?"

He shook his head. "Whoever he is, I think he should have remained in hiding. The master says that his presence in the past did more harm than good."

I narrowed my eyes. "I just bet he did."

Of course Thierry would say something like that to help take any attention off the obvious—to *me*, anyhow— similarities between him and the Red Devil.

Barry raised his chin. "You should know that the master is seeing someone new."

"I know." My eyes narrowed. Even though I knew it was only a cover, it still bugged me. "How do you like her?"

His lips thinned. "She is a crude and sharp-tongued woman. I don't know why he would choose her so quickly after the end of your . . . *relationship* . . . when his preference is typically for solitude and reflection."

"Thierry *is* a party animal, isn't he?"

"I wouldn't say that."

"I was being sarcastic."

"What a surprise." He eyed me. "I will say I was surprised by what happened between you and the master.

While I didn't feel that you would be together very long, I didn't think it would end so soon, given his questionable infatuation with you and your abnormal stubbornness."

I smiled at him. "I think that's the nicest thing you've ever said to me. Give me a hug?"

He took a step back from me. "For a moment, despite your numerous flaws and issues, I think he was . . ." He cleared his throat. "*Happy* is much too large of a word, really. But perhaps . . . hmm, I'm not really sure. Perhaps *not unhappy* would be a better way to describe his mood of late."

"Please stop. All of these gushing compliments will go to my head. If I hear from Amy I'll tell her you're looking for her, okay?"

He nodded stiffly. "Very well."

As I walked away from him, I touched the gold chain I wore—the *Carastrand*—and thought about what Veronique had said earlier. Maybe she was making it up. Maybe she'd heard wrong or had forgotten the details after so long. If she was right and the magic holding my nightwalker back was a fading thing, then I was going to be in bigger trouble than I already was.

Gideon said the grimoire was mine if I handed over the Red Devil so he could have a challenging kill to keep his mind off his problems.

Obviously that was out of the question. Thierry might have pissed me off a lot lately, but I wasn't selling him out for an easy answer to my issues.

The eradication wasn't an option for me because of the memory issue. It was worst-case scenario only, and the kid who'd do it wouldn't agree to go through with it even if I wanted him to.

There had to be a third option. I hoped the *strand* would hold out long enough for me to figure out what it was.

Too many eggs to juggle at the moment; it was inevitable that some of them would end up broken. The only question was, which ones?

When I got back to George's bungalow, there was something on my doorstep I hadn't been expecting.

It was pasty, stringy, greasy and it wore a "Death Suck" concert T-shirt.

The Darkness was waiting for me.

The Darkness did not look happy.

Chapter 9

The Darkness had somebody with him—a middle-aged woman with red hair who had him by his upper arm so tightly that even from a distance it looked painful.

I walked up the driveway and gave them both a guarded but curious look. How did he even know where I lived?

"Looking for me?" I asked.

The woman shook the kid. "Tell her."

"Fine. *Fine*, okay? Geez, Mom, let go of me."

She unhanded him. "Don't make me tell you twice."

The kid hissed out a breath and looked at me. "It was wrong of me to take your money yesterday. I'm really sorry. I've come to return it to you."

After another poke from his mother, the kid extended his hand, which held the thousand-dollar retainer from yesterday. I walked up to them, studied them to see if there were any catches or tricks, and then took the money.

"Thank you."

"Whatever. I got another job that pays way better anyhow."

"Yippy for you."

The kid absently scratched at a pimple on his chin. His pasty gothboy skin was sickly looking under the cloudy skies. Terrific. This was the person I was relying on for my tenuous Plan B? It was a good reminder how desperate I was.

"Okay, Steven, we need to get going." His mother's voice was firm.

"I have to take a leak. I had that Big Gulp and I can't make it all the way back home or I'm going to explode."

"Feel free to use my bathroom," I said. "It's the least I can do."

They followed me inside. George was sitting on the couch watching TV and he looked over at us.

Steven's mother frowned. "We rang the doorbell several times, you know."

"Yup, I heard you," George said. "But your kid makes me jumpy."

Steven clutched his lower region, and he looked very uncomfortable. I pointed him in the right direction and he disappeared down the short hallway.

"I'm very sorry about my son." The woman extended her hand. "I'm Meredith Kendall."

I shook her hand. "It's not a problem."

It was a problem, but I didn't want to go into any further detail because I had no idea how much she knew about what her son was capable of. Finding out your son was a wizard who practiced black magic was a little higher on the parental panic scale than finding out he smoked cigarettes.

"This isn't the first time, you see," she said. "And it

doesn't always turn out quite so well in the end. There have been . . . *issues*."

Yeah, I bet.

"Really," she continued, "I suppose it should be common sense not to hand over large sums of money to children, but vampires have different morals than the rest of us normal people."

Alrighty then. So she knew what I was and wasn't screaming or whipping out a wooden stake. Except for the veiled insult, that was encouraging.

"Obviously you're very savvy about this sort of thing." I decided to ignore her ignorance instead of educating her about what vampires actually were. There were only so many hours in the day. "How did you find out where I lived?"

"Steven did a location spell. I allowed the small bit of magic because it is important that he learn his lesson." She wrung her hands anxiously. "I thought that moving out of the country might curb his interest in the occult, but I don't think it's going to be as easy a solution as I'd hoped. He's beginning to remind me a great deal of his father."

"He said his father had passed away," I said.

She let out a long, shaky sigh. "*Vanquished* is the correct term, actually."

That made George sit up straight and give us his full attention. "Vanquished? Are you trying to say that his father was a . . . a . . . *demon*?"

She nodded gravely. "I'm afraid that's where Steven is channeling magical ability from—the demonic energy that already exists within him. That's why we're moving."

"You're moving out of the country so—"

"So his father can't find us again. He wants joint custody." Her expression soured. "Over my dead body. I'll do whatever it takes to protect my darling son from that jerk."

"I can't imagine having a demon for a dad would be a good thing," George said. "For one thing, the commute between Toronto and hell during rush hour would be . . . well, *hell*."

"It's got nothing to do with his being a demon. The creep cheated on me when we were together and I want him to suffer eternally." Her bottom lip wobbled. "Sending him back to hell wasn't a good enough punishment, in my opinion."

I heard the toilet flush, and a few moments later, Steven rejoined us. I looked at him a bit differently now.

Demon spawn.

I was seriously going back to church. ASAP. And not just for Easter and Christmas.

"Steven, let's go," his mother said sharply. "We have more packing to do."

I opened the door for them. Meredith went out first with barely a glance at me. Steven paused and extended his hand.

That seemed rather polite, considering how ornery he'd been in the past. I took it to be a good sign and hoped very much that he'd washed up after using the facilities.

I shook his hand. I wouldn't have minded talking to him in private about my eradication options, demonic or otherwise. "When did you say you were leaving for Germany, again?"

He didn't answer me. His hand was cool to the touch and his grip tightened so much that it hurt.

I grimaced. "Hey, you can let go of me now."

Steven raised his gaze to mine, and I couldn't help but gasp in surprise. His eyes had turned red again—dark red with no whites showing.

"Let go of the nice vampire lady," his mother snapped. "*Now.*"

"We're close to the end now," Steven said. "And if you don't step aside when the blood begins to flow it will devour you whole."

His voice didn't sound like a teenager's at that moment; it was deeper and raspier and filled with darkness.

"Let go of me," I managed. My fingers were turning white.

But he didn't let go. He grasped my other wrist, his gaze fixed on my own. "You should have died long ago—immediately after you were sired. But fate shifted that night."

I didn't think it was Steven who was doing the talking anymore—it was a *demon*. Just an educated guess. Cold fear slithered through me.

"Uh," George approached us. "What exactly is going on here?"

Steven narrowed his red eyes at George, who staggered out of the door as if he had been shoved by a large, invisible hand. He now stood beside Steven's mother on the front step.

Then the door slammed shut.

"Okay—" My heart rate was going twice as fast as normal. "Party's over. You can leave now and there won't be any problems."

The demon currently hanging out inside Steven tilted his head to the side as he studied me with those freaky eyeballs. "You cause nothing but problems, vampire. The fact that you still exist is a problem."

"You're actually not the first one to say that. You don't know somebody named Barry by any chance, do you?" I tried to keep the tremor from my voice but was failing miserably.

The demon brought his face close to mine, and he sniffed along my neck. "Your blood runs thick with power. I don't think I like that."

"You and me both."

"A witch has touched you. She left a trace of her magic on your skin."

"You make it sound way sexier than it was."

His red eyes went to my gold chain. "Such a tentative hold you have on the eternal darkness inside you. Perhaps it would be easier for you if you simply embraced your true nature."

I tried my damnedest to pull away from him but he was, not surprisingly, *supernaturally* strong. "My true nature isn't being a nightwalker, if that's what you mean."

"Then, in the end, this flimsy object you wear will mean nothing." He smiled and I felt it chill my insides. "We shall see if darkness or light will be the stronger force for you."

"Who are you?" I gasped.

"Someone with a great interest in the choices you will make."

"How about a little hint about what I should do? Pretty please with fire and brimstone on top?"

"Very well." The cold smile widened. "He who kills

your kind, but gives you diamonds, holds a clue in his hand—a glimpse of a betrayal you would never expect. One has already stepped too close to the flames and your choices will decide if they will burn."

"What in the hell is that supposed to mean?" I asked, then lowered my voice. "Are you talking about Gideon? Something he holds in his hands? He was burned by hellfire."

A smile twisted up the side of his mouth. "His and your destinies are now bound together."

"I'm not in love with him. I love Thierry."

The demon's eyes brightened with intensity, and I could have sworn I saw the flicker of flames inside. "Love is not enough to save you."

Before I could respond to that, the smile fell away from his pimply face and in the blink of an eye his hands shifted to my throat. He squeezed hard.

The door pounded as George tried to get back in. I heard Steven's mother yelling his name.

I clawed at his hands, trying to get away from him. This wasn't the grip of somebody who just wanted to give a friendly squeeze. I was strong enough to peel a few of his fingers back until he finally released me completely and I gasped for breath.

I held a hand to my tender throat. "What are you trying to do?"

"I'm trying to help."

He backhanded me so hard that I spun around and smacked my head against the wall. Everything went black.

The fact that it was only a dream didn't mean I wasn't going to enjoy myself.

After all, the wedding gown I wore was stunning Vera Wang. The full-length shard—an expensive mirror especially meant for vampires—I stood before reflected me from head to designer stiletto.

"You look gorgeous," a familiar voice said. I looked to my left to see George. "I didn't think white was for you, but color me wrong."

"It's off-white. Just like my virtue. And I'm wearing a black bra just to keep everything balanced."

He grinned. "Are you ready for your big day?"

I nodded, finding it hard to not smile. "I've been ready for a long time."

"Come on, you've kept him waiting for a very long time." George held his arm out for me and I took it. He led me out to a hallway where there was a railing that looked over into the church itself.

At the front of the church stood Thierry, wearing a tuxedo, and he looked mouth-wateringly delicious.

"Shouldn't I be down there? I'm going to miss it."

George shook his head. "Trust me, it's way safer up here."

Someone was making her way down the aisle—a woman with shoulder-length brown hair and a beautiful white gown that matched the one I wore. She glanced over her shoulder and I realized it was . . . *me*.

An odd sensation of dread filled me.

The other me looked up at where I stood on the balcony. Her eyes were pitch black. Her neck was bare—she wasn't wearing the gold chain.

Then the nightwalker dropped her bouquet and grabbed hold of Thierry so she could sink her fangs deeply into his throat. He didn't even try to fight her. I screamed but no sound came out.

The masked Red Devil now stood beside me.

"Why didn't you try to stop this?" His angry voice was low and raspy. He shook his head with disappointment.

A glance downstairs showed the nightwalker-me letting Thierry drop heavily to the ground, where his body immediately disintegrated.

Another groom stepped into his place—it was Gideon. The nightwalker hooked her arm through his and she and Gideon began to recite their vows. I stared down with horror as Gideon kissed nightwalker-me after we were proclaimed husband and wife. He glanced at the balcony and winked at me, smiling wide enough so I could see his brand-new set of fangs.

"Thank you for everything, Sarah," he said. "I'm sorry about the mess we made. It couldn't be helped. But we're together now. Forever."

"I love you, Gideon," the nightwalker said.

He kissed his bride and I realized he was now kissing me and I wasn't doing anything to stop him—in fact, I had my arms around him and was pulling him closer to me.

Next to where I now stood at the altar with Gideon, the Red Devil was gone as well, the red mask the only sign that he had ever existed. It lay next to the dead bodies of all of my friends.

I began to scream.

Chapter 10

There was something cold and wet on my head. I slowly opened my eyes to a blast of pain and realized that George held a cool cloth against my forehead. He looked worried.

"The Darkness totally knocked you out," he informed me, as if I didn't already know that tidbit of information.

I blinked painfully and noticed I was sprawled out on the sofa. "Where did he go?"

"After he put out your lights he let us back in. He seemed majorly freaked about the whole situation. Him and Mommy Dearest left. Are you okay?"

I guessed the demon had gone back where he came from. His message, cryptic though it was, had been successfully delivered. I wondered if I should tell George, but decided to say nothing for now. I didn't know what it meant. Besides, saying anything would mean a bigger explanation about Gideon was required, and I wasn't prepared to go there.

George was still dabbing the cold cloth against my

forehead, and I pushed his hand away. "I had a disturbing dream that you gave me away at my wedding, but my nightwalker killed Thierry and instead married Gi—" I bit my tongue. "Married *somebody*. I couldn't see his face."

"What was I wearing?" he asked very seriously.

I tried to focus on his face. "For a dream, you looked great. Fabulous suit. I'm thinking Armani. Dream George has good taste."

He nodded. "Nice."

I tried to shake off my episode of Touched by a Demon and the subsequent nightmare it launched me into. "I have a lot of dreams about Thierry dying. However, I'm not usually the one to kill him. I hope it wasn't a prophetic glimpse of the future."

He stood up and tossed the soggy cloth on an old newspaper on the coffee table. "Since it was a dream about you two getting married, it was obviously just a figment of your imagination. You two are history, after all. Right?"

Right. He didn't know about me and Thierry and I'd prefer to keep it that way. For his own good.

"By the way," he continued, "I can't believe you're back with Quinn and you never told me a thing. Amy sent me the photographic evidence of your tongue-twister match at the café yesterday. How could you keep this sort of juice from me?"

"Sorry." I shrugged. "It's pretty new news. And you've been busy."

"I forgive you. Barely." His bottom lip actually wobbled. "But only because you're currently nursing a concussion."

I studied him for a long moment, trying to ignore the

pulsing throb of my rattled brain. "Are you actually upset about this or are you just having an emotional day?"

He sniffed. "I'm fine. Just fine."

"You're acting kind of funny."

"Funny strange or funny ha-ha?"

"Strange." I touched his arm. "I'm sorry I've been obsessed with my own issues, but if there's something wrong you can tell me. We're friends."

He glanced at me, then moved away from the couch to stand in front of the window. "It's nothing you have to worry your pretty little brunette head about."

I propped myself up on the couch with my elbows. A small wave of dizziness came over me but passed quickly. "I think I know what it is."

"You do?"

I nodded. "It's me living here. I've been mooching off you for far too long and I'm sorry. I've just got a few more things to take care of, starting with my brand-new head injury—" and ending with curses, Thierry's secret identity, siring Gideon, and my new insight into the fun and exciting world of demons "—and then I'll get my own place. Just know that I really appreciate what a great friend you've been to me during my pathetic, self-pitying time of neediness."

"Sarah, it's not—"

But I'd gotten up during my speech and made a slow, staggering beeline across the living room to give him a tight hug. "You rock, you know that?"

He disengaged from my clinginess as best he could, then went to the closet to grab his jacket. He gave me a quick peck on the cheek. "I have to go out for a bit, but you stay here and rest. And chill out. And try to stay out of trouble, if that's possible."

"Not sure that's possible."

"Try, anyhow. After all, I only have so much house insurance."

Without another word, he left.

Maybe there'd been an Invasion of the George Snatchers lately. In any case, I'd have to remember—despite my multiple other dramas—to keep an eye on him. There was nothing worse than a potentially depressed vampire. I speak from personal experience.

I groaned and rubbed my tender scalp. Demon-boy sure had a mean left hook.

George wanted me to stay calm and rest up after being batted around like a fanged punching bag, but how could I relax? That teenager had been *possessed*.

"He holds a clue in his hand—a glimpse of a betrayal you would never expect."

I was fairly certain he'd been talking about Gideon. And if I was going to be betrayed then I'd really love to know all about it.

What did he hold in his hand? A remote control? A piece of fruit? Some of my butt last night when he'd kissed me?

Another thought occurred to me.

Maybe the demon was talking about Gideon's *Black-Berry.*

That made a whole lot of sense, actually. I'd already thought about what secrets might be inside it—names and contact information. Schedules. Meeting places. Text messages and e-mails. It seemed too simple an answer, but it was possible it could be helpful to find out who was on call to help him blackmail me to do whatever he wanted.

Maybe no one had to get hurt. If I could get my hands on his BlackBerry I could use the information on it against him. Make him know that he didn't hold all the power.

Then if I still decided to sire him he'd see I did it without any duress. I'd prove to him once and for all that vampires didn't deserve to be staked. And then he could take his newfound, benevolent view of the paranormal world back to his cronies and get hunters to stop hunting. It would be a whole new world.

The Disney song by the same name started playing in my head.

Okay, I wasn't a total ignoramus. I knew it wouldn't be that simple. But it was something to start with. Something solid.

Then he'd give me the grimoire, no strings attached. Because that's what friends do. They help each other out.

Gideon Chase = my buddy.

Obviously my concussion was worse than I'd thought it was. Thank God I had vampire-strength healing abilities now.

I'd start with getting the cell phone away from him and take it from there. Baby steps. Tomorrow night at midnight was when I was supposed to turn him into a vampire. I really hoped that deadline wouldn't contain too much "dead."

I grabbed my cell phone and scrolled to the last time Gideon had called me. Taking a deep breath, I pressed the button to redial his number. He picked up on the second ring.

"Good afternoon, Sarah," he said. "Are you feeling better today?"

We hadn't exactly parted on a good note last night, had we? I remembered sinking my teeth into his tongue and him snarling some sort of threat at me when I refused his generous offer to have sex with him.

Best friends. It could happen.

"I want to talk to you about what happened last night."

There was a long pause. "So, talk."

I swallowed. "Not on the phone. I want to see you."

"Really?" He sounded intrigued. "I was under the impression you weren't happy with me."

"I slept on it. I think I may have overreacted."

"Then by all means, come here this evening. We can pick up where we left off."

That could mean many things. "Can't I see you right now?"

"No."

"Why? Got company?"

"Would that make you jealous?"

"No." My stomach lurched. Who was with him? I hadn't seen anyone with him since he first came to town. "I was planning to see Quinn today as well, so I guess I can wait."

"I strongly suggest you say nothing to him about me today. Can I trust you, Sarah?"

"Of course," I said quickly. Besides, I wasn't lying. I wouldn't say anything today. I'd already talked to Quinn about his old hunting buddy yesterday.

"When you come here, I also want you to tell me everything you know about the Red Devil."

I tensed. "I don't know much about him."

"You were seen with him last night. You know enough. I'll see you later."

The line went dead.

Somebody saw me and the Red Devil last night? A shiver went down my spine. Who'd seen us? It didn't matter, it just proved to me how closely I was being watched.

I wanted to call Thierry. I wanted to talk to him. But I had no idea how to do that without raising Gideon's suspicions. I couldn't get him any more distrustful until I, at least, had that BlackBerry of his in my hot little hands.

The plan that had seemed so sparkly a few minutes ago now seemed like a dull grasping at straws.

Since I had told Gideon I was seeing Quinn that afternoon, that's exactly what I did. I met him at Bodacious Bean an hour later and we spent the rest of the day together. We chatted about innocuous things that, if overheard by Gideon's seemingly invisible spies, wouldn't sound like anything except two people who liked each other spending time together.

Quinn and I strolled around downtown and window shopped in the Eaton Centre, the coolest mall in the universe. Then we wandered along the frozen streets of Yorkville—probably my favorite part of Toronto, with cute boutique shops and the possibility of celebrity sightings in the trendy neighborhood. Normally it would have been a great day, but obviously my concentration was elsewhere.

"Hey—" Quinn squeezed my hand. "Earth to Planet Sarah."

"Sorry." I swallowed hard. "I'm a bit scattered today."

"Just today?"

"Ha ha." I gave him a look. "I guess I'm perfecting my craft."

"It's going to be okay. You know that, right?"

"It is?"

He nodded firmly and grinned at me. "We're both going to get everything we ever wanted. We'll both find the happiness we've been searching for. And you know how I know that?"

"Please share with the class."

His smile grew. "Because we've damn well earned it."

I eyed him. "You smoking crack?"

"No drugs necessary. Why, don't you believe me?"

I breathed out and watched the air freeze into a cloud. When I was a nightwalker that wouldn't happen. I didn't have to breathe, and being outside in the cold would lower my body temperature. "I'm not sure what I believe anymore."

"Then I'll have to believe enough for the both of us."

"Since when have you become the motivational speaker of the group?"

He shrugged. "One of us has to be and I guess today it's me. You've lost your optimism."

"I think I just misplaced it somewhere." I chewed on my bottom lip. "If you had the chance to be human again but it came with a heavy price, would you take it?"

He thought about that for a moment. "I've done my share of chasing after easy answers to hard questions. Nothing worked out how I thought it would. But if somebody presented me with a special pill today that would make me the way I used to be." His brows drew together. "I don't think I'd go for it. I'm okay with who I am now."

I took a deep breath and let it out slowly. "What if you were cursed?"

"I felt like I was for a time after I got bit. Now I know I was blessed."

I rolled my eyes. "I think I liked you better when you were angst-ridden."

"Oh, trust me, I still am." He smiled and squeezed my hand. "But life presents us with lots of forks in the road. We never know what the right one is until we walk that path and see where it leads."

"Please stop."

"Sorry. I can't help myself." His smile fell away and a shadow moved over his expression. "I think somebody's following us."

I tensed. "So what do we do?"

"Just act natural."

The sun had set. It was almost completely dark and not long before I could go and see Gideon.

"Look at us, having fun together," Quinn said tightly, loud enough for any passersby to hear.

"Totally," I agreed. "So relaxed and calm and ready to enjoy our wonderful lives. Together. Quinn and me. La la la."

His jaw tightened. "That didn't sound very natural."

"My acting abilities aren't what they used to be."

He pulled me off the sidewalk and against the wall of a high-end fashion boutique. "This is for appearances only."

"What is?"

"This." He kissed me. I was surprised, but knew it would definitely help show anyone who might be watching that Quinn and I were together romantically.

I'd kissed Quinn a few times before, and there had been some great chemistry between us in the past. But this? This was just for show, and the attraction I'd once felt for him was all but completely gone.

Still. The ex-hunter had some amazing lips on him.

He finally pulled away enough to whisper in my ear. "Sorry about that."

"Sorry?" I managed. "Don't be sorry."

"I wonder if the Red Devil witnessed that one as well." I felt him grin against the side of my face. "I know he's keeping tabs on you. Must have given him quite an eyeful just now."

Well, that was possible.

I knew then, without a doubt, that along with anyone Gideon had tailing me, the kiss had also been witnessed by Thierry. I concentrated enough to feel his presence through our vampire/sire connection.

Quinn had always brought out his jealous side. Served him right.

"I have to go," I told Quinn. "I have an appointment."

"Do you want me to come with you?"

I shook my head. "I'll catch up with you later, okay?"

It took a bit more convincing, but I managed to part ways with Quinn, and just before seven o'clock I approached the Madison Manor. My steps slowed the closer I got to Gideon's hotel as I tried to calm myself.

This will go just fine, I tried to tell myself.

I could handle Gideon Chase. He was putty in my hands.

Sure.

I heard a voice from the shadows.

"You're seeing Gideon again?" the Red Devil as played by Thierry de Bennicoeur asked. "What a surprise."

I put a hand on my hip. "He's just so charming I can't stay away."

"I see. So you feel the only way to get rid of a temptation is to yield to it?"

I'd taken an English Lit course the year I'd been in university. I recognized a good Oscar Wilde quotation when it was sarcastically thrown in my direction.

Or maybe he was just being truthful. I tried to see the situation from his point of view. I knew Thierry didn't want me to put myself in harm's way by seeing Gideon. He'd told me as much to my face. And yet here I was merrily prancing into Gideon's hotel room again as if it was no big deal.

Also, I do believe I admitted last night to the "Red Devil" that not only did Gideon kiss me, but I might have enjoyed it. *Whoops*.

"Do you think I'm having an affair with Gideon?" I asked.

There was a long stretch of silence. "Are you?"

"I can't believe you have to question that."

"That wasn't a clear yes or no answer." His voice was tight. "But it's really none of my business either way, is it?"

"Now that you mention it, I guess it isn't." I pushed my annoyance away and turned around to spot him in the shadows to the side of the hotel a little off to my right. "Why don't you just go ahead and tell me who you are? I've never been a big fan of game playing, unless it's Twister or spin the bottle."

I'd give him a chance. This was his big opportunity to come clean with me once and for all.

"It would be best if you kept your distance from Gideon," he said quietly, without even attempting to answer my question. "I don't need to tell you he's a very dangerous man."

"So are you. In fact, Gideon tells me you're basically a vampire of mass destruction."

"He said that, did he?"

"My words, but that's what he meant."

There was a pause. "And what do *you* think of me?"

"The jury is still deliberating. All I know is that Gideon will hand over the grimoire so I can break my curse if I hand you over to him. So I'd watch my step if I were you."

"Do you plan to help him? Is that why you can't seem to stay far from his side?"

"I don't know what I'm going to do." All I could see in the darkness was the outline of his body and a slight glitter in his shaded eyes behind his mask. "There's a lot on the line for me at the moment and I feel like I'm all alone in the world."

"You're not alone."

"Sure feels that way."

"You didn't seem so alone this afternoon with Quinn. Perhaps there is still a chance you and he can be together if that's what you want."

There was a familiar unfriendly edge as he said Quinn's name. Obviously the kiss had not gone unnoticed. As much as I'd had it with the jealousy, I did feel a twinge of guilt. More than a twinge. It felt like lately I'd been gallivanting all over the city attacking the lips of everyone I passed. Thierry had a right to be questioning the fidelity of my lips or, for that matter, the rest of my body.

"I'm not in love with Quinn. Never was, never will be. Also, his fiancée would rip my head from my body with her new fangs. You know very well who I'm in love with."

"Do I?"

I sighed heavily. "Why don't you take the rest of the night off? I don't need protection from anyone right now, especially not somebody who hides behind a stupid mask."

"Perhaps I'm not protecting you as much as I'm protecting others *from you*."

I tried not to cringe. "Is that so?"

"You are a dangerous woman right now, currently treading a very fine line of self-control. You pretend you're normal when you're anything but."

"Yeah, well." I swallowed past the lump in my throat and absently touched my gold chain. "That's what I want to fix. Now if you'll excuse me."

I started to walk away but he grabbed hold of my hand.

"Sarah—"

"What?" Just as I turned to face him he let go of me and stepped back into the shadows.

A long moment of silence stretched between us. "Promise to be careful."

"I'll do my best."

Frustration again welled inside me. Why was it that Gideon told me everything about himself, but Thierry told me next to nothing? The balance seemed wrong there.

He'd had ample opportunity to tell me the truth. Did

he honestly think I didn't know? That I couldn't see past a flimsy mask?

But of course that's what he thought. If no one had ever seen past his masks in God only knew how long, then why would he expect me to? But I could. And I did. Despite our many differences I saw who Thierry truly was underneath it all even if nobody else did.

I was sure there was a metaphor in there for something.

Up on the fourth floor of the hotel Gideon was waiting for me. When he let me in, I scanned the room quickly and saw that the bed was unmade, the sheets in disarray.

"Had a fun afternoon with your visitor?" I asked dryly.

His lips quirked. "Just a relaxing afternoon nap."

"Right."

"Would you be upset if I sought affection elsewhere? After all, you did leave me in a state last night."

"Yeah. A state of denial." Then I had to remind myself that I wasn't there to insult him or make him mad. I was there to get that glorified cell phone of his. Sugar, not vinegar, was the main ingredient of the evening. "Sorry. I'm just tired, I guess."

"It's fine. Please make yourself comfortable."

I chose the armchair by the window and sat down uncomfortably in it.

He sat down on the edge of his messy bed. He was fully dressed in a designer suit even Thierry might envy. Half the buttons of the white shirt were undone so I could see a glimpse of his muscled chest—still free from any scars, thanks to his glamourizing wristwatch. And I was willing to bet the BlackBerry in question was in his suit jacket pocket.

"You had a visit from your young wizard today," he said after a moment. It wasn't a question.

My mouth went dry. Why was I surprised? He obviously had one of his spies stationed somewhere outside George's house. I was concerned enough about George's current state of mind without his finding out that every move he made was being monitored. I did get the feeling Gideon's spies were never close enough to overhear conversations, just close enough to witness who I was spending time with. At least, so far.

"He returned my money from yesterday. No big deal." And he'd also been possessed by a demon, but I didn't think that was information Gideon needed at the moment.

"He seems very powerful for his age."

I remembered his grip on my throat and the whack he'd given me that knocked me out. "You could say that."

"A talented witch or wizard is a rare breed. There are so few who can actually work the darker arts at their whim. Your—Steven, is it?—could prove to be very dangerous. You should be careful."

"I appreciate your concern." I tried to look comfortable and knew I was failing miserably. "Feeling better than yesterday?"

He nodded and gave me a dazzling smile. "Your blood worked wonders. It only confirmed what I already knew. Tomorrow at midnight everything will change and the ritual will work exactly as planned."

"You're sure you still want to go through with it?" I asked, my mouth dry. "I mean, you have your shiny new glamour Rolex and you don't have pain anymore. Why take the next step into a life of fangs and blood-drinking if you don't have to?"

"Because all of this—" he waved a hand over his face "—is only an illusion. Damage sustained from hellfire is not the same as any other injury. I'm looking for a more permanent solution."

"Immortality is just about as permanent as you can get. Almost as permanent as a tattoo."

"Exactly." His smile widened. "Sarah, I want to apologize for my behavior last night. It wasn't right to attempt to force my affections on you."

I shook my head. "I overreacted."

He raised an eyebrow. "Did you?"

"I guess I felt a bit overwhelmed with you and my curse and everything. And when you kissed me . . ." I cleared my throat. "Well, I felt a little confused. Obviously."

He stood up from the bed and closed the small distance between us in a couple of short steps. He held his hand out to me and I tentatively took it. "I want to show you something."

I forced myself not to pull away from him. *Honey, not vinegar.*

He led me over to the desk in the corner of the suite, slid open the top drawer, and removed a worn-looking, black leather-bound book with gilded edges. He flipped through the pages to show me that it was handwritten with diagrams and sketches.

I couldn't believe my own eyes. "The witch's grimoire?"

"It is." He turned toward a page in the middle. "All of

the evil spells she used to ruin people's lives are in here. Here's the one she must have used on you."

With wide eyes I looked down at the book to see the small, precise handwriting of the crazy-assed evil witch who'd cursed me. It was titled with:

NIGHTWALKER (DARK VAMPIRE) CURSE

The writing itself looked to be Latin, but that was only an educated guess from all the supernatural TV shows I watched. She'd drawn a picture of a happy face with sharp fangs and a small notation in blue ink: "Perfect for Sarah Dearly."

She'd obviously been thinking ahead.

"This is unbelievable," I managed.

He turned the page. "And here is the incantation to remove your curse."

And, yes, it was actually titled:

NIGHTWALKER (EVIL VAMPIRE) CURSE **REMOVAL**

This one was illustrated with an unhappy smiley face. With fangs.

The witch may have been crazy, but she sure was organized.

I reached out for the book, but Gideon slammed it shut on my hand.

"Ouch." I pulled my hand back.

"Sorry. But I can't give all my secrets away that easily." He grinned. "Not before you help me track the Red Devil."

I inhaled sharply. "Right. About that."

"You are reluctant to tell me anything about him, aren't you? Even with the grimoire as your reward."

"It's not that, I . . ." I shook my head. "I don't know."

"I understand," he said.

I looked at him with surprise. "You do?"

"Of course. You don't want to hurt anyone. I admire that, Sarah."

"You do?" I said again.

"Yes, I do. However, it doesn't change anything. The Red Devil must die. And you're my link to find him while he's still in the city."

"And if I don't, you won't give me the grimoire."

"I can give you so many things." He stroked the hair back from my face. "Anything you desire. I'm a very rich man—even if everyone thinks I'm dead."

"I don't want your money. Or any gifts. I just want the grimoire."

"And I want the Red Devil."

"I'm sure he'd be flattered."

He slid his hand down the side of my face to my throat and neck, where he drew a line with the tip of his index finger along my gold chain. "I don't think you should break your curse at all. Do you know what being a night-walker really means?"

Gideon was way too close to me, our bodies were nearly touching. I could feel the heat coming off him in waves and smell the scent of his skin. Humans did smell like food to vampires when they got too close—warm, edible, and delicious. I was thankful that, while my chain was on, I had control over my thirst. I'd mostly stayed away from humans since I was sired and replaced my casual acquaintances and friends from my old job with new vampire friends. It was a bit disheartening how easily they'd accepted that I'd moved on to a new social group, but it was safer that way.

However, Gideon tended to get a little too close for comfort.

Close enough for me to feel the hard outline of his BlackBerry in the pocket of his pants.

At least . . . I think that was his BlackBerry. Or maybe he was just happy to see me.

Or both.

Damn.

Maybe I should answer his question, I thought. *And stop focusing on what he has in his pants.*

"Being a nightwalker means I'm an out-of-control monster who needs to be staked before I hurt somebody," I finally said.

He shrugged and drew even closer to me until my back was pressed firmly against the wall. "Or it means you have oceans of power at your fingertips. Along with your special blood, you could take your curse and make it an asset. Maybe you shouldn't try to stop the inevitable. Don't you believe in fate?"

"I believe in not using humans as chew toys. It's kind of been a rule of mine."

"So well-behaved for a vampire." He lowered his head so we were eye to eye and slid his hand around to the small of my back. "Do you ever think about how it would be if you just let go of all that control? I bet you'd find it very pleasurable."

"As pleasurable as you found your afternoon . . . *nap*?" I asked pointedly.

"Jealousy doesn't suit you, Sarah."

I braced my hands against his chest. "I'm not jealous."

"Admit it—to yourself and to me. Despite who I am. Despite who *you* are. You *like* me." His lips curled to the side and he focused on my mouth for a moment longer than was polite. "And I bet your nightwalker likes me, too, doesn't she?" He touched my chain and let his finger trail boldly down the front of me. "The part of you that wants to be free and wild and unrestrained?"

Something deep inside me shifted and surged forward. It was a healthy burst of lust that agreed wholeheartedly and without reservation to what Gideon was saying.

He was right. My inner nightwalker wanted Gideon so much she was fighting me right now for control even with my gold chain on. She wanted to make his bedsheets even messier than they already were.

I thought back to what Veronique had said that morning about the Carastrand's magic only being a temporary thing.

If so, there was no time to waste.

"It's true," I said. "I do like you."

He raised an eyebrow at the admission.

I was so close. I wanted to slip my hand into his pocket and grab the BlackBerry and then run as far away from Gideon as I could get—he was much too dangerous to me on too many levels.

"That's right," he whispered approvingly into my ear as my hands slid lower on his body. "I knew you wanted me."

He covered my mouth with his and he kissed me. I kissed him back as I attempted to maneuver my way into his pocket to get what I'd come there for.

Unfortunately, despite his healthy libido, Gideon wasn't stupid. It would have been so much easier if he was. He knew what I was after. His hand clamped down on my wrist just as I felt the cool metal of the cell phone.

"Someone has wandering hands," he said.

"I thought you wouldn't mind."

"But I do." He stepped back from me and eyed me with sudden distrust. "I'm disappointed in you, Sarah."

I felt frozen. Caught. Exposed. And a little bit dirty.

"I . . . I don't know what—"

"Get out," he said quietly.

"But I thought we were—"

"Leave now before I get angry and do something I might regret." His eyes glittered and his hands were clenched in fists at his sides. "I will contact you about the ritual tomorrow."

Feeling defeated and embarrassed, I slunk out of his hotel room without another word.

Great plan, I told myself dejectedly. *Now he trusts me even less than he already did.*

Total failure.

What else was new?

I started walking along Spadina Avenue. I needed to clear my head and think things through even though I knew it wouldn't change a damn thing. Red Devil Thierry didn't come out of the woodwork again. He was probably pissed off at me, too.

Take a number.

I tried to make things better and they just got worse. It was a talent, or something. I should teach classes at the Learning Annex.

After ten minutes of wandering in the cold night air with only my self-deprecating thoughts to keep me company I passed the entrance to Darkside. Like any self-respecting secret vampire nightclub, it was completely nondescript from the outside. In fact, it appeared to be a boarded-up used bookstore with a For Sale sign in the front window. If I concentrated and used my stronger vampire senses, I could hear the dance music from inside, but the insulation was very good. No humans, including hunters, would be any the wiser.

The bouncer—the same one from the other night— stood outside with his back to the club. To anyone who didn't know better he looked like some guy loitering all alone and definitely unapproachable if you knew what was good for you. He smoked a cigar and eyed me as I passed. I remembered the last time I'd seen him, when he'd let me run after the fledgling-in-distress because he wasn't paid enough to put himself in harm's way.

Still charming.

"Slayer of Slayers," he said with a grin.

I forced a smile onto my face. "Thought I told you that wasn't me."

"You told me but I don't believe you—I know who you are. Honestly, you should be proud of such a rep. *I'm* impressed."

"Then my work here is done." I looked up at the building. "I heard a rumor this place has been sold. Please tell me it's not closing down."

He shrugged. "No idea what's going to happen next. Nobody tells me nothing."

It would suck if the new owners shut it down. No more vampire clubs in Toronto would be a major bummer. Maybe I'd teach myself how to knit.

"Anyhow, good to see you again." I wanted to move along toward my comfortable bed and try to forget tonight ever happened, as if that was remotely possible.

"Yeah, you, too." He leered at me and it made me

uncomfortable enough to start walking, quickly, away from him.

Creepy men seemed to come in the fanged and non-fanged varieties.

After another minute I came to the alley where I'd nearly had a fledgling midnight snack, and I repressed a shudder at the memory. Would I really have hurt her? I had no doubt I would have bitten her, but would I have stopped before it was too late?

"Hey," the bouncer said, and I froze and looked over my shoulder. He'd trailed after me from the club. "Can I ask you a question?"

I swallowed, feeling more than a little uncomfortable. "Sure."

"How many slayers have you killed?"

"That's a bit hard to answer."

"That many, huh?" He gazed at me with obvious appreciation of my deadly prowess. "That's pretty hot."

"Oh, I don't know about that. Blood and guts is hell on a manicure."

"So, do you think you could take me in a fight?" he asked.

I eyed him. He was big and brawny and looked tough enough to smash beer cans against his forehead if he was so inclined. "Let's *never* find out, shall we?"

His expression soured. "You're not too friendly, are you?"

"The least friendly person I know, actually."

"I don't normally take any shit from women. My ex-wife used to cost me a fortune in alimony. She was a total bitch."

"*Was?*" I asked, tentatively.

"Yeah. *Was*."

"Look, I don't want any problems tonight."

"Do I seem the type to give somebody like you a problem?"

"Actually, yes." My heart rate had picked up. "Very much so and regularly. And I'm not in the mood to deal with any extra strife in my life so if you wouldn't mind leaving me alone so I can go home to my Slayer of Slayers lair, I'd really appreciate it."

"You didn't answer my question before," he said.

"What question?"

"Do you think you could take me in a fight?"

"I don't think so," I answered honestly, a chill going down my spine. "So why don't you go away now and I won't have to scream my head off for help."

"Nobody's going to help you," he said. "Nobody helps anybody anymore. It's everyone for themselves, dog eat dog. Kill or be killed."

"If you're thinking about mugging me, I think I have about five bucks in my purse. Hardly worth the effort."

He laughed. "I don't attack women. What kind of a monster do you take me for?"

I finally exhaled the breath I'd been holding. "You were seriously freaking me out. Then why are you acting like this?"

"Like what?"

"Like somebody who is going to attack somebody."

"I'm stalling for time."

I frowned. "You're . . . stalling for time?"

"Yeah. You walk really fast. I needed to let my friends have a chance to catch up."

"*Friends*," I repeated, feeling the churning, sick feeling

in my stomach begin to radiate out to the rest of my body.

He nodded. "I think they're here now."

I heard footsteps approaching from different directions and the outlines of several men appeared in the darkness.

"Good job," one of the men told the bouncer. "You definitely earned your finder's fee."

The bouncer looked at me. "Who says slayers and vampires can't be friends?"

I glanced at the other two hunters who already had their stakes in hand.

Three hunters. One me.

Those weren't very good odds at all, were they?

Chapter 11

Right. So here we were again. Cornered by vampire hunters. The story of my life. Did I deserve a stake through my heart for making questionably intelligent choices?

Probably.

Was that what I was looking for every time I wandered outside after dark?

Maybe it was. My actions did seem to speak louder than words.

I'd been staked before. Obviously I'd lived, since it hadn't hit my heart, but it still hurt like hell and added to my selection of nightmares from my subconscious juke box.

If these losers were going to try to kill me, I sure hoped they had better aim than the last guy.

"She's so quiet," one of the other hunters observed. "All reflective and shit. Is she going to fight us or what?"

"Not sure," the bouncer replied. "But if you wouldn't mind settling up, I'll leave you to your mayhem."

"You have been mighty helpful, Bruce."

The bouncer smiled widely. "And for the right price I'd be happy to be helpful in the future as well."

My throat was dry. "You're selling out vamps just to make some pocket change?"

Bruce the bouncer shrugged. "Survival of the fittest. Blood ain't cheap, you know."

My hands felt sweaty. "How much did I go for?"

"A thousand." Bruce looked at the hunter.

A thousand? A measly thousand bucks? If I wasn't so scared I'd be insulted.

"You know—" my voice shook more than I'd like it to "—I once knew a vampire who sold out other vamps to hunters for money."

Bruce snorted. "Yeah? And I care about that, *because*?"

"Because now she's dead."

He mock-shivered. "Ooo, scary. Let me guess . . . you killed her?"

I shook my head. "Hunters don't exactly make the best business partners."

He raised an eyebrow. "Oh, yeah?"

Then he gasped.

The hunter next to him had taken the opportunity to sink a stake into his chest. "The lady's right. Make sure you don't make the same mistake twice, okay, chum?"

"Damn." Bruce the bouncer dropped to his knees and looked down at the sharp piece of wood protruding from his heart with wide eyes. He pulled it out a moment before he disintegrated into a dark puddle of goo.

"Are you going to kill me now, too?" My voice sounded oddly emotionless.

The hunter studied me for a moment. "Have to say

you're not making this half as much fun as I thought it would be, given your reputation and all. Are you positive you're the real Slayer of Slayers?"

"That's what it says on my business cards."

He cocked his head to the side. "Why did your eyes turn black all of a sudden?"

"Because that's what happens when I take off my accessories." I slid the gold chain I'd removed during the slayage of Bruce the bouncer into my pocket.

Sure, I perhaps had a bit of a death wish now, but I wasn't a total victim. Desperate times called for desperate measures, after all.

I exhaled the last breath I actually needed and felt my head clear of any racing, frightened thoughts. My heartbeat came to a slow and sudden stop. The night around me ceased to feel even slightly cold and my vision narrowed in on the three weapon-carrying vampire hunters facing me.

"Leave me alone," I said evenly. "And I won't have to star in any of your future nightmares."

The first hunter laughed and looked at his buddies each in turn. "Do you hear that? I'm scared now."

When he returned his attention to me I grabbed him by the throat. "Leave. Me. Alone. Was that hard to understand? I thought I said it rather clearly."

With a shove I launched him backward. He hit the ground hard enough to knock the wind out of him. He coughed and sputtered, then raised his furious gaze to mine. I saw him in tunnel vision now. Just him. No one else. And his throat did look rather appetizing with my handprint on it.

"Vicious, evil creature of darkness," he growled. "The world would be better without you in it."

I cocked my head to the side. "Right back at you, sunshine."

He was about to rush me, stake held high, but a hand clamped down on his shoulder and he turned to face whoever was behind him.

A punch landed across the hunter's jaw and he spun back around. A thin line of blood and saliva flew from his mouth. Gideon stood there wearing a black scarf that partially covered his face—but not enough to shield his identity.

"You should leave my friend alone," Gideon said. He was talking to the hunter.

The hunter looked up in shock, holding the side of his face. "My God. Gideon Chase? Is that you?" He shakily got back to his feet and glanced at his two friends. "I can't believe this. You're supposed to be dead!"

"I am, aren't I?"

The hunter nodded. "I went to your funeral."

"Thank you for that." Gideon cast a quick look in my direction and then at the other two surprised hunters on either side of him. "I assume it was a good turnout?"

"Of course." The hunter nodded enthusiastically. "Very fitting for a great man like yourself." He looked at me. "We cornered the Slayer of Slayers. Do you want to do the honors?"

"No. As I said, Sarah is my friend. Or at least—" his eyes narrowed on me "—I *thought* she was. I'm not so sure anymore."

My nightwalker was very excited to see Gideon again.

She wanted to run to him and throw her arms around him. I firmly muzzled and restrained her.

The hunter frowned then. "I don't understand. You're friends with a . . . a vampire? That doesn't make any sense. What happened? Were you injured in the fire?"

"You could say that."

"Your body wasn't recovered. You were presumed dead. You must come with me and we can tell everyone—"

Gideon's arm moved and I saw a glint of silver under the moonlight. The hunter clutched his throat and made a sick, gurgling sound as Gideon slit his throat. Dark blood welled between the hunter's fingers.

"Actually," Gideon said evenly, "I'd prefer you didn't tell anyone about my little secret if you wouldn't mind." He arched his arm and the next-closest hunter got the blade embedded in his chest. "That goes for you as well."

Both men fell to the ground dead.

Since I wasn't currently wearing my chain, the fear and shock I should have felt at witnessing these murders felt distant to me, as if I was watching this on television. But this was real. Gideon had killed two out of three of the hunters without even blinking.

In front of me was a great deal of blood that filled me more with hunger than fear. I raised my black eyes to the man in front of me.

"Aren't you going to thank me?" Gideon asked.

"For what?"

"For saving your life again?"

Thank you, Gideon, my nightwalker chimed inside me. But I said nothing.

They hadn't threatened him. One hunter had even wanted to help him.

"Just a moment." Gideon held up a finger. "There's one more for me to deal with, isn't there?"

But the third hunter wasn't there anymore. I heard the slap of hard-soled boots as he ran away down the street. However, there was another man standing in his place. This one wore a red mask.

"Your hunter is getting away," Red Devil Thierry said. "Shouldn't you be in murderous pursuit?"

Gideon smiled broadly. "See, Sarah? I had a funny feeling that if I followed you from my hotel tonight as I did last night there might be a chance I'd catch a glimpse of the elusive Red Devil again. But this is more than I'd hoped for."

I reached into my pocket with a shaking hand. I knew I had to get my chain back on while I still had some semblance of control. I couldn't feel it. Frantically I scanned the alley. There it was. On the ground a half dozen feet away. It must have slipped out when I tossed the hunter away from me.

My gaze tracked back to Gideon and Thierry, who studied each other intensely. For the first time in several minutes, my fear completely slipped through to the surface. My heart let out one small, barely noticeable thump.

"This doesn't have to happen," I managed. "Not here. Not tonight."

Gideon bent over and pulled his knife from the dead hunter's chest. "It was a little earlier than I'd planned, but I can adapt."

"I'm told you have a grimoire." Thierry still spoke in that low, raspy voice.

"Has naughty little Sarah told you all my secrets?"

"You will need to give me the grimoire and then leave her alone. Permanently."

"I need to, do I?" Gideon glanced at me. "Just look at her, though. How could you possibly want to break her curse? She's so powerful like this. Can't you feel it? She's better than a normal vampire. So unbelievably powerful. It would be a waste to snuff out all of that possibility."

"Give me the grimoire," Thierry persisted.

"I'd be happy to give it to Sarah if she still wants it. But first you need to die."

Thierry grabbed him by the front of his shirt and glared at him. "You first."

Gideon easily twisted around and out of Thierry's grip like the trained, athletic hunter he was. I watched, half entranced, half panicked at what would happen next.

"Stop this," I said, taking a step toward them. "Please. Nobody has to get hurt here."

"Stay back," Thierry said.

"Thanks to Sarah's blood last night I'm feeling much better than I was before." Gideon clutched his knife tighter. "That's why I sought you out—the infamous Red Devil. My last kill as a fully human hunter. Let's make it a good one, shall we?"

Thierry didn't have a weapon, but he lunged at Gideon anyhow, his fist connecting with the hunter's jaw. Gideon's head snapped to the side. I knew Thierry was very strong, a strength that had grown over all of his centuries. How did Gideon think he had any chance against him?

But Gideon was fast, and he easily ducked the next blow. The silver of his knife flashed bright a moment before it made contact with Thierry's chest, sinking in deep enough to make Thierry gasp in pain. He shoved Gideon back from him.

Thierry glared at him. "You missed my heart."

"True. A bit unsatisfying." Gideon glanced at the knife. "However, considering this silver blade is coated in dead blood I think I've done enough."

"Go to hell, hunter," Thierry growled.

Dead blood. I searched my memory for what I'd learned through my recent vampire research. The blood of a dead human could be used as a poison against vampires. But the hunter had only just died minutes ago. The blood on the ground was still fresh enough to be appetizing to me. I thought "dead blood" had to be much older than that.

Blood. My nightwalker self moved closer to the surface of my consciousness. *So much delicious blood.*

Thierry staggered back a few feet, now favoring his injured side. Seeing the sudden weakness, Gideon moved toward him again.

"You've definitely earned your grimoire, Sarah," he said, flicking a glance in my direction. "And my renewed trust."

He arched the knife toward Thierry's chest again, but I quickly moved toward him and grabbed his arm to feel the hard bicep underneath.

"What are you doing?" he snapped.

"Stopping you."

"Let me finish him."

"No."

He frowned at me. "Let go of me or you won't get your precious grimoire."

"You can shove the grimoire."

I clamped my grip down on Gideon's wrist until the pain made him drop the knife.

"Sarah, what are you—" He gasped in surprise when I wrenched his head to the side and sank my fangs into his throat as the dark thirst swept over me. He weakly pushed back against me as I pressed him up against the brick wall—our positions the opposite of those we'd had in his hotel room.

My mind went blank to everything except the salty tang of blood that spilled into my mouth.

Almost blank. My hand sought out the pocket of his pants and I pulled out the BlackBerry. I slipped it into the pocket of my jeans. He didn't feel a thing. After all, he was a bit preoccupied dealing with my teeth in his neck.

Only a short taste, unfortunately—and not nearly long enough to transfer the vampire virus to him.

Thierry hauled me off him so forcefully that I staggered across the alley to whack my head against the hard wall, and I fell to the ground. It was the second time that day I'd hit my head.

But this time I wasn't knocked unconscious. Something else happened. Thanks to the pain now ringing through my skull, the nightwalker fog cleared a little. Enough to allow me the chance to crawl on the ground until I found the gold chain. I scrambled to put it back on as quickly as I could, and my head immediately cleared.

I gasped for a breath of air. My heart began to beat again.

Thierry crouched next to me. His gray eyes behind the mask were filled with concern.

"Are you all right?" he demanded. "Did I hurt you?"

I blinked rapidly. Did he hurt *me*? Is that what he asked?

"I'm okay," I managed. My eyes widened. "Gideon—"

I looked over to where I'd chomped on the hunter in question only to find that the alley was empty now except for the two of us.

And the bodies of the two hunters.

And the dark stain of Bruce the bouncer.

Thierry got to his feet before helping me to mine, and then grimaced in pain. He held a hand against his injured chest just under his heart. I could see the blood. There was a lot of it. Instead of hunger, my stomach twisted with concern.

"Gideon said the dead blood on the blade—"

"It's fine." It was the first time I'd ever heard that much pain in his voice. "It won't heal as quickly as normal, but it's fine."

"You're lying."

He looked over at the bodies. "I need to call somebody to take care of this mess."

He took a step back from me and faltered, then braced himself against the wall.

A sharp line of panic sliced through me. He *so* wasn't fine. At all.

"Then call somebody," I said. "But you're coming home with me."

That earned me a glare, but not an argument. I felt sick at the thought that Gideon had managed to hurt Thierry, but why was I surprised? That had been his goal—to kill the Red Devil—just as it was his goal for me to turn him into a vampire tomorrow at midnight.

The man had a lot of goals.

In one fell swoop I'd betrayed his confidence and attached myself to his jugular—as well as siding with the Red Devil and thus diminishing my chances of ever getting my hands on that grimoire. Not a great way to win friends and influence people.

I wouldn't think about what the repercussions would be just yet.

One thing at a time. I had to make sure Thierry was okay, whether or not he'd ever admit his true identity to me. Then I'd deal with Gideon. Because if he still wanted me to sire him tomorrow, he'd just experienced a sneak peek.

Despite his assurances that he was feeling just peachy keen—my words, not his—by the time he'd made a quick phone call to whoever might be the local go-to guy for corpse clean-up and we'd made our way back to George's house, the "Red Devil" was very pale under his red mask. He even leaned on me slightly as we walked up the driveway. I knew he wouldn't do that unless he was feeling pretty badly. After all, the closer he got, the more likely it was that I'd discover his big fat secret.

Obviously, Elvis had already left the building on that particular subject. Thierry just didn't know it yet.

My head still ached from bashing it against the brick wall, and I also was dealing with the taste of Gideon's disturbingly delicious blood still in my mouth, but Thierry's current state of health was my number-one concern.

Fortunately, George wasn't home. I knew he had his first shift at the strip club that evening and hoped he was getting over his odd mood enough to rake in the tips.

Serving alcohol to a sea of horny human females amongst a bunch of half-dressed muscled men helped to get the cash flowing. I might know that from personal experience. No admissions here.

I nudged the front door open and helped Thierry inside. A small table light was on, but the overhead wasn't so I made a move for the light switch. He took my hand in his to stop me.

"No more lights," he said.

I looked at him through the near darkness. "Why? You want to make sure I don't see you? Want to keep your identity a secret?"

"Something like that."

I hissed out a breath, annoyed by his typical stubbornness. "Then keep your stupid mask on, but I need to see your wound."

"Forget my wound. I'm fine."

"You look like you're going to keel over."

He braced a hand against the wall behind him. The other hand, now dark with his blood, was pressed to his chest. "I've felt better."

"The blood of a dead human is like a poison for vamps," I stated the obvious. "But the guy was barely dead. Why would it affect you this badly?"

His jaw clenched. When he raised his gaze to mine I could see the uncertainty there as well as the pain. "If the freshly dead blood was consumed orally it wouldn't be as great a risk, but a silver weapon tipped with the same blood will have a more deadly result."

"*Deadly*," I repeated, feeling cold.

"I need to leave." He made a move toward the door, but I easily blocked his way.

"Is there somebody who can help you? A doctor that knows how to fix this sort of injury?"

His throat worked as he swallowed. "I'm afraid it's too late for that."

I felt a flash of panic. "What do you mean?"

His lips thinned. "Gideon may have gotten his wish tonight."

"Don't tell me you think you're dying."

"Then I won't tell you that." His pale expression shadowed. "But there is no cure I'm aware of to reverse the effects of such an injury."

He braced himself against the wall behind him and slid slowly to the floor. The blood on his hand was slick and shiny even in the darkness.

If it was a regular knife wound it would be healed already. I remembered when I was staked and Thierry got me to drink from him afterward to help me heal up quickly with his master vampire blood.

According to Gideon, my blood was even more powerful than that. It had even taken his pain away. A magical cure-all.

"Wait here," I snapped at him.

I was all bossy when I was scared. And I was. He was dying. It was slow but every moment that passed I could see the life leaving him bit by bit.

In the kitchen I grabbed the sharpest knife I could find and then went back into the living room.

"You need to drink some of my blood," I told him. "If I can heal Gideon, maybe I can heal you, too."

"Sarah—"

I waved off any protests he might make. "Gideon wants my blood because it's supercharged with energy

and healing properties. I'm like a can of medicinal Red
Bull right now."

I took the knife and held it against my forearm, tensed,
and then dragged the sharp edge across my skin. *Ouch.*
The blood welled up and I sat down on the floor next to
him and held my arm out.

His eyes darkened, *literally*, but he turned his face
away. "No, Sarah."

"Drink."

He shook his head. "I can't."

"You can't, or you won't?"

"I won't. It's . . . it's complicated. I don't want to hurt
you."

Stubbornness, thy name was Thierry de Bennicoeur.
Yes, he had an addiction to blood and whenever he got a
taste he went a bit insane. It had happened once or twice
with me—he'd tasted me and lost control. Now this might
sound kind of hot, but it wasn't. It was scary and dangerous and he'd almost drained me dry.

At the moment, I was tempting fate by waving myself
like a big juicy steak in front of a starving lion. But there
simply wasn't any other choice.

"Stop being a baby and drink my blood." Definitely not
a phrase I used every day.

His eyes had turned completely black with hunger.
"You don't know what you're doing. You don't know who
I am."

Wrong, devil-boy. I knew exactly who he was. He was
the man I loved, despite his being the most impossible,
stubborn, secretive jerk on the planet and currently under
the impression I was cheating on him with the leader of
the vampire hunters.

I brought my arm another inch closer.

"Sarah . . ." His voice lowered further, into a low tone that gave me goose bumps.

"Drink," I insisted for what felt like the millionth time.

His hands moved to grip my arm and he gazed at the line of blood presented to him. After hesitating for another long moment, he lowered his mouth and slid his tongue along the wound and without any further protests, he drank. His eyes closed and he gripped me very tightly.

Sure, I was worried that I wouldn't be able to stop him. When he drank blood he lost that part of himself that helped him stay in control. Sort of like me losing my gold chain. He'd promised to work on this little problem of his, but as with an alcoholic, it was probably best to stay away from the drug of choice.

Blood was Thierry's drug. Which, as a vampire, was not exactly convenient.

After a minute or two, he pulled his mouth away from my skin and looked at me, his eyes as black as death itself. I forced myself to stand up and he followed. He trailed his hands around to my back, and he pressed me against the wall with the weight of his body.

"I don't think your *boyfriend* would appreciate this." His voice was low and sexy and very much not like the normal bloodless Thierry.

"You're probably right," I managed, my body tingling everywhere he touched me.

"And yet you're not pushing me away." One of his hands moved downward again to explore my body in a very non-first-date sort of way. I bit my bottom lip as a hot line of desire raced through me.

Black-eyed Thierry had a tendency to be way more aggressive than regular-eyed Thierry. And while part of me feared this, another part really . . . well . . . *liked* it. A lot.

I know. I had issues.

He stroked the hair off my neck and pulled my shirt off my left shoulder. He did the same thing with my bra strap, and then he caressed the now-exposed skin there.

"You were right. Your blood has healed me, but I want more," he growled, and I felt the brush of his fangs on my throat. "I need more."

"You need more of my blood?"

He licked along the curve of my ear as he whispered, "I want to sink into you, Sarah. I want to taste you so deeply . . ."

"Is that your best pick-up line? Because it's totally working."

I tensed at the sudden pain as his needle-sharp fangs pierced my skin. But, instead of pushing him away, I wrapped my arms around him and let him drink. I wanted him to have my blood. I wanted him to be okay.

After a minute, he pulled away from me. His expression was tight and haunted. His chest moved with labored breathing. "I can't do this. I can't take too much." He pushed back from me until there was a good six feet separating us. "I'm surprised at you. Why didn't you stop me?"

"I didn't want to."

"Even with your recent interest in Gideon, I was under the impression that you were more loyal to the one you proclaim to love."

I held a hand to my neck. He was able to stop all by himself. That was major progress! "I *am* loyal."

"It doesn't seem like it to me." There was a hard edge of anger to his words now.

I eyed him. "I guess you don't know me very well at all, do you?"

"All I know is that you let me touch you, that you let me taste you, with no protests. I don't think that's very loyal behavior."

"No, it definitely isn't." I began to unbutton my blouse and took a small thrill at the shocked look he gave me. "Actually, neither is this."

"What in the hell do you think you're doing?"

"Seducing you."

He took another step back from me as I approached. "You've given me enough of your powerful blood to heal my wound and I thank you for that. But this isn't right."

"Because you're the Red Devil, a vampire of mystery and intrigue?"

"Because you're in love with another. Or is that no longer the case?"

I let my blouse fall to the ground. I wore a really nice black lace push-up bra underneath. It had a little pink bow in the front that I knew probably wouldn't make it through the first wash. I never sorted my delicates. It was a lazy habit and it tended to cost me loads in new lingerie.

Not that my laundry habits were even remotely important at the moment. I'm just saying.

"I love you," I said evenly.

His eyes widened and I watched them slowly change from the black of a hungry vampire back to his cool, gray gaze. "No, Sarah—"

I walked directly toward him and kissed him, feeling how tense he still was. His cold mask shifted a little against my face.

With a low groan, he pushed me back from him. "Why would you say something like this to me?"

"Because it's true. I love you." I crossed my arms. "I'm breaking it off with Thierry to be with you. I love you, Red Devil. You can bite me any time. Thierry and I are through, he just can't get it through his thick head."

He stared at me for what felt like a very long time, studying my face and body language. Suddenly, a clear realization came over his expression. It was amusing enough to almost salvage the entire messed-up day for me. *Almost.*

"You *know*, don't you?" he asked slowly.

I smiled at him. "That the Red Devil and Thierry de Bennicoeur are one and the same? Of course I know. *Duh.*"

Chapter 12

Yᴏu can take the mask off any time now." I finally flicked on the light and the living room became painfully bright.

He looked stricken. "How did you know?"

"I just knew." I put a hand on my hip. "Also, that's not exactly the greatest disguise in the world. It's just a mask. I mean, how has no one else ever figured it out? *Veronique* doesn't even know."

He shook his head, still holding that expression of shock in his eyes. "Nobody has known."

"Not even Barry?'

"Not even Barry."

I shrugged. "I guess I'm just special. It's like Superman when Lois Lane never figured it out—his disguise was a pair of glasses, for Pete's sake. Ditto Wonder Woman. I mean, maybe Batman had a reason, since his costume was a bit more involved, but still, a jaw line is a jaw line and I could tell—"

"When did you know?"

"The third time I saw you. Or, rather, saw the *Red Devil*."

He tentatively reached up and slowly removed the mask. His handsome face was pale behind it. "Why didn't you tell me?"

"I was waiting for you to come clean and tell *me*." I raised an eyebrow. "I've been waiting for a while."

"I thought . . . when you let me touch you thinking I was another man that our time apart had added problems to our relationship."

"No more problems than we already had." I crossed my arms. "Like the wife who won't give you an annulment? That's a problem. Like the fact that we can't see each other in public or let anyone know we're still together? Another problem."

"Like Gideon Chase's interest in you?" he added.

"Definitely a problem. A big one." The reminder of the hunter sent a chill down my spine, especially after what had happened in the alley. "But the fact that I like you with or without the mask? That's not a problem."

"I must have lost more blood than I thought. You had me completely fooled."

"I'm obviously a brilliant actress."

"Of course." He cleared his throat. "Does anyone else know?"

I shook my head. "Just me. And I have no idea how Veronique couldn't have clued in. By the way, I'm supposed to set you and her up together. She wants to be *lovers*."

"When Veronique couldn't see past my mask I assumed that my disguise was good enough and didn't give it another thought. She had known me for hundreds of years before she met the Red Devil. She should have known."

"But she didn't."

"No." His gaze moved over my features. "But you did."

"By the way, I'm fairly furious with you and I have about a billion more questions, so if you wouldn't mind—"

He kissed me and it took me by surprise, but not in a bad way. I wrapped my arms around him as the kiss deepened.

"I've missed you very much," he murmured then. "I've wanted to see you but I've been fearful for your safety. I've wanted to touch you but I couldn't."

I smiled against his lips. "Well, you're here now. And my blouse is currently on the floor. I think that's probably a good sign that even though I'm still mad at you right now, touching is allowed."

He leaned back and placed his hands on either side of my face. "This will work out. All of this. I won't let anything bad happen to you."

"Promises, promises."

"It's a promise and a vow." His lips brushed mine again.

I unbuttoned his shirt and pulled it away so I could inspect his chest. I ran my fingers over the now rapidly healing wound. Only a small pink mark remained from where the knife had made contact. I kissed it before looking up at him again.

"See?" I said. "All better."

"Your blood is as powerful as Gideon claims it is." His expression shadowed. "It worries me deeply."

I felt another chill as I remembered the look in Gideon's eyes as I turned against him. He'd looked angry and disappointed with me—not a good combination.

I pressed my index finger against his lips. "Let's think about that later, okay?"

"Why? Did you have other subjects for us to address at the moment?"

I nodded this time. "Actually, I do."

He didn't protest this time when I kissed him, no more talking about Gideon, or my curse, or anything like that. He was alive. He was okay. He knew I knew who he was and he knew how much I loved him.

But just to make sure, I led him to my microscopic bedroom and showed him. Twice.

Um. Make that *three* times.

He told me again how much he loved me as his mouth and body took me to the edge and back . . . however, he very politely kept his fangs to himself.

I didn't care if he was old enough to have had the chance to see Romeo and Juliet performed on stage for the first time sitting next to Shakespeare himself, the man I loved had the stamina of a thirty-year-old.

Afterward, he held me in his arms and I explored his chest: muscled but lean, with a familiar old three-inch scar from where he'd been injured as a human. So faint that it was hard to see if you weren't looking for it. I traced it with the tip of my finger.

"Now, no more secrets," I said. "Tell me about the Red Devil. Let's start with the main points."

He threaded his fingers through my hair and pulled me closer to him. "I wasn't the original Red Devil. It was Marcellus, Veronique's lover from before I even met her. The night Marcellus died I learned his secret, and he entrusted me to destroy his papers, his identity. But I knew that the Red Devil couldn't die. I wanted to continue with the same name and try to . . . try to—"

"Help others," I finished for him.

"That was the original plan."

"Does Veronique know this about Marcellus?" I'd heard enough about the guy from her before. She claimed he was her one true love. All her multitude of lovers since had paled in comparison to this Valentino vamp.

"I don't think so. At least, she never gave any indication."

"It's all very Zorro. Very solitary Musketeer."

"If you say so."

"And you funded this all yourself? Without telling anyone?"

"No one has known." He swallowed. "Until now. Obviously I'm very rusty after being out of commission for so long."

"I think I still would have known."

He looked at me incredulously. "I still cannot believe it."

"Believe it. Why did you stop? You haven't done the mask thing for a hundred years, right?"

His jaw tensed. "It was after what happened with Elizabeth."

I remembered the name. Elizabeth was Thierry's friend's wife who wanted to have an affair with Thierry a century ago, but it didn't turn out the way she'd planned. When she used her own blood to try to seduce him, it backfired—due to his blood addiction—and he nearly drained her. She ran from the bloodthirsty Thierry into a pack of hunters who killed her without a second thought. Thierry felt it was his fault, and the guilt had stayed with him all of these years.

"It was then I knew that the Red Devil caused more harm than good. That perhaps it was safer to stay hidden than charge headfirst into danger."

"Not safer for you, safer for others, you mean."

He wouldn't meet my gaze anymore. "That's right."

I studied his tense, haunted expression. "What's the problem?"

He shook his head. "No problem. I don't usually share so much."

"Tell me something I don't know."

"There are so many things that I regret in my life."

I touched his face and made him look at me. "Which totally answers the question of why you're always so serious."

He finally met my eyes directly. "Actually, I was serious even as a human."

"Figures."

I kissed him again before he pulled back to look down at me. He stroked the hair off my forehead.

"I keep waiting for you to be so disgusted by my past that you really, truly want to leave me. And your spending a great deal of time with Gideon while keeping it from me has done nothing to ease my mind."

I sighed. "Damn. I never knew master vampires could be so needy."

His lips twitched with amusement. "I'm *not* needy."

"So needy. And jealous. And possessive. But just for the record, I'm not giving Gideon anything other than my time."

"You kissed him."

"It was nothing. Seriously." I cleared my throat. "So what would you like me to do about Veronique wanting to become the Red Devil's lover? Seriously. She's so into the guy that a little drool messed up her Chanel lip gloss when she was talking about him. It was kind of sad."

"Are you trying to change the subject?"

"Yes, I am. Now, Veronique and the Red Devil. Your thoughts?"

He raised a dark eyebrow. "I'm afraid having an affair with my estranged wife is not something that interests me."

"Come on, now. The woman is beautiful. She's powerful and savvy and you guys have a lot of history together."

"This is all very true."

I cringed. If Thierry and Veronique were Internet dating, they'd definitely be matched up together. Me? I'd be put with the guy who still lived with his parents and enjoyed an unhealthy relationship with video games.

"Then what's the problem?"

He sighed. "You're serious about this?"

"No. Forget it. I really don't want to know."

He shook his head. "You asked and I'll answer. Why wouldn't I embrace the chance to be with Veronique again? Being that she's so—as you believe—perfect?"

"Did I say that?"

"Numerous times."

"Okay, then why? Why would you put up with everything we've been through? Everything we're probably *going* to go through, when the simple, perfect choice has been right in front of you all along?"

"Why would you choose to be with me when you're obviously better matched with Quinn?" he countered.

I blinked at that. "Well, I'm not in love with him, for

one thing. Also, Quinn's engaged to a really scary blond chick now. I probably wouldn't touch him with a ten-foot pole even if I wanted to."

His expression darkened significantly. "Except for kissing him in public earlier today. And admittedly kissing Gideon as well and not wanting it to be a topic of conversation between us."

I swallowed hard. "Gideon showed what kind of person he was tonight when he slit two hunters' throats and nearly killed you."

Thierry sat up, swung his legs over the side of my bed, and proceeded to get dressed without another word.

"Where are you going?" I asked.

"In twenty-four hours you're supposed to sire Gideon. Now that I know that your blood is as powerful as he believes it to be, I'm very worried what this will mean."

"So I sire him and he leaves us alone. That was the original plan, wasn't it?"

He shook his head, his brow deeply creased with worry. "You don't know what the implications could be when someone like him is given the power and strength equivalent of a master vampire."

He was right, of course. I let out a shaky breath. "I know, this is bad. I'm sorry."

"Please don't apologize." He slid into his black jacket. "And if you really want to know how I could possibly choose you over such a perfect woman as Veronique— just know that such perfection is highly overrated."

He slid his hand into his jacket pocket and pulled something out. Something small that sat easily in his palm. "Know that I carry this with me every day with the hope that I'll earn the right to be able to give it to you again."

It was a ring studded with diamonds around its circum-
ference. An eternity band. He'd given it to me a couple
of weeks ago and I'd given it back to him when I'd been
forced to break things off with him. While it wasn't an
engagement ring—hard to be engaged to somebody who
was already married—it symbolized Thierry's wanting to
have me in his life.

My heart swelled to the size of a hot-air balloon. "Can
I have it back now?"

He closed his hand and shook his head. "I'm going to
hold on to it for safekeeping."

"You carry that with you everywhere?"

He nodded.

A smile began to spread across my face. "You are such
a romantic."

I gathered the sheets around me and kneeled on the
side of the bed. He sat down on the edge and touched
my face, stroking the hair out of my eyes and tucking it
behind my ears.

"I love that you saw through my disguises to who I
truly am." His voice was thick.

"Bad disguise. Really flimsy." I smiled as he brushed
his mouth against mine. "But I love you anyhow."

He raised an amused eyebrow. "Now, I must go. Before
tomorrow night I have to figure out how best to deal with
Gideon without jeopardizing the safety of anyone."

His words worked like a splash of cold water in my
face. "Oh, my God. I can't believe I forgot!"

"Forgot what?"

"I wanted to grab Gideon's BlackBerry tonight in his
hotel room, but it totally fell through," I said, choosing to
limit the details, including being pressed up against the

wall by the BlackBerry owner in question as my inner
nightwalker rubbed against Gideon like a cat. "I'd hoped
it would show me who his contacts were—the men he's
assigned to do his dirty work. If I could get that we'd definitely have an advantage."

"But you weren't able to get it?"

"Not then. But in the alley when I was . . ." I chewed
my bottom lip as I flashbacked to what happened earlier. ". . . doing my Gideon Chase taste test I managed
to grab it."

"You did?"

I leaned over the side of the bed and grabbed my jeans,
pulling the small black device out of the front pocket. "Ta
da!"

He raised his eyebrows. "Why didn't you say anything
earlier?"

I shrugged. "I was a bit busy dealing with the Red
Devil dying on George's living room carpet. And then I
was distracted by—" I smiled at him "—*other things*."

"Definitely the highlight of the evening for me." He slid
his warm hand along my arm before he frowned. "The
'other things' you speak of, not dying on the carpet."

I grinned. "I figured that's what you meant."

He took the BlackBerry from me, pressed the on button,
then scrolled to the list of sent and received messages.

I saw a long line of my cell-phone number from when
Gideon had contacted me or I'd contacted him.

"You have been in constant contact with him, haven't
you?" he said unpleasantly.

"He is blackmailing me."

"Of course."

There was only one other number listed several times.

It was a number I recognized all too well.

I shook my head. "No, there has to be more."

"This is all there is. The device has only kept a record of the past five days."

Breathing was beginning to be difficult as my heart slammed against my rib cage. I couldn't believe that number. I *knew* it. I'd dialed it myself many times before.

"He holds a clue in his hand," the demon possessing the teenaged wizard had told me. *"Of a betrayal you would never expect."*

"No, it's not possible," I managed.

Thierry regarded my stricken expression. "What's wrong?"

I tried not to throw up right then and there.

A betrayal I'd never expect.

He frowned and touched my face with concern. "Sarah, who is it? Who is Gideon's informant?"

I swallowed so hard it hurt. "It's George."

Chapter 13

It was nearly two o'clock in the morning when George got home.

He jumped when he saw me waiting on the couch for him and put a hand to his chest. "Okay, that was creepy. Are you lying in wait ready to pounce on me?"

"I'm like a ninja." I eyed him. "A dangerous, pissed-off ninja."

"I'm glad you're still up." He threw his coat into the closet and untied his black bow tie, which, along with his tight black pants, was the sum total of his new waiter's uniform. "I think I was fired. I'm officially morbidly depressed and I really need a friendly face right now."

He'd come to the wrong place for that. "Why would they ever want to fire a great guy like you?"

He didn't seem to notice the seething sarcasm attached to the words.

He rubbed his temples. "It's very possible I spilled an entire tray of drinks on a bachelorette party who then decided to take up their squelchy disappointment with the manager. She, in turn, yelled at me for being distracted on the job and threw me out. It wasn't pleasant."

"I bet." So he was distracted, huh? I guessed not telling your friends you're spying on them had a tendency to weigh heavy on one's mind.

"I'll find another way to make some extra cash."

"Oh, I'm sure you will." I patted the seat next to me. "Come sit. I want to have a little chat with you."

He looked at me warily. "Everything okay? You seem a little, what's the word? *Freaky*?"

"I'm queen of the freaks right now."

His brows lowered. "You're still wearing your chain, right? Not feeling like biting anybody?"

"I'll keep my fangs to myself. Promise."

Hesitantly, he did as I asked and sat down next to me. I searched his handsome face for a definite sign that he was a liar and a traitor—like somebody I trusted more than almost anyone else in the whole world, but who would betray our friendship like a dirty rat bastard.

He had his hands clasped together tightly and a tense, frozen smile on his face. "So . . . what's up?"

"Is there something you've been keeping from me?"

"What do you mean?"

"Something important that has been affecting your moods and causing you to spill drinks on unsuspecting women?"

He let out a shaky breath. "Yes. But, I can't say anything."

"Really?" I cocked my head to the side. "Why? Is it a surprise? My birthday isn't until October."

His bottom lip wobbled. "Look, I know I'm acting

strangely. But you . . . you just have to trust me. And don't ask me any questions."

"Trust you?"

He nodded. "Sometimes I have to keep secrets. If I don't, then people will get hurt."

This wasn't exactly the reaction I'd been expecting. "What are you talking about?"

He grabbed my arm. "I love you, Sarah. In a completely nonsexual way, of course. But whatever happens, I want you to remember that. And I love Amy. And I love Barry . . . although not nearly as much as I love you and Amy." He glanced off to the armchair next to where we were seated. "Oh, hi, Thierry. I love you, too."

"Hello, George," Thierry said.

George must really have been distracted to not see him sitting there the whole time.

His frown deepened and he looked at me. "What's he doing here? I thought you broke up."

I shrugged. "That was actually a lie. We're still together, but nobody knows."

George clasped his hands over his ears and his eyes widened. "Do *not* tell me things like that! Please!"

"Why not?" I glanced at Thierry. "It's good gossip, isn't it?"

Thierry nodded. "I'd say so."

"That's the problem!" George got up from the couch and paced to the other side of the room where he peeked through the curtains to the street outside, before spinning dramatically around to face us again. He wrung his hands. "Okay . . . I can't believe I'm going to do this, but I *have* to. I've been keeping a secret so big that it's literally been killing me."

Thierry leaned forward a little. "Do you mean the secret that Gideon Chase is still alive and you've been working as his informant?"

I tensely studied George's reaction. It didn't come right away.

"You know?" His voice sounded strangled.

I nodded. "We both do."

Instead of immediately trying to escape the house or explain it away in a rush of words, he let out a long, loud sigh of relief. "Thank God you know! I've been dying inside a little bit each day with this. You don't know what it's like to keep a secret this freaking big!"

"Actually—" I began, but George rushed back to the couch and grabbed me in a tight bear hug that squeezed the breath right out of me. He kissed me hard on the side of my face.

That was not the reaction I'd expected. At all.

George then hugged a very reluctant Thierry before sitting down hard on the floor and crossing his legs. "Gideon has been blackmailing me. He said he'd kill you, Sarah, if I didn't keep him informed about everything you're up to."

Even though I'd already mostly figured it out, the confirmation still managed to stun me. George was Gideon's spy. That's why he always knew where I was going and who I was with.

But, hold on a minute . . .

"He said he'd *kill* me?" I asked, surprised.

"Yes! And he said he'd kill Amy, too. I swear, I never would have helped him if I had any other choice. But I had to protect my girls." He paused. "And myself, of course."

Thierry stood up and came to sit next to me. He took

my hand in his. "So you've been in touch with Gideon daily about Sarah's whereabouts and activities?"

George nodded. "I only told him the bare minimum. Things like Quinn being back in town and dating Sarah." He glanced at us each in turn. "Two men again, Sarah? Still impressed. I'm currently mortified, humiliated, and unemployed, but I'm very impressed."

"Forget about Quinn," I said.

He raised an eyebrow. "Perhaps I should be telling you the same thing."

"Why didn't you tell me what was going on?" I'd been so ready to hear the worst—that George had betrayed me over a stack of money, or something petty like that, but he wasn't a good liar. He was telling the truth right now. I knew it. And it was such a total and complete relief I nearly burst into happy tears.

"Gideon said if I breathed a word he'd kill you and Amy."

I shook my head. "I can't believe he said that."

"*Gideon Chase*," George said the name shakily. "The *leader of the vampire hunters*? Hello? He's crazy. Certifiably insane, I think. And angry. And tall. And he had a lot of scars and then, *poof*, he didn't have any scars anymore. What's that all about? He threatened me and, based on his history of death and destruction, I wasn't exactly in a position to argue with him."

I nodded in agreement. "He's desperate, sure. The pain from the hellfire made him do some fairly crazy things in the beginning, but I don't know if I'd call him *insane*. Nicolai was insane. Peter was insane." A vampire and a hunter, respectively, who'd both died when trying to kill me. "But Gideon is just . . . I don't know . . . *focused*."

George, who didn't have any idea of my connection to the hunter, just stared at me with confusion. "What in the holy hell are you talking about?"

"Why are you defending him?" Thierry asked me quietly.

"I'm not defending him."

"It sounds as if you are."

I swallowed. "I'm just saying that he's made a lot of mistakes in his life and the rich, hunting family he was born into didn't exactly help. Maybe this situation—getting burned and now being turned into a vampire—is what he needs to finally change his ways."

"You witnessed him kill two hunters tonight in cold blood. And he almost killed me."

"I know that."

"And even though he's obviously lied about having any assassins or spies on call—other than his connection to George—he's threatened the people you love with death." Thierry's face had gone expressionless.

George's eyes were very wide. "What's going on here?"

Thierry raised a dark eyebrow. "It's obvious. Despite what she might want me to believe, Sarah is smitten with the hunter."

"I really hate that word," I said, feeling sick to my stomach. "And I'm not. At all."

"Gideon is very intelligent. He knows how to manipulate others to get what he wants. In George's case he wanted to use fear against him with threats. With you, Sarah, it began with threats, but obviously changed into something else he found more effective. Perhaps gifts? Compliments? Did he use his infamous charm on you?

Is that why you enjoyed the kiss you shared the other night?"

"Hold on," George cut in. "Sarah kissed Gideon? What the f—"

"Forget it, George." I crossed my arms, feeling very uncomfortable suddenly at how perceptive Thierry could be. "It was nothing."

"This is why you wouldn't do the eradication, isn't it?" George said. "Maybe you didn't want to forget the softer side of Gideon?"

"Eradication?" Thierry repeated.

"Didn't you tell him?" George asked. "Yeah, Sarah and I went to see this wizard kid a couple of days ago. He could remove her curse, but it would also have made her human again and wiped six months of memories out of her pretty little head."

My face felt frozen. "Did I neglect to mention that?"

"It didn't come up." Thierry's voice was cold. "But perhaps you discussed it with Gideon instead."

I glared at him. "I don't need this right now."

"What?"

"This jealousy bullshit. I don't feel anything toward Gideon. Just let it go once and for all, would you?"

He nodded and stood up. The warmth I had seen in his eyes when he looked at me before had been replaced by something frostier. "I think I'm going to go now before I say something I might regret. There are things I need to take care of."

"In case I need to remind you," I looked up at him, "you haven't exactly been around lately. Who was I supposed to share my problems with? The Red Devil?"

Thierry's eyes narrowed at the mention of his alter ego.

"I will see you tomorrow, Sarah." He didn't give me another look as he left the house.

George also stood up and went into the kitchen where he fixed two quadruple martinis made from his dwindling supply of moonshine—a mysterious liquid that helped to inebriate even those unfortunate creatures, like vampires, whom regular alcohol no longer affected. He downed one glass in a long gulp and handed me the other. I tossed it back.

"That's a start," I wheezed.

"Please tell me that you're not in love with Gideon Chase," George said. "I don't have enough moonshine to get me through that revelation."

"I'm not." I hissed out a long, frustrated breath. "I love Thierry, even though I want to punch him sometimes. But—"

"But what?"

"I can't help that there's a part of me that cares what happens to Gideon even after everything he's done. I'm supposed to sire him at midnight tomorrow. And yes, he's used his charm as well as a whole bunch of threats to get me to agree to what he wants. But—"

"But what?" he persisted.

I shook my head. "I don't know."

"That's not very helpful."

I sighed heavily. "Tell me about it."

I slept. Dreamlessly, except for a nightmare about Thierry trying to stake me before I staked him first. Pretty standard stuff, lately. Terrifying and disturbing, but to-tally standard.

I remembered when I used to dream about shoes. Like, literally, trying them on to find that they all fit me per-fectly. I think Prince Charming was in those dreams as well. And, possibly, a chorus line of cute, singing mice.

The unfortunate reality was that the shoe didn't always fit no matter how perfect it looked on the shelf. I could squeeze my foot into it and wear it, but it would be un-comfortable and binding.

Hard to run for your life when your feet hurt. Even vampires got blisters.

I woke to a strange sensation—a buzzing by my cheek. It took me a while to figure out what it was and in my half-conscious state I thought I had a pillow full of friendly bees.

But it was Gideon's BlackBerry. I'd taken it to bed with me for safekeeping like a cold black teddy bear.

I eyed the screen.

UNKNOWN NUMBER

After a few more moments it went silent. I sat up quickly. Who would be calling Gideon? Thierry had seemed convinced now that he didn't actually have any assassins on speed dial. I knew it wouldn't be George—not if he knew what was good for him.

And it definitely wasn't me.

When it buzzed again, I moistened my dry lips with the tip of my tongue and pressed the answer button. I held it to my ear with a trembling hand.

There was silence on the other end. And then, "Sarah? Are you there?"

The chipper female voice was immediately recognizable. "Amy?"

"Yup. It's me."

"Where are you?"

"No idea whatsoever, actually. I'm supposed to talk to you for a moment. How's it going?"

I felt incredibly confused. "Why are you calling me at this number?"

"It's the number Gideon gave me." There was a pause. "You know, after everything I'd heard about him I was expecting something totally different. But he's actually super nice, isn't he?"

My throat closed and I found it difficult to breathe. "Gideon has you?"

"He picked me up yesterday when I took a break from work. I was a bit surprised at first. I may have screamed a little bit when he grabbed me, but then he gave me something to relax me."

I had a death grip on the phone. "He drugged you?"

"Dunno what it was, but I'm all mellow and groovy now. Totally chilling. Tell Barry I'm okay, okay? I know he worries."

There was a shuffling sound. I waited, my hand twisting into the bedsheets until my knuckles were as white as the linen.

"Sarah—" Gideon's deep voice greeted me. "How are you this morning after our exciting evening?"

"What are you doing? You grabbed Amy yesterday morning? That was way before what happened last night."

"I like to cover my bases just in case. As you can hear, she's perfectly fine."

"Only because she's drugged." I struggled to breathe normally. "Let her go."

"Why would I do something like that?"

"Because it doesn't have to be this way."

"Unfortunately, it does. You proved last night once and for all that even though I want to, I can't trust you." I could hear a strange edge of disappointment in his voice. "I can't let anything get in the way of what I need. And if I must use your little blond friend to ensure that everything runs smoothly tonight, then that's exactly what I'll do."

I shook my head. "You can trust me."

"You tried to seduce me in my hotel room to steal my BlackBerry—"

"I wouldn't really use the word 'seduce.' "

"Then you underestimate yourself. And then you took it away from me in the alley at your first opportunity. Did it give you the information you were looking for?"

Being that I was speaking to him on the device itself, I couldn't very well deny I had it. "You must have dropped it. I was going to return it to you. Oh, and by the way, really sorry about what happened there. I didn't mean to . . . to . . ."

"Bite me?" he finished. "When your nightwalker takes over you become a very different woman entirely, don't you?"

I exhaled shakily. "Now you can see why I have to find a way to break my curse."

"Just the opposite. With the right nurturing and guidance I'm now convinced your darker side could be an asset. I envy you that other self, Sarah. I wish I had something similar."

My jaw tightened. "Then I guess it was a mistake for

you to kill the witch who cursed me. She could have set you up with a nice shiny inner nightwalker of your own." My honey was starting to turn to acid. "You need to let Amy go. *Now*."

"You're just a girl who can't take no for an answer, aren't you? So let me ask you this . . . did you discuss everything with my good friend George? I assume since you slid your talented little hand into my pants last night to steal my phone you know we've been in contact."

My back stiffened. "Maybe."

"You can have George—provided you tell him nothing further. Consider his life a gift from me to you since you refuse to take jewelry from me. Besides, I don't need to use the false threat of shadowy assassins anymore, do I? I have something much more tangible now—Amy."

"What do you want, Gideon?" I asked.

"What I've always wanted. For you to sire me at midnight."

"I'll do it."

"Of course you will. And you'll also come to my hotel room right now. There's something important you need to see."

The line went dead.

Chapter 14

When I arrived at Gideon's hotel room—hoping for the best but expecting the worst—the door was open and a housekeeping cart was out front. I sidestepped it to get into the room.

The suite's fireplace currently cast a warm glow on the rich décor. The bed was made and on the brocade bedspread I noticed some photos. I walked directly toward them.

When Gideon had first revealed himself to me—so to speak—he'd shown me these photos. At the time I'd assumed he'd hired a private investigator to follow me and my friends and family around, but now I had a funny feeling that Gideon had been the shutterbug himself.

There were pictures of Thierry leaving the nightclub he used to own. There were pictures of my parents up north in my hometown of Abottsville. Pictures of Amy and Barry going about their newlywed lives, and pictures of George. The shots all looked familiar even though I'd been in a fog when I'd first seen them. At the time I'd been dealing with the beginning stages of my nightwalker curse.

There were new pictures as well. They made my stomach sink lower and lower.

The first was a picture of me talking to the Red Devil after he'd stopped me from chomping the fledgling. A picture of Veronique and me having coffee from yesterday. And a picture of Thierry leaving George's house in the wee hours last night after confronting George and our subsequent argument about my misplaced loyalties.

A cold line of perspiration slid down my spine.

Okay, so he officially knew I'd been lying to him about seeing Thierry. So what was he going to do about it?

The thought that my secret was out made me feel very ill. But even with my secrets laid bare in the photos, Gideon Chase still *needed* me. That fact alone would keep Amy safe.

This could still turn out okay.

It could. Leave me to my delusions, please. Luckily, things couldn't really get much worse than they already were.

The maid emerged from the bathroom and she touched her hand to her chest when she saw me. "Goodness! You scared me."

"The . . . the man who was staying here. Where is he right now?"

"Checked out. I'm making up the room," she said. "Left me a real mess to clean up, too. It's going to take forever to get whatever that is out of the fireplace."

I turned slowly to look at where she pointed. I'd never stayed in a hotel room that had a fireplace. Usually for me it was a bed, a desk, and a bathroom. Maybe some generic shampoo and a tiny bar of soap if I was lucky.

I tilted my head. "What is that?"

The maid shrugged. "Looks like he's burning a big book of some kind. Guess it wasn't a page turner. I like some Stephenie Meyer, myself."

My mouth went dry. I grabbed a poker from a stand at the side of the fireplace and poked at the large rectangular object.

"What are you doing?" the maid exclaimed as I dragged the book out of the fire and it landed in an ashy heap on the floor.

It was the grimoire.

Or, at least, it *had* been.

Now it was no more than a black, charred excuse for a once-magical book of spells. The pages were seared and blackened. I pushed it open with the tip of the poker to the middle and found that the pages were ruined and unreadable. It had been burning for a while.

Liar, liar. Your grimoire's on fire.

"What is that, a phone book?" the maid asked curiously.

"You don't know any magical incantations that will unburn a book, do you?" I asked, mostly to myself.

"Magical incantations?" She now gave me a wary glance. "You'd better get going so I can finish up in here now that you've given me more to clean up. I don't have time for nonsense."

Gideon had burned my grimoire. He had destroyed my chance to break the curse.

I take it back—things could always get worse.

The maid moved around to the side of the bed. "You're not Sarah, are you?"

I looked over at her. "That depends on who's asking."

She snatched an envelope off the desk. "This is addressed to a Sarah."

I made a beeline to her and took the envelope, slicing it open with my thumbnail and reading the inside quickly.

You will find me at the nightclub you frequent lately. It's nice and quiet at this time of the day. Tell your master vampire lover nothing about this. Please don't disappoint me again. Be there by noon.—G

Well, at least he said please.

Yes, he was definitely having a hissy fit. On anyone else I might be able to brush it off, but Gideon Chase was a different story.

I'd been reading the wrong translation of that story for some time now. The real Gideon was no one to mess with, no one to flirt with, and definitely no one to underestimate. I wouldn't make that mistake again.

The sun was extra bright when I emerged on the sidewalk, and I slid my sunglasses into place and got my bearings. My cell phone rang. I had both my Pink Razor and Gideon's BlackBerry on me now. I went through cell phones like I used to go through panty hose.

A glance at the screen told me it was Thierry. I answered it.

"Where are you?" he asked.

"Downtown," I said simply.

"I was worried. George said you left without saying anything. Quinn has been looking for you as well."

"I had something I had to do."

"Something to do with Gideon?"

I huffed out a breath. "I can't talk right now."

"Sarah, please tell me what's going on."

I swallowed past the lump in my throat. "Can't. Busy, busy."

"I'll come and get you. We can deal with Gideon together."

Yeah, and if I showed up at Darkside arm in arm with Thierry, Amy would be picking out her angel wings.

"Sorry, Thierry. I'll have to take a rain check on that."

"I can be there in minutes. Tell me where you are; where you're headed." He sounded worried.

"I need to clean up this mess myself. If there was any other way then we'd do it that way, trust me on that. I . . . I have to go."

"Sarah—"

I ended the call and slid the phone into my pocket, ignoring it when it began to buzz a few moments later. He was calling me back. The man was persistent with or without the mask.

If I'd been feeling hunky dory about everything it would make me smile. Thierry pursuing me, insisting he be by my side—even after we'd had a fight.

Talk about a one-eighty from where we'd come from. Honestly, he'd been the most standoffish guy I'd ever met in my entire life. I figured that it had a lot to do with living for so long. He'd been hurt, both emotionally and physically. A lot. Badly. Therefore there was a ton of armor he carried around with him. He didn't trust people and he didn't open up. Keeping his Red Devil secret was only one example of this. He'd pushed me away so many times

that it was only out of sheer stubbornness and questionable intelligence that I hadn't walked away and not looked
back. He'd been silent and moody and sullen and unbelievably bossy.

But for some strange reason that totally did it for me.
Who knew what a masochist I was?

I'd kept digging and digging until I'd found the real
Thierry. He was a bit dusty, to say the least. But beyond
that dusty, moody exterior was my Mr. Right. Nobody believed we fit together except for me. Everyone was all too
ready to accept that we'd broken up.

But I didn't care. I loved him.

I was all stubborn like that.

Darkside was closed for business when I got there, but
the front door was unlocked, so I summoned my courage
and went inside, past the false front of a used bookstore.
It smelled musty and dusty and had paperback novels
stacked from floor to ceiling and several tables with stacks
of mysteries, romances, and thrillers.

The interior of the club seemed completely empty as
well, but I knew it wasn't.

"You're here. Right on time, too."

I turned to face Gideon, who stood behind me with his
arms crossed. "Where's Amy?"

"Somewhere safe."

"I want to see her."

"I'm sure you do. But there's a little business we need
to take care of first."

I scanned the dark nightclub but didn't see anyone but
Gideon. "Business? I thought that the ritual wasn't until
midnight?"

"It's not." He cocked his head to the side. "I wanted

to give you the chance to apologize for lying to me about ending your relationship with de Bennicoeur."

"I think you burning the grimoire makes us more than even on that subject."

His expression shadowed. "Perhaps I acted a bit rashly."

A bit rashly? "You think?"

"Do you like this place?" Gideon turned away from me and looked at the interior of the nightclub. "I know you come here a lot lately."

"Sure, I like it. It's recently been sold, though."

"I know. It was sold to me."

My eyes widened at that. "You bought a vampire club?"

He nodded. "I did."

"Why?"

He leaned against the bar. "You wouldn't take the earrings I wanted to give you. I thought I might give you something a bit more practical."

I blinked hard. "You bought me a nightclub? Because I said no to some earrings?"

"I got a very good deal on it. The papers are in your name. The transfer of ownership will be next week. It's a gift to thank you for helping me. Do you like it?"

"If I say no will you get me a private jet instead?" I drew in a slow breath. "I don't want gifts or money. The only thing you had that I wanted was that grimoire and now it's gone." I felt sick to my stomach as I said it. "I just want you to leave me and my friends alone after tonight."

I was about to say something else when he tensed and

his face convulsed. He let out a gasp and grabbed hold of the side of the bar top. A shudder went through his body.

I resisted moving any closer to him. "What's wrong?"

"The pain from the hellfire has returned even worse than before," he managed. "Your blood wasn't strong enough to keep it away for long."

Every muscle in my body was tense. "What does that mean?"

"It means your blood may be strong enough for some things, but not strong enough to fully heal my particular injuries during the ritual."

"Unfortunately I don't offer a money-back guarantee."

"No, I'm sure you don't." He remained hunched over for another minute before he slowly straightened up. There was a sheen of perspiration on his forehead. "Come with me. I have someone I want you to see."

"Who is it?" I asked, my mouth feeling very dry.

Gideon turned and walked away without giving me a detailed description of our destination. He moved across the dance floor and toward a hallway leading toward the restrooms. I followed him at a safe distance, and he glanced over his shoulder at me.

Gideon used a key to unlock a door and push it open. The small storage room held a woman whose dark eyes flashed with anger. Her left wrist was shackled to the wall. Otherwise, she looked as composed and beautiful and, well, *perfect* as she always did.

Veronique's gaze moved to me and widened.

"Sarah!" she exclaimed. "What are you doing here?"

My eyebrows shot up with surprise. "I was about to ask you the same question."

"Gideon kidnapped me. I assumed he meant to hold me for ransom for a large sum of money."

Gideon braced himself against the doorway, still weakened by his blast of pain. "Not exactly."

My stomach really couldn't sink any lower than it already was. "Why can't you leave my friends alone?"

"You consider this one a friend?" he asked with mild surprise.

I glanced at Thierry's wife, a woman who'd given me a huge pain in my neck—no vampire pun intended—from the moment I first met her. "Sure, she's my friend."

Veronique smiled. "What a dear, sweet girl you are. We really should spend a great deal more time together, yes?"

A wave of pain shadowed Gideon's face for a moment. "I've suspected your blood isn't strong enough to fully cure me. So, I want to make sure it is."

I really didn't like the way that sounded. "Which means what?"

"Your blood is filled with power because, as a developing fledgling, you've drunk from two master vampires. Today you'll drink from a third."

Veronique and I exchanged a glance.

"I'm not really all that thirsty right now," I said weakly.

His jaw tensed. "Despite her youthful appearance, she is one of the most ancient vampires in the entire world."

Veronique's cheeks flushed and her eyes narrowed. She tapped her stiletto-clad foot angrily. I don't think she was upset that he was suggesting that I drink her blood. No, I think he just made her feel old. Well, she *was* seven hundred. Whether she needed Botox to retain her late-twenties appearance was another issue. Maybe her wrinkles were only on the inside.

"I'm not biting Veronique." My stomach churned at the horrible thought.

Gideon's eyes narrowed with pain and frustration. "You should thank me. Other than the vast power her blood will give you, this is the woman who keeps you from a commitment with your lover for her own selfish reasons. This is your opportunity to drain her. After all, dead wives don't stand in the way of true love."

Veronique frowned. "Sarah and my husband have ended their relationship."

"All lies." Gideon raised an eyebrow at me. "They've been keeping their continued affair a secret, even from you."

Veronique made a small, annoyed sound at the back of her throat. "I thought we were friends, my dear. You could have told me."

I shrugged. There were more important issues on the table at the moment than keeping a secret from her. I wasn't biting Veronique. It wasn't in my nature to gnaw on necks 24/7. I wasn't going to do it and he couldn't make me.

Unless . . .

"If I refuse to drink from her, will you hurt Amy?" I asked quietly.

He shook his head. "Of course not. What kind of a monster do you take me for?"

Hope swelled inside me again. "You won't?"

"Of course not." He brushed the dark hair off my forehead and pushed it behind my ear before stroking my cheek gently. Then he smiled at me. "I'm saving your little blond friend for tonight. If you give me any more problems, I will slice her open from bottom—" he moved his hand down to my stomach as I stood frozen in place, and then skimmed his fingers up between my breasts to spread around my throat "—to top. But that's then, and this is now."

I swallowed hard. "Gideon—"

"I know this whole situation is difficult and I'm sorry for that." He brought my hand up to his lips and kissed it. "Let me make it easier for you."

In one smooth motion, he tore the gold chain that held my nightwalker curse at bay off my neck and then shoved me into the room with Veronique.

The door slammed behind me.

Chapter 15

I clamped my hand over my throat and felt for the chain that wasn't there anymore. Gideon had taken it from me. No, he hadn't just taken it. He'd ripped it off. He'd *broken* it.

Oh, shit.

According to what Veronique had told me yesterday, even if I got it back, it wouldn't work for me anymore. And I no longer had the promise of the witch's grimoire to break my nightwalker curse.

Veronique's eyes were filled with worry. "Sarah, my dear. Are you all right?"

For a moment I felt completely fine, figuratively speaking, of course. But after I took in my next deep breath, I realized I didn't need it anymore. I pressed my hand against the wall as my heart came to a slow, commanding stop.

"I'm not so good, actually," I admitted.

I quickly moved toward her to inspect her bindings. It was a set of silver handcuffs that locked her in place. Her left wrist was already red and raw from the contact with the metal, which was also attached to the shelving unit.

Vampires and silver didn't go together very well. While we might have the strength to break the metal, especially a master vampire like Veronique, silver was dangerous to us. If she pulled against the cuff, she ran the risk of severing her hand. Even the slightest contact with it hurt like hell.

I felt that pain as I tugged on the cuffs and pulled my hand away to shake it out. "I don't know how to get you loose."

She sighed. "I wish you could have felt comfortable enough to tell me the truth about you and my husband. I feel that it's something I had the right to know about."

Frustration rose up inside me. "Why do you do that?"

"Do what?"

"Always have to call him your husband?"

She looked confused. "Because that's what he is. What difference does it make right now what I call him?"

"It's just . . ." I exhaled shakily, thinking about the fact that she'd never recognized that her "husband" was the Red Devil. "Whenever you say that you just remind me that he can never be mine and it hurts. A lot. I guess we're having a camel-and-straw situation here, and I'm close to having a broken back."

"It's only a word."

"No, it's more than that. It's . . . it's a title. A *brand*. He's 'your husband.' " I even made air quotes. "You won't sign the annulment because he's yours and that's all there is to it."

"I don't think this is the time or place to discuss this."

"You're absolutely right."

She studied me for a long moment. "Do you hate me for not signing the papers?"

I raised my gaze to hers. "I wish I did sometimes, but I don't. Having this nightwalker curse has taught me a lot. It's taught me to value the times when I do have control over my life. And obviously now that my chain is gone those times are about to come to a stuttering end in the next few minutes." I fought against the sting of tears. But I couldn't lose it right now—I had to stay calm. "I don't know what to do."

Her expression turned fiercer. "You will do what I have always done and what I continue to do. You will survive. You will do whatever it takes to see another sunrise."

"Nightwalkers don't get to see sunrises."

Her expression fell. "Oh, my dear—"

"And stop calling me *dear*." A dark wave of violence swelled inside me.

Uh oh. That was not a good sign. I had to remain calm. I didn't want to go Dark Sarah on Veronique. Like I said, I didn't hate her. I didn't want to hurt her. And she was currently in a very precarious position—trapped in a room with a potential monster thirsty for the blood of a master vampire.

Her blood would be so sweet and rich, my nightwalker commented excitedly. *Filled with power . . . running down my throat . . . delicious and nutritious . . . yum!*

Thoughts like that were *sooo* not going to be very helpful at all at the moment.

"Did I ever tell you the story of how I met my true love, Marcellus?" Veronique asked.

That was the vamp Thierry told me was the original Red Devil before he became the man behind the mask. "Do you really think this is the best moment for a random stroll down memory lane?"

"I think this story is relevant to this particular situation, so if you will permit me to continue."

I glanced back at the locked door. I couldn't hear anything beyond it even if I strained my vampire ears. I figured Gideon was waiting patiently outside while I chowed down. I was still in shock from losing my gold chain. How would I ever be normal again? I hadn't realized just how much I counted on getting that grimoire until it was no longer an option.

Geez, forget the grimoire, would you? my nightwalker said. *You never wanted to break the curse in the first place. It's too much fun being me.*

I would not think about blood. And I would not notice the slow but steady pulse at Veronique's throat.

Admitting you had a problem was part of the solution, right? It was. I had a problem and I didn't think hearing Veronique yap wistfully about her dead lover was going to help very much.

"Before I met Marcellus," she began when I didn't say anything to stop her, "I lived a privileged, but boring life with my mother and father and many servants in France. I was thought to be a great beauty and my hand was sought after by many."

Here we go. "Sounds pretty good to me."

"My parents had arranged for me to marry a wealthy man but he was very old and ugly. I told them I wanted to marry for love, but people didn't marry for love until relatively recently. They married for much more practical reasons such as fortune or title. But then I met Marcellus."

"Wasn't he rich, too?" I asked. I wouldn't look at her throat and the promise of master vampire blood beneath her skin. I *wouldn't*.

"Oh, yes. He was very wealthy and handsome. I fell deeply in love with him at first sight and ran away with him. This wasn't something proper young women did back then. I knew there would be no returning to my family, but that was all right. As long as I was with Marcellus I feared nothing."

The flawless white length of her neck was becoming more distracting the longer she spoke, and she must have noticed my shifting attention because she cleared her throat.

"Sorry," I said. "I . . . I'm having a hard time concentrating. Any way you can get to the point so we can deal with the problem at hand?"

"You truly have no control over your nightwalker?"

I guess we'll find out soon enough, won't we? my nightwalker snarled inside me.

"I'm trying." I felt my fangs lengthen and sharpen in my mouth and I ran the tip of my tongue over them. My stomach growled with hunger.

"Marcellus revealed himself to me as a vampire the first night we made love," she continued, undeterred. "He was ashamed and afraid of what I might think—that I'd leave him immediately in fear and loathing. But I didn't. I asked him to sire me and he did. Since he was already a master vampire I was very strong from the beginning and he taught me how to survive." She sighed at the memory. "How I loved him."

"And then Marcellus left you and took up with a younger fledgling. I know this already, Veronique. And then the loneliness and solitude you felt during the Black Death caused you to sire Thierry and the rest is history. Uh . . . *ancient* history, actually. Gideon wants me to drain you so I can become stronger. Doesn't this bother you even a little?"

"Of course it bothers me," she said sharply. "But I have dealt with many more dire situations than this. I have survived to this day by doing whatever I must. And yes, Marcellus left me." Her voice caught. "That betrayal still stings. But after everything that happened between us I know that he loved me as much as I loved him. He sacrificed himself to save me in the end. That was true love."

My vision had slowly closed in and her voice became a tinny buzz that I had an easy time ignoring. "That was a lovely story. What was the purpose of it again?"

"If Thierry loves you so much, where is he now?" she asked.

"Why? Do you think he'd sacrifice himself to save you like Marcellus did?"

There was still no fear in her eyes, only pity. For me. "I've lived a long time without anyone coming to my rescue."

A slow smile stretched my lips. "Honestly, Veronique, you really should have signed those annulment papers and headed back to your fabulous life in Europe. Washed your hands of this whole mess. But *no*, you had to hold on to Thierry—a man you don't love—with both hands so somebody else didn't get him."

"Then perhaps Gideon is right. Maybe you should take this opportunity to kill me. There are many ways to kill a vampire, even a master, if one is willing." She studied me. "Your eyes are black now, my dear."

"Maybe I need to accept the fact that I'm a nightwalker."

"It's only an unfortunate curse. It's not what you truly are."

"You're not the first one to say that, but I feel like a nightwalker, I act like a nightwalker. The odds of my ever getting rid of this side of me are now slim to none. It's real."

"No," she said firmly. "This is only magic and magic is not the same as reality."

"All I know is that Gideon isn't letting either of us out of here until I do what he wants me to do. And oddly, it's becoming easier and easier the more you talk."

I was very thirsty. Parched. Dying from the need for blood. Something I'd fought against since becoming a vampire—something I thought was really gross and monstrous and unhygienic. It was one thing to drink blood from a keg at a vampire club, but it was another thing to get it straight from the source itself. Shifting morals—one was good, one was bad. One made me normal, one made me a monster. It was still blood.

All my attention narrowed down to the pulse on Veronique's throat—a pulse that had been pulsing away for seven hundred years. The beat had gone on. And it suddenly became the only thing in the world that existed for me.

I reached out to touch that pulse, feeling the blood coursing just below the surface of her skin. I felt the power emanating off her in waves. Gideon was right about so many things. If I drank from her I would become more powerful.

If I drain her, my nightwalker said as I brought my mouth closer to Veronique's throat, *it will solve so many problems.*

Yes, I thought. *Maybe you're right.*

Suddenly, Veronique slapped me very hard across my face with her uncuffed hand.

"Step away from me," she hissed.

I grabbed the front of her shirt and narrowed my eyes at her, baring my sharper-than-normal fangs.

She slapped me again. Even harder this time.

"Ow!" I yelped and moved back from her.

Her dark eyes flashed. "Honestly, Sarah, you're stronger than this."

I shook my head. It was foggy and cloudy and completely confused, but there was a small bit of myself still there. "I don't think I can stop this."

"Of course you can."

"I can't!" I moved toward her again and got another stinging smack for my efforts. That was enough to clear my head enough to think half straight.

"Think of Thierry," she said harshly. "He wouldn't want you to be like this. He'd find it most unseemly."

She was right. I tried to hold on to the image of Thierry in my head.

"I'm trying."

Her jaw set. "It doesn't get any easier, my dear. It never will. There are no simple answers in the life of a vampire. There will always be hunters, there will always be danger, there will always be those who wish to hurt us, but you must not let them defeat you. Survival should be your number-one concern. Just as it is mine."

I was getting the gist: Be strong. Don't wimp out. "I need to get us the hell out of here."

"Again, you are not understanding me." She brought her right forearm to her mouth and bit her wrist. "You may drink from me on *my* terms. I don't think Gideon realizes that my blood is strong enough to give you back some of the control you are currently lacking. It won't change the fact that your chain is gone, but it will help for a while."

My eyes locked onto her wrist. "Veronique . . . I don't know."

"Do it," she said, so sharply that I, well, *did it*.

I was so hungry, thanks to my curse, that her blood was like a Big Mac combo after two weeks of stale bread and water. I drank greedily—half of me thrilled, the other half scared to death.

It wasn't a good mix of emotions.

My face still stung from where she'd hit me, but instead of trying to ignore that I hung on to it. The pain kept me grounded. I drank from her until she pushed at my forehead with her chained hand.

"That's enough," she said.

"I feel . . . *better*." I pulled away and looked at her. "Are my eyes still black?"

She nodded. "They are."

I turned toward the locked door and kicked it, feeling a bit surprised but satisfied when it splintered open on contact thanks to my extra nightwalker strength. I stalked down the hallway and back into the main club where Gideon waited by the bar. I made a beeline toward him and grabbed his throat before he had a moment to defend himself.

"Sarah—" he choked out. "Don't."

"Don't what?" I asked, cocking my head to the side. "Don't pop your head off like a dandelion for being a total, manipulative dick?"

I brought my other hand to his throat and squeezed harder. His eyes bugged out and I saw sudden fear behind his gaze. His face began turning an unpleasant shade of purple.

Don't hurt him, you bitch! my nightwalker yelled.

I frowned and tried to ignore my evil inner voice.

Then I felt a hand close around my upper arm and I couldn't hold on to Gideon any longer. My eyes widened when I saw it was Veronique. She pushed me—just a small shove, but her strength was great enough to make me stagger backward and fall on my ass on the empty dance floor.

I had no idea she was that strong.

The wounds at her wrists—from where she'd offered me her blood and from being secured with silver—were already healing.

Gideon coughed and sputtered and touched his tender throat.

"Not so happy with me anymore, Sarah?" he managed after a moment. "I suppose I can understand that."

I scrambled up off the hard floor and moved toward him again, but Veronique stepped into my path to stop me.

"What are you doing?" Her strange behavior was really throwing me off. "And how did you get out of the handcuffs?"

"With a key," she said simply, her expression unreadable.

"A key? What key?"

"The key Gideon gave me earlier." She said it very matter-of-factly. "I'm sorry. But as I said before, survival is my only goal."

"What are you talking about?"

Gideon came to Veronique's side. He took her hand in his and brought her healing wrist to his lips to kiss it. "Poor Veronique. I'm sorry about the pain."

"It is nothing."

My vision had grown shaky, but that might be because I was trembling all over. "What in the hell is going on here?"

Gideon smiled at me. "Do you remember the woman I told you about? The vampire who seduced me years ago to save her own neck?"

"Best sex of your life?" I did recall that little fable. Then my gaze shot to Veronique as I remembered Gideon's rumpled bedsheets from yesterday afternoon. I shook my head. "No. I don't believe it."

"I'm sure you won't understand," she said simply, "but Gideon is very powerful and will only become more so after he is sired tonight, along with having a new outlook on what it means to be a vampire. As I said before, survival is my only goal. How can I not align myself with him, especially now? No one has to get hurt. You never would have drunk from me without duress if you thought I knew about all of this. This is the best decision for everyone involved. Trust me, my dear. I don't do this to hurt you or anyone else."

Veronique was with Gideon? I could understand, although only partially, sleeping with him in the past to distract him from killing her—he *was* pretty hot—but to do so willingly now?

I was stunned, but as the moments ticked by it made more sense to me. Veronique was always selfish. She valued her existence. She was one of the oldest vampires in the entire world. She was a survivor—no matter what it took.

And I knew firsthand how very charming and convincing Gideon could be when he wanted something.

Even though I resented her role in Thierry's life, I'd believed in her. Hell, I even looked up to her a bit. Like a much, much . . . *much* . . . older sister. I was disappointed in her.

"I have to get out of here," I said shakily. "If I wanted to deal with a major daytime drama I would have set my TiVo."

Gideon shook his head. "It's the middle of a very sunny day. Without your chain, I don't advise that you go anywhere until after sunset."

I stepped slowly toward him again. He didn't flinch away from me.

"Are you going to attempt to kill me again?" he asked.

"No." I reached down to take his hand in mine. "I was a bit upset about you breaking my chain and, you know, burning my chance to break my curse. But killing you or getting mad about that won't help, will it?"

"No, it won't."

With one quick yank, I pulled off the magically glamourizing watch from his wrist. A pulse of light moved across him and an instant later his scars had fully returned.

His eyes narrowed. "Give that back to me."

"This?" I held the watch out to him for a second, but then stepped back out of his reach, dropped the timepiece on the floor, and stomped on it with the heel of my shoe. "Oops. Sorry, about that. I slipped."

It was petty, but it felt so good.

He reached up to touch his scarred face and cringed. Veronique looked at him with shock.

"*Now* I'm leaving." I backed away from them toward the entrance. "Are you going to stop me?"

His jaw tightened. "Sarah, don't do this. Stay here. Don't put yourself in harm's way just to prove a point."

"Screw you, Gideon."

Yeah, real eloquent. I know.

Without another word, I turned my back and walked out into the used bookstore.

"I'll find you, wherever you go," Gideon called after me. "The ritual will go on as scheduled. A simple glamour won't matter then. My scars will be healed for real when you sire me."

A tear of anger and frustration trickled down my right cheek as I pushed open the front door, but it was burned away the moment I emerged onto the sidewalk outside the club and the blazing sunlight hit me full-on.

Chapter 16

If I can explain what it feels like to be a nightwalker out in bright daylight it would be like this:

Sheer agony.

Multiplied by a billion.

It might sound like an exaggeration, but I assure you, it wasn't. Sun and nightwalkers *do not* go together. At all. Prolonged exposure, and we're only really talking ten to fifteen seconds, would be enough to make me burst into flames and run around flailing my arms until I turned into the contents of a dirty ashtray to scatter over the sidewalk. And even then I'd probably still be screaming.

So when I emerged from Darkside into the hot death sunshine, I pulled my shirt up over my head and ran like an Olympic sprinter toward the nearest subway entrance. I staggered down the stairs into the blissful darkness and tried to ignore the strange stares I was getting, for a moment, as my skin glowed red and wisps of smoke rose into the air.

"Lady, you okay?" someone asked.

"Fabulous," I gasped. "Never better. Thanks so much for asking."

My hair was slicked to my forehead with the perspiration that poured out of me in buckets. I reached up to touch my eyebrows to make sure they hadn't been singed off because that would really suck. They were still there. For now, anyhow. I stood in place, my back against the wall of the station until I came back down to room temperature like a sweaty soufflé that had been removed from the oven.

Veronique was with Gideon. The thought swirled continuously through my head.

I seriously couldn't believe it. Sure, I knew she was selfish and self-involved, but was this what being a survivor really meant to her?

She was so getting voted off the island, as far as I was concerned.

And the worst thing was she hadn't seemed to realize what she was doing was wrong.

Well, okay. It wasn't the *worst* thing.

If I had to find one good thing about the whole situation, it was that her blood had given me some temporary control over my curse. Normally, at this point of being without my gold chain, I'd be wandering around sniffing the neck of any human that passed me trying to figure out who'd be the tastiest.

But I wasn't sniffing anyone. I could smell them, sure—dozens of humans brushing past me on their way to catch the subway. And it wasn't only the disturbing scent of food they gave off. It was deeper that than. The smells helped me pinpoint their mood—if they were stressed out or scared or angry.

It smelled . . . *delicious*.

But my fangs didn't lengthen at the moment. After all, I'd just had a very satisfying meal.

God, what had happened to my life?

Before the curse I had resented being a vampire. I always fought against the label of being a "monster." I thought being turned into a vampire would change me, but it didn't. I felt the same as I always had; that's why it was so hard to understand why all of a sudden hunters wanted to kill me just because of what I was.

But now I understood. Hunters would have been very necessary back when nightwalkers roamed the earth. This was the kind of vampire that people should be afraid of—what I was right now. Hiding from the sun, coming out at night when they were very hungry. Not being able to stop. Not *wanting* to stop.

I was now the kind of vampire that deserved to be staked. An out-of-control bloodthirsty monster.

I swallowed hard. I was in such deep shit.

Deep.

But it was good that I was still thinking straight. The gold chain had been great—a miracle, really—but it was gone now. Losing the chain had always been a possibility. It sucked. Hard. But it was gone and I had to make do without it.

I could stay in control. I could.

Dammit. Who was I trying to kid? Let's stick with the "I'm in deep shit" direction of thinking.

I needed to find Thierry.

Thierry. His difficult-to-pronounce French name alone gave me courage—a teensy bit.

I pulled my cell phone out of my purse and speed-

dialed his number. It went directly to voice mail. *Dammit.*
I shoved it back in my bag. I'd cooled off, both literally
and figuratively, enough to start walking. One foot in
front of the other. I got on a subway and took it to Union
Station.

Once I got back to George's I'd deal with everything
else. I wasn't sure how I'd get all the way there, but I'd figure out a way. Without setting foot outside again. *Sure.*

I'd channel the little vampire engine that could. I could
do this. One thing at a time.

I think I can, I think I can.

I forced myself to find something good in this situation. It was hard, but I actually came up with something.
Now that I'd reached Union Station, I'd entered the PATH
system of downtown Toronto—sixteen miles of under-
ground passageways that connected the transit system and
a whole bunch of the buildings in the business district. It
was possible to never have to go up to the surface level.
Like, *ever.* There were shopping, theaters, and restaurants
galore all below street level.

A total nightwalker's paradise.

Still, the thought wasn't much comfort. While the
PATH was great to have in case of shopping and commut-
ing emergency, it didn't make potentially never seeing the
sun again a pleasant prospect.

I knew the PATH. I used to take it daily when I worked
for an honest living. But now . . . everything started to
look the same. My head felt foggy. I put one foot in front
of the other and headed north, glancing at some people
as I walked past them. They all gave me strange stares
in return.

Maybe I looked like hell. I felt like it so why shouldn't I look like it, too?

"Excuse me," I asked a blond lady with a kid who looked around three years old. "Can you help me with some directions?"

Her eyes widened and she took a step back from me. "Uh . . . I don't know."

I looked down at the kid and smiled at him.

The kid started to cry.

I slapped a hand over my mouth. I'd probably just flashed him my fangs, which were longer—not to mention *sharper*—than normal.

Sarah Dearly's my name. Scaring innocent children's my game.

"Are you . . . are you wearing funny contact lenses?" the woman asked shakily.

"Contact lenses?"

Oh, *shit*. My eyes were still black. And my fangs were sharp. And I was a sweaty, skanky, runny mess. I glanced around to see that I now had the attention of several people, who looked at me like I was about to whip off my jacket and reveal a braful of dynamite.

Then I glanced over to the wall next to us to see that it was mirrored. It reflected everyone in the vicinity of the donut store I stood in front of.

Everyone except yours truly.

The woman also noted this, and she began to shriek and point at me, while her kid started to howl even louder.

I started walking again. Faster. I didn't really care what direction I was headed in anymore as long as it was away from screaming peanut-butter-scented people. A glance over my shoulder showed that a few were tentatively following me, but I wasn't sure if they were hunters who'd been alerted to the lost vampire or if they were simply curious onlookers. I couldn't think straight so I couldn't figure it out. The best thing to do was to run, which is exactly what I did.

I turned a corner and found there was suddenly a solid figure in front of me. Tall, dark, and blurry. But familiar. And he held me in place by my shoulders, looked down at me, and stroked the stringy hair off my face.

"Sarah," Thierry said with concern. "Please, try to calm down."

I had to admit, it did take a moment.

He pulled me into an embrace and held me there in the middle of the PATH while I slowly got hold of myself.

"H-how did you find me?" I managed after a moment.

"I've been searching for you since you hung up on me earlier," he said. "I'm able to sense your location if I concentrate, thanks to the sire-fledgling bond we share."

He wasn't my true sire but he was close enough. After my blind date from hell had been staked, it was Thierry's blood that helped me not die. That sealed the deal in giving us the bond—which until now I thought only I had.

"My chain is gone," I said shakily. "Gideon broke it."

His jaw clenched. "*What*?"

"And Gideon burned the grimoire."

"I see."

"Are you going to tell me you told me so? About him?"

His expression was grim. "No."

"You should. I deserve it."

"Nothing I say will help to make this any better."

He was right about that.

With an arm around my shoulders, he directed me down the corridor and we walked and walked for what felt like forever until we got to a parking garage.

"I've kept this in a central downtown location in case we needed it," he said, nodding at a white van.

When I first discovered that I was cursed and sunlight had the potential to burn me to a crisp we'd had to use a similar van. It wasn't a very pleasant drive, but it did the trick. Transport the sun-fearing nightwalker from point A to point B.

"What am I going to do?" I asked him.

He stroked the hair off my forehead and kissed me there softly before holding my face in his hands and gazing down into my black nightwalker eyes.

"You're going to get into the back of the van and we're going to George's."

"But—"

"No. One thing at a time, Sarah."

"Are you going to tell me that everything's going to be okay?"

He tilted his head to the side. "Do you want me to say that?"

"Only if it's true."

"Then I think we should hold off any such proclamations for a while until we decide what to do next."

He couldn't hide the worry that slid behind his gaze. He couldn't convince me that all was well with the world. Out of everyone I'd known in my life, Thierry was the biggest realist. He'd seen a lot of years and it had definitely dampened any optimism he might have had. Some people saw him as Mr. Doom and Gloom, but now I knew. He was right. He didn't put on a happy face when things were going to hell in a hand basket. He dealt with it and then he moved on.

I had to be dealt with.

I climbed into the back of the van. He let go of my hand and without saying another word, slammed the back door shut and I was plunged into darkness. There were no windows, no pretty view, because that would let in the sunlight.

He'd prepared for this without telling me. He'd known this could happen—that it *would* happen.

He might not be an optimist, but he definitely could have been a Boy Scout.

I pressed my back against the cool side of the van as it started moving. From where we were, wherever we were—I'd kind of lost track—it took less than fifteen minutes to get to George's house.

I heard a knock on the back door, which warned me it was about to open. I scooted back and the door swung open. The light didn't touch me but it seared my vision. Just a taste of the pain waiting for me outside the van.

Thierry had a black blanket in his hands. A thick one. And he held it up.

"Come," he said. "George is waiting."

Summoning up what little courage I had left, I threw myself into his arms and he covered me with the blanket. We ran as fast as we could to the front door. Only twenty feet but it was not a pleasant sprint.

From the tiny peephole I had, I could see George standing there at the threshold wringing his hands anxiously.

"I invite you into my house, Sarah Dearly!" His voice was pinched.

Oh, yeah. I'd forgotten. I couldn't enter people's private homes anymore without an invitation.

That would be very inconvenient.

I'd experienced hitting a threshold before, and it was like a thick glass wall. Invisible but impenetrable. Luckily George had said what he needed to and I swept right past him with Thierry at my side into the blissfully dark interior. All the shades had been drawn.

I tried to ignore the smoky wisps that drifted upward from my skin. It was minus zero on the last day of February, but that didn't seem to make a bit of difference.

Thierry was frowning at me. "Sarah, are you well?"

Was I well? I didn't think I could be less well if I tried. My vision was narrowing. Darkening. The room spun in slow circles.

When nightwalkers existed, they tended to sleep through the day. Best way to avoid the sunlight was to be unconscious during it.

"She's very pale," George said, studying me. "Pasty is definitely not the new black."

Then my eyes rolled back into my head and I fainted dead away.

Chapter 17

A dream. It had all been just a dream. Thank God.

"Yoo hoo, Sarah. Are you awake?" a voice penetrated through my unconsciousness.

I opened my eyes.

George stared down at me. He had a cool, wet cloth pressed firmly against my forehead for the second time in two days.

Not a dream. *Damn.*

"Wh-what?" I managed.

He waved a hand over his nose. "Yikes. Hello, morning breath. And it's not even morning anymore. Or afternoon, even."

"How long was I out?"

"All day. The sun has set. I figure that's why our little Miss Nosferatu has arisen at last."

I pushed up enough to see that I was in my bed fully dressed, except that my shoes and coat had been removed. "Why didn't you wake me up earlier?"

"We tried. You were dead to the world, and I mean that

literally. You don't breathe and you have no heartbeat. You're lucky we didn't embalm you."

I let myself collapse back onto my pillow. "Maybe you should have. It would solve a lot of problems."

His expression turned wary. "Now that the chain is gone, are you still feeling . . . *normalish*?"

"Normal is a very relative term." I swung my legs out of bed. I felt weak and shaky, but there was no immediate need to attach myself to George's jugular like a brunette leech. "Where's Thierry?"

"He was by your side all afternoon."

"He was?" The thought gave my room-temperature body a little inner glow.

George nodded. "Obviously he wasn't aware of the morning-breath situation. Mint?" He presented me with a couple of Tic Tacs.

I took them. I could take a hint. "Thanks."

"Right now he's on the phone with Barry about Amy being missing." His brow furrowed. "Did she mention anything to you about leaving our favorite little maître d' for another man?"

I swallowed. "Gideon has her."

He paled. "Any man other than that would have been okay with me."

"He's going to use her to make sure I sire him tonight."

His jaw tightened. "That bastard."

"George, please give Sarah and me a moment alone." Thierry was at the doorway looking in.

He turned. "Gideon has Amy."

Thierry nodded gravely. "I heard you."

George looked frantic. "This is horrible. I feel completely useless just waiting around to see what's going to happen. There has to be something I can do to help."

"I could use some coffee," I said.

He nodded. "Excellent idea. I'll make coffee."

He turned and left us alone.

"Amy's not the only person Gideon has right now," I said evenly. "He's also got Veronique."

Thierry's eyes widened a fraction. "He's kidnapped her as well?"

I shook my head. "She's with him more in the mattress-testing capacity. She doesn't seem to see that there's anything wrong with that. He's a powerful man and she's a survivor. End of story."

I couldn't read his expression, but it darkened significantly. "I'm very disappointed to hear that. I would have expected more from her."

"Me, too."

"I'm well aware of her selfishness, after all, I've known her for a very long time. But this? To learn that she'd rather aid a man like Gideon, whose family has been nothing but death-bringers to vampires for centuries . . ." He exhaled. "I am disappointed."

"She also gave me some of her blood. Gideon thought that drinking from a third master vampire like Veronique would make me an even more powerful sire for him."

"I fear he may be right about that."

I rose from the bed and moved toward him, but not too close. I was still very awkward after everything that had happened. The whole situation positively sucked. "Sucked" actually wasn't a strong enough word.

Really sucked.

"Veronique's blood was powerful enough to give me

control. At least for a little while. I'm still thirsty . . . it's like I'm always thirsty now, but I can control it at the moment. I don't know how long this is going to last." I turned away from him when my throat thickened up. "I'm so sorry."

He touched my back and the warmth sank into my cold skin. "What are you sorry about?"

"For everything. Things haven't gotten easier. They've gotten worse. And worse. And it's all my fault. You probably wish you'd never met me."

"If I had never met you I would have ended my existence three months ago."

Oh, yeah. I forgot about that for a little while. I had a quick flashback to a tall bridge and a man in a long dark coat who felt he had lived too long. He'd wanted to find peace that night. Instead he found me.

Maybe he should have jumped when he had the chance.

"I'm sorry," I said again.

"Please, stop apologizing." He pulled me against him and hugged me tight to his chest. "You are right about many things. It *hasn't* gotten any easier for us. But I don't wish I'd never met you. I cherish the moment you entered my life."

I shook my head and couldn't help but smile a little at that. "Then you're even crazier than I thought you were."

"Perhaps I am." He held my face in his hands and leaned over to kiss me chastely on the lips. "Now you must stop this so we can decide what must be done."

"It's simple. I'm going to sire Gideon at midnight so he'll let Amy go."

Thierry was quiet for a long moment. "That can't happen."

"What?"

"Last night you proved to me that your blood was strong enough to heal even the deadly injury that I sustained. What kind of a vampire will it turn Gideon into now that you're even stronger? And what level of power will you transfer to him? It's too much to risk."

I licked my dry lips. "He gave me the impression he was looking at life a little differently. That he might change."

"And now what do you believe?"

"I believe he broke my chain and burned my grimoire. I hate him."

"And yet you still want to help him tonight." He glowered at me. "How curious."

"This has nothing to do with having the hots for his body. He has Amy."

A dark eyebrow raised.

"He has Amy," I said, more firmly.

His face tightened and his eyes narrowed. "How do you know he'll free Amy once you do as he says?"

"I'm not seeing any other choices here." My bottom lip trembled and his hard expression softened significantly.

"I apologize for my frustration." He exhaled. "I normally can find my way through unpleasant situations, and this—with Gideon, with your curse—it has me at a disadvantage."

"I know." I hugged him and he brushed his lips against mine again. I swallowed and looked up at his tense expression. "What time is it right now?"

"It's seven o'clock."

If I currently had a heartbeat it would speed up at that. Ditto breathing. "We have five hours until the ritual's supposed to start."

"There's something else you need to know," he said softly and wouldn't meet my gaze.

"Please tell me I won the lottery. I could use some good news right now."

He shook his head. "It's . . . it's the Ring. They've contacted me."

"The pow-wow at Barry's house the other morning?"

"They called me today personally. It's about your curse. They know about it. They already knew about your reputation of being the Slayer of Slayers—"

"*False* reputation," I corrected.

"Of course it's false. But it's lasting, and speculation is growing. They already considered you a potentially dangerous member of vampire society, but now, with the curse—" He looked at me then, a searching gaze over my face. "They've ordered your elimination."

My mouth went dry. "But you convinced them that I'm not evil and everything's okay now?"

"They wouldn't listen. They feel I'm too close to the situation to give an objective opinion." He looked away from me and at my full-length shard mirror that hung on the wall. The mirror able to reflect vampires showed both of us from head to toe.

I felt ill. "So what happens now?

"If we can't find a way to break your curse—" His normally steady voice betrayed a hard edge of stress. "You'll change. I've seen it. Your eyes—in the alley when you attacked the fledgling. It wasn't you anymore."

My jaw tightened. "You're right."

"Without the gold chain as protection that darkness will now begin to soak through to your true self."

A chill went down my arms. "I can already feel it getting stronger."

His eyes were filled with barely controlled anguish. "If you become like that permanently I know what I'll have to do."

"It's obvious," I said, surprised by how calm I sounded. "You'll have to kill me."

He shook his head. "No, there's another answer. I can take you somewhere. Somewhere that isn't populated. I can keep you safe and away from others."

"Locked up in some castle like a hunchbacked monster?"

"It won't be like that."

The more Thierry spoke, the more distraught I saw he was becoming over the problem that is Sarah Dearly, the more I knew the answer to this situation—the only answer there was.

It was simple, really. Crystal clear.

"Listen to me, Thierry." I placed my hands against his cheeks and made him look at me instead of at the floor. "I need you to make me a promise. If I become total Dark Sarah all the time and there's the threat of my hurting anyone, I want you to stake me."

"Sarah—"

I shook my head. "If I can't live a long, healthy, happy, immortal life with you, then I don't want to live at all. And I don't want to be hunted down like a rabid dog by the Ring's assassins. When I go completely nightwalker, I'm not me. The real me will have already died. You have to kill me."

He shook his head. "I won't do it."

"Thierry," I said it more sharply than I'd ever said his name before. "I'm serious. I know this sucks. I'm not exactly asking for flowers and jewelry here. Or a temporary loan of cash, which actually I could really use at the moment." I tried to smile, but it was a lost cause. "I know you'll do it quickly. It won't hurt."

He didn't say anything for a very long time. "We'll find another way."

"Stop being so damn stubborn and just promise me this. Please."

"Damn it, Sarah."

I raised an eyebrow. "If you won't do it, I can always ask Barry. I know he won't have a problem with this request."

His silver eyes glistened as he looked at me long and hard. "If this is really what you want—"

"It is."

"Then I promise. But only if there's no other possible solution."

He crushed me against him so hard it took my breath away. That is, it would have, if I still needed to breathe. His body warmed me up a little and I sank against him, wrapped my arms around his neck, and kissed him softly.

I'd just totally asked my boyfriend to stake me. And he'd said yes.

I had no idea why I felt good about that.

But I knew it was the right thing to do. Out of every decision I'd made recently—both the good ones and the questionable ones—I knew this was right.

Dying wasn't my first choice. Or my second, either. Hell no. Part of me fought forward, wanting to beg him to forget everything I'd just said, but I pushed that cowardly part of myself back down where it belonged.

I didn't want to live if I was a nightwalker. She was

a different person entirely—a mean, nasty, black poison that ran just below the surface of my skin. A monster lying in wait, ready for the chance to take over my life.

She had to die.

I'd fight like hell to find another solution to this monumental problem, of course, but a girl always has to have a Plan B just in case.

"I don't want to lose you," Thierry murmured into my hair. "I've only just found you."

I was wrapped in his arms and his warm scent embraced me as well. He always smelled so good. Behind it I could smell him, the warmth of his skin. I could even smell the distress he felt at the moment. I slid my hands through his dark hair and propped myself up on my tiptoes so I could look him right in the eyes. Then I kissed him, gentle at first, but it grew and grew until his mouth opened to mine and I swept my tongue against his, tangling and sliding together, and it only made me want more.

I silently thanked George for the well-timed breath mints.

Anxiety moved away from me like heavy clouds parting to show the sunshine and I drank him in, his taste, his scent, the feel of his body against me. Strong arms, a firm chest, his heart pounding against my silent one. I took that heartbeat and concentrated on it, tasting it as I tasted him, and it filled me with a deep aching need.

"I want you, Thierry," I whispered.

"This is not the time," he said, but his body didn't seem to agree. He wanted me, too. Hard to hide something like that.

I smiled inwardly and shut off any more protests with another kiss he didn't resist at all. His hands dropped down to the small of my back as he pulled me tighter against him.

However, he did jump a little when I bit his tongue and tasted his blood. The world around me—it really didn't exist anymore as far as I was concerned—had faded and fogged and grown warmer with every moment that passed. I sucked on his tongue and he let out a deep groan of desire from the back of his throat.

I bit my own tongue so he could taste my blood as well, and as he did, his breathing increased.

He'd been able to stop last night when he'd drunk some of my blood. He'd been practicing his restraint, but this was still a dangerous scenario I was in. Playing with fire.

Big no-no.

If that was so, then what in the hell did I think was I doing?

Ah, but that's the problem. *I* wasn't doing it anymore. My nightwalker had been so sneaky I hadn't even felt her creep up behind my subconscious to take me over. She welcomed Thierry's addiction, she nourished it, she wanted to feed it, groom it, and pet it. She liked pushing him over the edge. She found him much more interesting when he was out of control.

I worked my cool hands up the front of his black shirt to touch his hot skin, feeling his fast heartbeat against my flattened palms. I slid my hands down his abdomen.

"Please," he groaned, and I wasn't sure if it was a "please stop" or a "please don't stop."

Probably a mixture of the two.

Nice.

"Do you want me?" I asked in a low, throaty voice that sounded very unlike the real me.

"Yes," he hissed.

He pulled back just enough to show that his eyes had turned to black. Just like mine were—as a quick glance at my shard confirmed. I pulled the hair off the side of my neck, baring it to him. He lowered his mouth to me and slid his tongue up the length of my throat. I shivered at the wet warmth left behind and it made things low in my body wake up.

"What are you doing to me?" he said. "I can't control this. Don't make me do this to you."

I wasn't making him. It wasn't as if I had any mind control over other vampires as a nightwalker, like what Amy called my "thrall" over weak-minded humans.

Amy.

I pushed the distant thought of a friend in need away, concentrating only on the feel of Thierry's mouth as he tasted me—his fangs grazing my neck but not quite piercing the skin. He was fighting for control. The memory of almost draining me that night not so long ago was probably still very vivid for him.

At the moment all I wanted was to make him bite me again. Why did I have to be alone? I could still be with Thierry. If he embraced his monster while I embraced mine . . .

Then nothing else mattered.

My nightwalker thrilled to that idea, but there was a small piece of me that disagreed—the weak and dying part of Sarah Dearly who wanted to stop this before it was too late.

"Thierry—" There was something in my tone now, something more than desire or lust. It was a thread of panic. It made him pull away from me to look into my dark, dark eyes. Intelligence came back to his glazed expression.

My hands still roamed very freely over his beautiful body. My mouth still sought his lips for another kiss. Or, forget his lips, I nuzzled instead against his throat, tasting the skin there, trying to find the best place to sink into. But I forced myself to clench my teeth, trying to grab hold of the control that danced away just out of my reach.

"You need to slap me," I told him after a moment. "Veronique was able to stop me from biting her when she slapped me."

He swallowed hard. "I can't."

"You can't or you won't?"

"I won't hit you," he said firmly.

"Don't say I didn't offer." I sank my sharp fangs into his throat and his blood spilled into my mouth—so unbelievably delicious and addictive and just plain yummy. I drank him in, literally, and felt my untapped power increase even further, like a glowing light at my core getting brighter and brighter—a sun that wouldn't hurt me, that would only make me stronger.

Thierry pushed at me. Even though I knew he didn't have a problem with my bite, as evidenced a few times before in our relationship, he was now trying to stop me.

"Slap me," I begged him again. "Before it's too late."

Then I felt someone's hands on my back and I was pulled off Thierry where I had him pinned to the bed. My eyes widened at that realization. When did we get to the bed? I turned with a hiss at the unexpected interruption.

Janie Parker stood behind me. "Hey there. How's it going?"

Then she hauled back and backhanded me so hard my ears rang.

Chapter 18

Did you say something about slapping you?" Janie whacked the other side of my face even harder. "I'm only trying to help."

Half of me wanted to lunge at her and tear her throat out—well, we'd never really been bosom buddies—but the pain from the slap helped me gain a little control back. I skulked over to the far side of the room and glared at her from the shadows.

Quinn was behind her with an expression that was part worry, part disgust. Harsh judgment from a former vampire hunter who once upon a time had the hots for me. Just super duper.

Thierry held a hand to his injured neck for a moment until it healed as if by magic. His expression was unreadable. "Thank you for intervening."

Janie shook her head. "When a woman gives you explicit permission to slap her around, you should take her up on it."

His eyes narrowed. "Perhaps Quinn wouldn't have had a problem striking you, but I refuse to harm Sarah."

"Don't drag me into this." Quinn sent another wary glance in my direction.

Janie surveyed the room with a sweeping glance and then pulled a wooden stake out of her shoulder bag.

"Don't even think about it." Thierry's brow lowered.

"Hell, maybe this is for you. After all, you're looking a little out of control yourself, stud."

Quinn put a hand on his fiancée's tense arm. "That won't be necessary, Janie."

"She's a nightwalker," she reminded him with a nod in my direction. "I've read the stories in the history books."

"Sarah's got a curse," Quinn explained. "You already know this."

"Doesn't make her any less dangerous."

"She's different."

"Doesn't look all that different to me." She studied me for a moment. I refrained from hissing at her, since I didn't think that would go over well. After another moment, she grudgingly put her stake away.

I could still taste Thierry's blood. I wanted more, but there was that part of the real me still fighting like hell to stay in control.

"I need to speak with you," Quinn said. For a moment I thought he was talking to me, but his attention was on Thierry.

Thierry's eyes had returned to their normal silver shade. After a searching glance at me that also held a heavy dose of guilt, but saying nothing further, he turned and left the room with Quinn.

Janie stood there, blocking the door, which at the

moment was my only escape, with her arms crossed in front of her.

You can take the mercenary out of the girl but you can't take the girl out of the mercenary.

Or something like that.

"So—" She gave me a weary grin. "Are we having fun yet, or what?"

"I'm going to have to go with what's behind door number two."

"Feeling any better?"

"Microscopically."

"I thought for a moment we'd walked into an explicit love scene. But then I noticed you both still had your clothes on and your teeth were stuck in his neck. Kind of a tip-off to trouble."

"You're very observant."

She exhaled. "You're way different than the last time I saw you. A little less with the happy."

"It's been a busy month." I blinked slowly. "For both of us. I still can't believe that you and Quinn are together."

"Believe it."

"Care to share how you two hooked up?"

"I was assigned by my demonic boss to get a magical artifact Quinn had a map to in Arizona. Then I was supposed to kill him. We ended up working together to defeat the bad guy. Then I almost got killed and he had to sire me so I'm now a card-carrying member of the fang gang. You want more details, you can buy my memoirs."

Janie was always more of a smart-ass than even I was. Well, marginally. But I knew down deep—very deep— she had a good heart. She had saved my life before. That counted for something with me. She'd had a hard life and had fallen in with some questionable people, but in the end she made good choices. Including Quinn.

My control was now back up to at least 60 percent. "Quinn's a great guy."

She made a sound. Not a happy one.

"Don't worry," I said. "I'm not going to try to steal him away from you. He already told me what you'd do to me, which I believe included death and dismemberment."

"I'm not the jealous type," she said firmly.

"Good to know."

She paced over to my messy bed and then back toward the closed door. "But you don't know what we've been through together. I know it's fast, but I love him so much. And I know he had a thing for you and the only reason you're not together is that you chose Thierry."

Great. Vampires with issues. There are so many of us I think I should start a chat group.

"You're right." I shrugged. "Maybe I should have chosen Quinn. He is pretty cute."

She gave me a dirty look.

I couldn't help but smile, despite everything. "I'm kidding. Seriously, Janie, the guy is head over heels for you. Besides, Quinn was never really in love with me, and all I felt for him was a deep friendship."

"Really?"

"Then again, he is an amazing kisser."

"I think I'm going to kill you."

Even though she said it half-joking it worked to sober me up a little. "About that . . ."

"Killing you?"

"Yeah."

"Go ahead. I'm listening." Her lips turned up at the sides until she realized I wasn't kidding. "What is it?"

"My curse isn't getting any better—as you just witnessed. In fact, it's heading straight downhill into the Village of the Damned."

"You don't think you can learn to control it?"

I shook my head. "Not forever. I have a small grasp on it right now because I'm . . . well, let's just say I'm *well-fed* at the moment. But as soon as my stomach starts to grumble, I'd suggest that everyone should clear out."

"So what are you going to do?"

"All I can do is try to protect the people I care about. Hell, I need to protect the people I *don't* care about, too." I took a long shuddery breath that I didn't really need anymore. "I've asked Thierry to stake me if we can't find a solution to this. If I turn totally bad, then there's no other choice."

Her eyebrows went up at that. "You asked him to kill you? And he agreed?"

I nodded and tried to hold back the sudden surge of panic. It did sound horrible, but there wasn't any other way. If he didn't stake me personally, the Ring would send their people in to do it, and I'm fairly certain their method wouldn't include attacking me with fluffy bunnies.

"I have another idea about what you should do," Janie said.

"What?"

"Stop being a damn chump. Stop accepting all of this bullshit that's being thrown at you and start fighting for your life."

I frowned at her. "Is this tough love?"

She shrugged. "It's my opinion. Take it or leave it. I just

think any kind of action is better than sitting around and waiting. In fact, Quinn and I are going to try to find where your buddy Gideon has Amy hidden away right now."

I felt the reminder of my friend's impending danger like a third slap in the face. "How did you even know about that?"

"George filled us in when we got here. Since he knows where Gideon's hotel was, we're going to start there. It's better than nothing." She turned away from me toward the bedroom door.

"Listen, Janie . . ."

"Yeah?"

"If things take a serious nosedive and Thierry can't . . . well, *you know* . . . then I want you to . . ."

The silence weighed heavy for a moment between us.

She nodded firmly. "You won't even feel it. It'll be like getting your ears pierced."

"We are talking about the same thing, aren't we?"

"My staking you when you turn completely black-eyed, batshit, crazy evil?"

"Yeah, but I remember getting my ears pierced hurt like hell."

She shrugged. "What can I say? I'm not great with the pleasant analogies. I'll make it quick, though. Don't worry."

Don't worry? Sure. Easy for her to say. "Well, good. Thanks."

"Janie," Quinn said from the doorway. "We're going to take off and start looking. You're coming, right?"

"Yeah," she replied. "Be right there."

Quinn looked directly at me, and I saw that the dis-

gust and uncertainty in his gaze had been replaced with
concern. "You okay?"

"I'm doing my best."

He nodded. "You need anything, just ask."

Well, I just asked your fiancée to stake me, I thought.
How's that for a favor?

"I'll do that," I said instead.

Janie reached forward without hesitation and touched
my shoulder. "You *are* going to make it, you know."

"You think so?"

"I know so. You want to know why?"

"Why?"

"Because you're invited to our wedding." She smiled.
"And FYI, cash is preferred since we're not registered
anywhere. Between running for our lives and getting used
to being a vampire, I simply didn't have the time."

"Totally understandable."

She took Quinn's hand. With a last look at me he
turned and they left my room. Had I known I'd be having
a parade come through there today I would have spent a
little time cleaning up. Luckily I was too distracted to be
embarrassed by my messy tendencies, which I just noticed included a pink bra hanging precariously from my
closet doorknob.

I stood there for a few minutes thinking about what
Janie had said.

"Don't be a chump" was the general theme.

I emerged from the bedroom in time to see George,
Janie, and Quinn head out the front door and off on their
wild goose chase to try to find Amy.

How odd that they'd leave Thierry and me alone after

what had happened earlier. Did they trust me again so easily?

But no, when I turned around I saw the reason for their mass exodus. Barry sat on the couch. He stared at me with a dark expression of grief on his face. There was no doubt in my mind that he already knew what had happened to Amy.

"She's going to be okay," I told him.

"This is all your fault." There was a catch in his words that made me feel worse than I already did. He sounded more upset than angry.

Also, he was right. This was my fault.

"I know. And I'm sorry."

Barry frowned. Maybe he didn't expect me to come right out and admit it.

"If Amy dies—" he began.

"If Amy dies then you have permission to stake me since I won't want to live anymore," I finished.

So that was three people I'd given permission to do the deed. I really should start an Excel spreadsheet to keep track.

"That won't be necessary," Thierry said. He stood by the front door, his arms crossed over his chest. He wasn't making eye contact with me at the moment, in fact, he seemed to be avoiding looking at me at all after our little make-out session from hell. "I have faith that Quinn, Janie, and George will be able to locate your wife."

"But what if they don't?" Barry argued. "We have no idea where she is. And if that bastard harms a hair on her head . . ."

"Can't you sense where she is?" I asked. "If you concentrate really hard? I mean, you're her sire, right?"

He shook his head. "That is a very rare bond that Amy and I are not lucky enough to share. I love her so much, but I can't find her. I . . . I can't help her."

Even though the two of us didn't get along very well, it made my unbeating heart ache to see him in such distress over the woman he loved.

"It'll be okay," I said simply. "I'm leaving now to find Gideon, too. When I sire him he'll let Amy go. It's simple."

"No, there's nothing simple about it." Thierry grabbed my hand before I made a move toward the front door. "It's too dangerous."

"It's too dangerous if I stay." I shrugged away from his grip.

"And what will you do after you follow his wishes and make him possibly one of the most powerful vampires who ever existed? Do you think that he'll give a damn who lives or dies? Gideon Chase is a selfish, self-serving hunter who is thinking of nothing more than his own survival."

"He's in pain. The hellfire is burning him alive."

He glared at me. "After everything that's happened, why the hell are you still making excuses for him?"

I felt a rise of anger. "You're overreacting."

"Am I?" he replied dryly.

"Yes, you are."

"But, master," Barry said. "We can't simply sit here and wait helplessly."

Thierry crossed the room to stand in front of Barry. "It's too risky to send Sarah out there alone in her current condition."

"She's willing to go."

"Sarah is obviously not herself right now and can't be trusted out on her own." He eyed me, and I knew he didn't mean to sound cruel, he was telling the truth. After what had happened in the bedroom I couldn't very well blame him.

Barry eyed me and for one of the few times since I'd first met him—it felt like an eternity ago but it was only three months—there was none of the usual distaste in his expression, only fear and worry. "What do you think, Sarah? You're Amy's best friend. Will she be all right?"

I shook my head. "I . . . I don't know."

I felt the nightwalker at the edges of my consciousness. She was chomping away at my control, little by little, like a bloodthirsty Ms. Pacman, but I held tight—the latest infusion of master vampire blood had helped again.

"You don't know?" Barry's face reddened. "That's not good enough."

There was stony silence for a full minute.

"I'm going to prepare some of that coffee George made," Barry snarled. Without waiting for a response, he stood up from the couch and went into the kitchen. I could hear the cupboards and utensils slam and clank.

I took a step toward Thierry. "I seriously need to go."

"You can't." He held up a hand to stop me. "And please, Sarah. Don't come any closer to me. I'm still feeling a bit shaky from earlier."

I froze in place. "I took too much blood."

"It's not the blood, it's—" He raised his silver eyes up to lock with mine, and I felt the full weight of his gaze on me. "Your nightwalker brings out my own darkness. It disturbs me."

I cringed. "I know. It's disgusting."

He shook his head. "No. I find it disturbing because . . . because I *like* how it feels. When the darkness
takes me, everything seems much too simple. The worries
of the world fade away and there is only the darkness and
the pleasure it brings."

I bit my bottom lip. "That sounds kind of sexy, actually. But you're saying that's a bad thing, right?"

He made a small sound, almost a laugh. "I made the
decision a long time ago to avoid all that brings about that
darkness in me." His brows drew together. "No vampire
I've ever met has had the same problems with control I've
had. None that weren't nightwalkers to begin with."

"There are lots of vampires who aren't all that picky
about where they get their blood from."

"Yes, but their desire for blood is not so . . . *addictive*
as mine."

I turned over what he was saying in my head. "So you
think you might have a little nightwalker in you trying to
get out?"

"Perhaps." I could tell by the strained expression on
his handsome face that it had taken a lot for him to admit
this to me.

I shook my head. "Nope, not possible."

His frown deepened and he looked at me. "As one
who's witnessed my darker side more than many, I'm surprised you'd say that."

"Nightwalkers don't feel guilt when they've had their
midnight binge. You? You're all about the guilt. Nearly
seven hundred years is a long time to hate yourself. I bet
you were a self-loathing human even before you met Veronique, tending your sheep or whatever people did back
then for a living."

He quirked a dark eyebrow. "I wasn't a shepherd."

"Then what were you?"

"I was an innkeeper. I operated several inns and taverns before the plague came." His eyes got a faraway look for a moment. "Strange. I haven't thought of that in a very long time."

"So, you were a medieval Donald Trump?"

"I suppose you could say that."

That made me smile. "Seems fitting, actually." I reached out to touch him and he didn't pull away from me. "I know you had a hard time in the past. Being a vampire isn't the easiest gig in the world, is it?"

"You've handled yourself remarkably well."

"Are you kidding me? Do I need to pull a transcript of my past misadventures? I've fought tooth and nail against it since the night I was sired. I didn't want to be a vampire. I hated it. And just when I was finally getting used to it, it went and got worse on me."

"Sarah—"

I shook my head. "I can feel her right now, Thierry—the nightwalker who wants my life and my body. I can feel her clawing her way to the surface. I don't know how much longer I have but I want you to know one very important thing."

His expression was tense. "What is it?"

"That I don't want to be normal anymore. All I want is to be happy. With you."

He pulled me closer to him. "I swear, Sarah, I will do whatever I can to fix this."

"I can fix it, but I have to go now."

"No. You'll stay here." His grip on me tightened. "I will find Gideon and I'll do whatever it takes to stop him."

My stomach sank. "You mean you'll kill him."

"If that's what it takes." His eyes narrowed at me. "Would his death affect you? Would you mourn Gideon Chase after all he's done?"

I guess I didn't answer quite as quickly as he wanted me to.

"I see," he said, and his open expression closed off to me behind that annoying, cold brick wall he had.

"You don't see anything."

"Gideon's vision perhaps is much clearer. He seems to cherish your dark side while I restrict it. I suppose you'll have to decide for yourself which of us is correct."

A flash of anger pulled my darkness forward and I actually felt my eyes turn black as my vision narrowed and blurred at the edges. "Dammit, Thierry—"

Barry emerged from the kitchen with a tray of coffee and there was even one on there for me. "Here, master. Drink this."

Thierry absently took the mug of black coffee. "It's the way it must be, Sarah. Even if you disagree with me vehemently, it's much too dangerous for you to go to him. Especially being so close to the edge of your control."

I glared at him, fighting the fogginess inside me, and tried to calm down.

Thierry walked toward the window and glanced outside as he sipped from the steaming mug.

We were silent for a moment as I tried to figure out what to say or do next. I couldn't just sit around the house all night waiting for news. That was not in line with my "don't be a chump" advice from Janie.

There was a sudden crash as Thierry dropped his coffee mug and it fell to the floor, causing a dark stain on the light beige carpet that George would not be happy to see. He brought his hand up to his forehead.

I rushed to his side. "What's wrong?"

He turned slowly and looked past me at Barry. "What have you done to me?"

Barry's expression was unreadable. "You didn't give me any choice. I'm sorry, master."

Thierry collapsed to his knees and I caught him before he fell all the way to the ground.

"Sarah . . ." he whispered, then his eyes closed and he went limp.

I turned to look at Barry with wide eyes. "What did you do?"

His breathing was so fast his little chest went in and out like an accordion. "Odorless, tasteless garlic tablets. I put a few into his coffee."

Garlic. It was a myth that vampires were repelled by the cloves. Actually, garlic knocked us out cold. I'd encountered the stuff in darts that hunters used to hit their targets if they didn't want an immediate kill. It would render the vampire unconscious for a short time.

A harmless but very effective tranquilizer.

I touched Thierry's face and stroked the dark hair back from his forehead. He'd trusted Barry and the sneaky little bastard had used that to get the upper hand.

I was so impressed!

"You need to go," Barry said. "Before he wakes up."

I eyed him. "He's going to be furious with you about this."

"If it's the difference between saving Amy and sitting here powerless, then I'm willing to take that risk. Now will you go, or what?"

"Bossy, much?"

"I know the master only wants to do the right thing, but he refuses to see logic when it involves risking your safety. You've quickly become his blind spot."

He was right. Thierry couldn't see past his desire to keep me safe. He'd never let me leave the house tonight even if it meant we were risking Amy's life.

Also, he obviously didn't want me anywhere near Gideon again.

I leaned over and kissed Thierry softly on the lips, praying that that wouldn't be the last time I ever kissed him.

Then I got up and looked at Barry. "Wish me luck."

"There's no time for luck. Just go."

"Sheesh. It's not like I asked you for a hug or something."

He glowered at me. "Why are you still here? The master will not be unconscious for long."

Good point.

I turned and pushed the door open and left the house, hoping that everything would work out perfectly. I'd had enough experience to know that was an impossibility, but a girl could dream, couldn't she?

Chapter 19

I headed to Darkside, since that was the last place I'd seen the billionaire vampire hunter in question.

No one was there. The club was closed for business and deserted.

My cell phone rang three separate times and I knew by the call display that it was Thierry. I didn't pick up. He was probably furious with me for leaving. Probably? Make that *definitely*. I understood his point—my being out on the streets in my current chain-free condition wasn't the best decision.

Another understatement.

Who cares what he thinks? my nightwalker said. *That guy is such a drag. He never lets you have any fun.*

"Is that so?" I said aloud. "Not that I'd take any advice from you."

I am you, stupid. And I know what you want.

"And what's that?"

To be free. To have fun. You used to have fun, but ever since you met Thierry you've been miserable.

"That has nothing to do with Thierry. That has to do with being a vampire."

You know who's fun? Gideon. He is so sexy and exciting and life with him would be so wickedly awesome.

"Wickedly awesome?" My evil inner voice sounded like a Valley Girl.

Yeah. You liked Gideon, didn't you? You felt sorry for him. More than you should have. And there was something else there as well—a spark of something more. Are those feelings all gone now?

I gritted my teeth. "They're gone. He was using me— trying to manipulate me."

And it totally worked. You left your "true love" lying on the floor unconscious so you could run out to find Gideon. You're going to give him exactly what he wants from you.

"Only to save Amy."

Mmm hmm. Sure. Yeah, I believe that. Vamp tramp.

My jaw tightened. "I don't care what you think."

Well, you should care. As soon as I have the chance, I get to make the decisions, sweetheart. I'm so sick of your taking the lead. I want my moment in the sunlight. Figuratively speaking, of course. No real sunlight. It stings like a bitch, doesn't it?

"You can shut up anytime now."

Great. Now I was having full-fledged conversations with my inner nightwalker. That wasn't a good sign. She wasn't feeling any angst about this situation. She was happy to let the darkness take over completely. She wanted to find Gideon for reasons different from mine. And she couldn't care less about Amy.

Is that really how part of me felt? Or was my nightwalker a separate identity completely from who I actually was?

I guess we'll soon find out, won't we? she said inside my head.

She was a total bitch.

Hey, no need to be rude.

I shouldn't be on the streets in my condition. It was like drinking and driving—risky, dangerous, and insanely stupid. But I held on to one thought: *Amy.* It was like waiting until after Valentine's Day to break up with somebody. I had to make sure she was safe before I could let my nightwalker take me over completely.

Unfortunately, she seemed to want to get an early start. I pushed back at her whenever she raised her ugly head.

Thierry's words from earlier rang in my head. *"Gideon cherishes your dark side while I restrict it. I suppose you'll have to decide which of us is correct."*

Was he just being jealous, as he used to be with Quinn? I already knew which was correct. It's not as if I was conflicted about what side I was going to take. I loved Thierry. I hated Gideon. It was that simple.

Yeah, right, my inner voice chimed.

"Shut. Up."

Where the hell was Gideon? And how was I supposed to find him in a city of two and a half million people?

How about a location spell? my nightwalker suggested helpfully.

"Last time I checked, I was a vampire, not a witch."

A few people on the Front Street sidewalk where I now briskly moved along glanced at me warily as I kept talking to myself like a crazy woman.

A location spell. A person's exact location could be pinpointed if you knew someone who could work some hocus-pocus. What's his name—wizard-boy Steven, aka

The Darkness—did a location spell to find out where I lived, didn't he? Just before he was possessed by a demon and threw me into a wall, that is.

However, it might be worth it if I could find him.

But how was I supposed to do that? I didn't have his phone number. I had no idea how to contact him. And time was running out.

Check it out, my nightwalker said. *A falling star. Why don't you make a wish, you loser?*

My evil inner voice wasn't very nice at all.

I looked up at the sky, dark but clear, showing a full moon and stars like a thousand sparkly diamond rings.

Normally, I'd wish for a million dollars. Tonight I'd make an exception.

"I wish I could find Gideon Chase," I said aloud to the brightest star I saw. "Pretty please."

The star moved to reveal that I'd just wished on an airplane.

Well, that sucks, my nightwalker said.

At least we agreed about something.

"Hey, lady." Somebody poked me in the arm. I turned around to scowl at my attacker. "Need concert tickets?"

"Concert tickets?" I repeated. "That's one thing I actually *don't* need right now."

"C'mon. They're cheap. Concert's already started. You can have 'em for fifty each."

The man's breath smelled like a cross between Cuban cigars and a used litterbox. Pleasant it wasn't.

"Not interested," I told him.

"Death Suck is the hottest heavy metal band out there. You look like you could use a little excitement tonight."

He waggled his eyebrows. "Forty each. C'mon. Take them off my hands."

I was about to open my mouth again to tell him exactly where he could shove the tickets when I froze.

Did he say *Death Suck*?

Did I not already know Death Suck's biggest fan in the entire Northern Hemisphere?

Why, I think I did. And Death Suck's biggest fan just happened to be a teenaged wizard who liked to be called The Darkness, who I already knew had expressed a very keen interest at being at the concert this evening.

I looked up at the path of the plane I'd wished on and said a silent thank you. Wishing on stars was obviously overrated.

"Give me the tickets," I said.

"Forty each."

I narrowed my eyes and held out my hand, reaching down a little into my nightwalker self to pull out my "thrall" ability as though I was searching through a cluttered purse. "*Give them to me.*"

His eyes glazed over immediately. "Sure thing," he said, and he handed me the tickets without further argument. "Enjoy the show."

I snatched the tickets away from him. I'd forgotten that the thrall was, hands down, my favorite side effect of being a nightwalker.

Not that there was anything good about the curse, mind you. But if there was, it would be the thrall. Wonderful, glorious thrall.

I focused on going into the domed Rogers Centre stadium, getting past security, who saw nothing suspicious about my strolling into a heavy metal concert more than an hour after it had already started. The scent of beer and pretzels and popcorn hit me, along with the very mild scent of weed.

Vampire nose at full capacity. *Check.*

The sound of twenty thousand screaming kids assaulted me, and the grinding whine of guitars and synthesizers hit me like a brick wall as I wandered the seating area, straining my senses, for any sign of the wizard I was looking for.

"Death suck!" the lead singer screamed into the microphone.

"Kill them! Stab them! Make them bleed!

"Tear their hearts out, THEN WE'LL FEED!

"Suck! Death! DEATH! SUUUCCKKK!"

Catchy.

Vampire hearing: not exactly an asset at the moment. *Check.*

A quick sweep of the place showed me nothing I could use. This was already taking too long. How would I be able to find him in a crowd of thousands of kids?

I kept searching until a glance at my watch told me it was just after ten o'clock. I'd already been wandering aimlessly around the concert for way too long.

Two hours left.

I made my way down the aisle trying to ignore the music, if you could call it that, and focus on finding Steven. I knew I couldn't find him the old-fashioned way. It would take forever to look at faces one by one. So I decided to do something a little risky.

Here we go again, I thought.

No, I could handle it. Really. I would slide into my nightwalker skin just a little, kind of like testing the temperature of water with your big toe. He'd touched me the last time I saw him. I vividly remembered him wrapping his hand around my throat and trying to squeeze the life out of me. We all had a dark side to deal with, didn't we?

"We're close to the end now," the demon speaking through Steven had told me yesterday, all red-eyed and scary. *"And if you don't step aside when the blood begins to flow it will devour you whole."*

When the blood begins to flow?

Still freaky. And yet, weirdly appetizing, which wasn't a very calming thought at all.

Oh, how I missed the days of Chinese food and chocolate cake. The only potential victims then were my thighs.

In any case, I had to find Steven's creepy, freaky little ass that I was totally positive was somewhere at this concert. If this didn't work, I'd just *thrall* my way past the security guards, grab the microphone from the lead singer, who looked like he'd just been released for a day pass from San Quentin Penitentiary, and yell out his name. I'd done karaoke before in my prevampiric life. I could belt out a little Bonnie Raitt if the situation called for it, no problemo.

I grasped the railing in front of me and closed my eyes, focusing on Steven's hand on my throat. The warm scent of his skin. The blood just underneath racing through his veins.

The stadium shifted after a moment to something more tangible, more alive. I could smell past the light odor of sneaked-in drugs, sweaty armpits, and expensive snacks to something deeper. Twenty thousand hearts beating, pumping blood through their young bodies.

Twenty thousand tasty treats.

No. I pushed past that thought as if it was seaweed hanging down in front of me, squishy and unpleasant, getting past that so I was able to focus on one teenager in particular.

Focus. Weaving my way through the crowd, my senses opening up and searching like fingers lightly brushing over the audience, checking and rechecking, and I knew I was close. So very close . . .

"Hey," somebody said.

My eyes snapped open and I looked to my side.

A man stood there checking me out. He wore a black T-shirt with a big white skull and the band's logo emblazoned across it.

"Hey, baby," he said. "Cool black contacts. They so rock."

"Oh, yeah?"

"Yeah. They rock like Death Suck rocks!" He thrust his fists into the air. "Wooooo! Death Suck! ROCKS!"

"Sit down," I hissed.

"Okay." His eyes glazed and he sat down heavily right in the middle of the stairway.

I fought against the fog that rolled over my senses.

I'd already fed from two master vampires that day. I didn't need more blood. I could keep my bitchy little nightwalker at bay for a little longer.

I had to. It's not like I had any choice.

Do or die.

Like, *literally.*

I opened my eyes to see that somebody was looking directly at me, somebody other than the über-fan who had made a lame-ass attempt to hit on me. Just on the other side of the aisle where the fan now sprawled was the very person I'd been trying to find.

"Hi," Steven said. "I was wondering when you'd show up."

He wore a T-shirt identical to the other fan's shirt, but Steven's was autographed, and he held a concert program under his arm.

I waded through the mental haze I saw him through. "You were wondering when I'd show up?"

He nodded. "I sensed you were near."

"Well, that's convenient, isn't it?" I drew in an unneeded breath and felt a wave of relief hit me. He was here. It was going to be okay, after all. "You have to help me."

"Oh yeah?"

"Yeah. I need you to find somebody for me. To do a location spell."

"Dude," another kid came up beside Steven. "Who's the black-eyed babe?"

My eyes were still black? Not good. Luckily I probably fit in around here. I'd just pump my fists and yell "Death Suck rocks!" if anybody gave me a hard time.

Or tear their throats out and bathe in their yumtastic blood, my nightwalker suggested.

Uh, wait. No, no, no, that wasn't a good thought, to say the very least. Let's stick with the first one. Only the first one.

"She's a client," Steven said.

"A client?"

"For my magic shit."

"You are *the man*." The friend eyed me. "What's your name, sweetness?"

I black-eyed him with distaste. "What are you, twelve? Get away from me."

"That's okay," he replied. "I like my women frisky. I can handle it. And, for the record, I'm almost fifteen."

I ignored him and looked at Steven. "So, can you help me?"

"*Oh, yeah.*" The friend leered at me. "He's going to help you, all right. Help you all night long, baby. Uh huh."

Maybe I could rip out *one* throat tonight. I'd promise to make it quick.

Wait . . . *no.* Not even one.

"Stop that," Steven told him. "She's old enough to be my mother."

That snapped me out of my nasty nightwalker funk. "Hardly."

"Steve, dude, I can handle older women. I'm all about that."

"I told you to call me *The Darkness.*"

"Don't be a wiener."

Steven scowled. "A wiener? I'm not a wiener. You're the wiener!"

I sighed. The fate of my best friend's life was currently in this wiener's hands.

The night was not looking up.

About three seconds later, Death Suck wrapped up their concert extravaganza and the lights came on. Thousands of blurry-eyed teenagers with damaged hearing began filing out through the exits.

"Come with me," Steven said to me.

His friend snickered. "Yeah, baby. Then you can *come* with me. Get it? Heh heh."

I looked at the kid and channeled my thrall. "Go home, little boy."

"Okay, bye." His eyes glazed. He turned around and left without another word.

I followed behind Steven, keeping a close eye on the back of his stringy-haired head as we moved through the thick crowd. Finally I managed to clamp my hand down on his shoulder to stop him for a second.

"Where are we going?" I asked. "Are you going to do the location spell for me?"

"Maybe. Follow me."

He started walking again.

"About what happened yesterday," I said. "When you were possessed—"

He looked at me and his eyes widened a bit. "Yeah. I told you the dark magic had touched you already. I guess it must have recognized you again."

"Will you still be able to do the eradication again if I have no other choice?" I asked. "You gave me the impression it might be possible."

"Forget it. Not going to happen." He shuddered. "In fact, I'd prefer never to go that deep again. No more vampire clients. Stupid demonic energy almost made me too sick to come to the concert tonight. Besides, I got a new job. Dude's paying me loads for my mad skills."

The crowd was thick and warm as it spilled outside and I forced myself to think about anything other than the collective scent of appetizing teenagers, all so vulnerable and tasty.

All in all, I was rather proud of my control so far tonight. Maybe it would be difficult, but not impossible, to keep my nightwalker at bay indefinitely. It was like a muscle I hadn't flexed very much. Maybe I could simply use those new muscles to push aside any dark thoughts like thick, sticky cobwebs.

Like a recovering drug addict, I could recite the Serenity Prayer to myself when things got tough.

God grant me the serenity to accept the things I cannot change;

Courage to change the things I can—

And, uh . . . etcetera.

Obviously I'd have to memorize that at a later date.

I kept following Steven as the crowd dissipated, everyone heading for public transit or the surrounding parking lots. Or off to a restaurant or bar to recover from the audial onslaught. The CN Tower stood tall and grand next to us, reaching up to the sky like something really tall and pointy and iconic.

Funny. I'd never before noticed how very much it resembled one big-ass, tall, wooden stake. I shuddered at the thought.

The hum and buzz of the crowd faded away. The fresh air helped me concentrate on things other than the scent of humans.

Don't you think it was surprisingly easy to find Steven? my nightwalker slid into my thoughts. *A little too easy, maybe? Makes one wonder, doesn't it?*

I frowned. "Actually, now that you mention it . . ."

"This way." Steven didn't turn around as he jogged down a short flight of stairs and through a little snow-covered parkette lined with benches at the base of the stake-shaped landmark.

"I can't believe I found you tonight," I told the back of his moving head. "It's amazing, really. I wished on a star . . . or rather an *airplane* . . . and then I just happened to be in front of the concert. Talk about fate."

"It's not fate," Steven said. "I summoned you."

I stopped walking for a second in shock and had to run a bit to catch up to him again. "You *summoned* me? What are you talking about?"

"My new client wanted me to find you. So I sent out some of my magic to draw you here. And, hey, it worked. Which is good, since I really don't want to piss this guy off."

I swallowed as Steven turned the corner leading to the street. "This client . . . what's his name?"

"Mr. Chase," he said simply. "You already know him, right? He said he found me because you came and saw me the other day and he was impressed with my magical abilities. Dude's paying me five Gs for tonight."

"That's why you found me? For the money?"

Steven cleared his throat. "Also, he's got my mom somewhere, but he promises not to hurt her. And he let me come to the concert, so obviously he's cool. Scary, but cool."

The back door of a black Lincoln Navigator idling at the curb opened up and a tall man stepped out. He was dressed all in black and even had a black scarf around his now rescarred face. I could see the physical pain in his green eyes as he watched me approach.

"See, Sarah?" Gideon said. "I told you I'd find you."

The nightwalker half of me was delighted to see him.

The rest of me hated surprises. I used to love them when they meant birthday parties and gifts and cake. Not so much anymore.

"Sorry for the scarf," he said. "It's a little overly dramatic, I know. But I happened to lose my wristwatch earlier this afternoon, didn't I?"

"I'm glad you found me," I said even though my voice sounded shaky. "I've been looking for you. I want to get this over with."

"You do?" He seemed surprised by that. "I thought you might give me a hard time. I was certain your master vampire lover wouldn't let you out of his sight anymore."

"He didn't. I basically ran away from home so I could find you."

I couldn't see the expression on his covered face but I got the impression he was smiling at that.

"Intriguing. I'd even say it was borderline romantic if I wasn't sure that you're not so happy with me anymore."

I tensed. "It's like you're psychic, or something."

"Do you still agree to sire me? Despite your newfound hate for me."

"It's not newfound."

"Perhaps I can make it up to you."

"I wouldn't be so sure about that."

His eyes crinkled at the sides so I could tell he was smiling. "I did buy you a nightclub."

"Right. Well, I'll hold off writing my thank-you note for now, if that's okay. At the moment, I really want to sink my fangs into your throat, Gideon. And I have a feeling you're okay with that as well." I looked at the car. "So let's get going."

"I appreciate your enthusiasm. But I can't take any chances, I'm afraid. Pardon my taking a few precautions."

"Precautions?" I repeated, but then I felt a painful sting. I looked down at my chest and pulled out the small garlic dart.

The stars flickered out as unconsciousness reached for me.

Chapter 20

arah, wake up!"

A familiar voice.

I slowly, grudgingly, opened my eyes. Coming back from a garlic-dart knock-out was never exactly a pleasant experience. It was like waking up with a hangover—headache from hell and general wooziness included at no extra charge.

I blinked a few times until a pretty face came into focus. Short blond hair. A cute red blouse I knew she'd recently purchased from Banana Republic.

"Amy." I pushed myself into a sitting position.

"Holy cow!" She grinned at me. "I thought you'd never wake up."

I blinked a few more times. "Where the hell are we?"

"Don't know."

I looked around. It was somewhere dark. There were a few candles lit, but otherwise there was no light. It smelled musty and old in there—other than the whiff I got of Amy's strawberry-scented perfume.

I looked at her, searching for some sign she'd been abused. "Are you okay?"

"Other than being a bit claustrophobic, I'm just fine and dandy. How's Barry?"

"Worried."

She waved a hand. "He doesn't have to be. Gideon is really nice, isn't he? Very polite." Her grin widened. "And I think he might have a little weensy crush on somebody I know." She poked my shoulder. "And by that, I mean *you*! It's like Romeo and Juliet. Only with more blood."

I blinked at her. "Have you been dropping acid in here?"

"No."

"Drinking buckets of moonshine?"

"Nope."

I remembered what she'd told me on the phone that morning. "Gideon drugged you to keep you calm."

"Oh, totally." Her smile was lopsided. "I normally don't like needles, but these ones are a-okay. It's all good, Sarah. No problem whatsoever. Life is fine and breezy and everything's gonna be all right."

A sedative. Terrific. I'd seen Amy freak out before. The last time had been when she'd found out that her best friend was a vampire. She'd run away from me screaming. But at the moment, she wasn't in freak-out mode at all. She looked like she was on vacation. Somewhere relaxing.

"Gideon's really handsome," she said. "With or without the scars."

"Gideon is evil."

She smiled. "He got those scars fighting a demon, Sarah. A *demon*. That's total alpha romance hero right there—*not* a bad guy. Can you judge a book by its cover?

I don't know. What is evil, anyhow? Are we born that way or is it the choices we make? It's so groovy just having the time to think about these things and turn them over and over in my head." She sighed wistfully. "Maybe nobody's really evil and nobody's really good. We're just sisters and brothers of the earth, whether we're vampires or humans or hunters. We need to hug each other. Make love, not war."

I blinked at her. "I think you're definitely dropping acid."

Her grin held, but her gaze moved down to my neck. "You're not wearing your gold chain. Naughty, naughty!"

"Gideon broke it."

"Really?" Her thin eyebrows went up in woozy wariness. "So are you going to bite me?"

"Wasn't planning on it." I looked at her throat. Well, now that she mentioned it . . . I bet her blood would be very sweet and tasty . . .

No, not going to happen. I was still in control and I had to stay that way if I was going to get out of here. Wherever *here* was.

I shakily got up from the floor and walked over to the faint outline of a door but there was no handle. I scanned the interior of the small room we were in. The walls were made of stone—smooth and cold to the touch. There was something chiseled into the wall. Names and dates.

"I'm thinking this might be a crypt," Amy said. "In a cemetery somewhere. Isn't that totally cool?"

My stomach sank. "Yeah, real cool. What time is it?"

She glanced at her wrist. "Ten to twelve."

Ten minutes.

I'm super excited! my nightwalker said. *Aren't you? So close to our moment of destiny. Tick-tock.*

My cheery inner darkness inched forward. I didn't want her to take over at the moment, especially not with such a helpless victim nearby.

I slammed my fist against the door. "Gideon! Where are you?"

Amy sighed contentedly. "Maybe Quinn will rescue us. A lot of vampire hunters are so gorgeous, aren't they? Who knew? Have I mentioned how excited I am that you two are together again?"

I rubbed my temples. "That was just a cover. Gideon made me break up with Thierry so Quinn and I acted like we were still together to throw him off. Didn't work very well."

She frowned. "So, you're still with Thierry?"

"Yes. Or, at least, I think so. He has some issues with my siring Gideon. Plus, the last time I saw him he was unconscious on the floor. I actually had to step over him to come and try to save your butt." I glanced around the crypt. "And so far, that hasn't worked out so well either."

She huffed. "You could do better than Thierry, you know."

I hissed out an exasperated breath. "I don't have time for a Thierry debate, thanks so much. I'm supposed to sire Gideon in less than ten minutes. It's kind of weighing heavy on my mind right now."

"I think you'd even be better off with Gideon than Thierry."

"Because everyone knows you have such fabulous taste in men that you can judge something like that. Now would you mind being quiet for a minute? I need to think."

She made an annoyed sound. "Oh, what else is new? It's all about you. Martyr Sarah, what a big surprise. You've been such a total drag since you got vamped, you know that?"

The darkness was eating away at my control. "Since you're currently drugged I'm going to let that slide."

She rolled her eyes. "I think you're jealous of me."

"Of you?"

"I've adapted to vampire life a billion times better than you. And I have a man who loves me no matter what. All you've got is that sullen, miserable—although admittedly really hot—old stick in the mud."

She gasped when I grabbed her throat and slammed her up against the wall. "You know what? I don't really care what you think. He's the man I want to spend the rest of eternity with." I paused, frowning. "Unless he has to kill me, of course. But in the meantime, you can take your opinion and shove it where the bats don't fly. Got it?"

"Y-yes." She wheezed her agreement. "Please . . . don't . . . hurt . . . me."

I frowned. Hurt her? Then I realized I'd raised her a foot off the ground and was holding her by only her throat against the wall.

The door scraped open behind us.

"Put her down, Sarah," Gideon said.

My eyes widened and I immediately lowered her. A glance over my shoulder confirmed that Gideon, with the scarf still wrapped around most of his face, stood in the doorway with Steven at his side.

"I need to get out of here!" Amy walked toward Gideon. "I'm so not feeling very groovy anymore."

"I'm going to need you to stay put. Why don't you have a little nap again?" Gideon shot her with a tranq dart.

"Oh, *poop.*" She pulled the dart out, then stumbled to the floor, where she promptly fell asleep.

"That wasn't necessary." I heard the growl in my voice.

"I'm afraid it was," Gideon replied. He was studying me intently. "Your control is very shaky, isn't it?"

"Are you afraid I'm going to kill you by mistake instead of just siring you?"

"I'd be a fool not to consider that possibility."

"What if I lose control completely? Turn totally 100 percent nightwalker on you? Can't control me very well then, can you?"

"Such control is highly overrated," Gideon said. "What makes you unsteady now and unable to maintain your composure is the fact that you're fighting it. Your two sides are battling and weary from the fight."

"Good versus evil," Steven said, nodding.

"I'm a much bigger supporter of the shades of gray theory, myself." Gideon's green-eyed gaze swept over me. "Everyone has both good and evil inside them all the time. It all depends which is more dominant. But even someone you may think is completely evil has some good in them—like me, for example. And someone you feel is good—perhaps like your master vampire lover—has a great deal of darkness as well."

"Well aware of that little factoid." I crossed my arms over my chest.

"So you accept Thierry's inner conflict, but you won't accept that I might be the same?"

"I think actions speak much louder than words."

"My actions have spoken very loudly. I saved your life. I gave you your gold chain—"

"Which you destroyed."

"You don't need it," he said firmly.

"That's very debatable. You threaten my friends and family to get what you want."

"And I have apologized for that. Desperate times call for desperate measures."

"You're a vampire hunter."

"I can't deny that. And yet here we are. Standing on one side of the bridge that will take me over to my new life."

"That's funny, I thought we were in a cemetery."

His eyes crinkled with a hidden smile, then shadowed over with pain. He staggered forward. "I think it's nearly time."

I looked at Steven. "Thought your job was to summon me, or whatever. Why are you still here?"

Wizard-boy looked completely miserable. "I have some other stuff to do as well. Mr. Chase was very specific."

"I need Steven's help during the ritual to help pass the strength of your special blood to me. It isn't a simple siring. It is a healing as well. Plus, I needed him for another reason."

"What?" I asked warily.

Gideon approached me. He looked very weary as he raised his scarred left hand and stroked my cheek. "It's better if you don't struggle against it. Let your darkness take over. You're more powerful as a nightwalker. More useful to me. It makes everything so much simpler."

Hell, yes, my nightwalker agreed wholeheartedly from inside me. *I like the way this guy thinks.*

I pushed his hand away. "Not going to happen."

He didn't move away from me. In fact, he got a little closer. He was totally tempting fate. I could reach up right now and tear out his throat and end this once and for all if I wanted to.

Trouble was, I didn't want to.

My nightwalker swirled and shifted inside me, growing larger and harder to control. The thick poison of my curse churned under my skin. It reached toward Gideon—it liked him.

A lot.

My nightwalker desired Gideon Chase, big-time. She was attracted to his darkness as much as, if not more, than she was attracted to Thierry's—the darkness she liked to pull out and play with whenever she got the chance. Only with Gideon she didn't have to seduce it out of him.

Gideon knew I was in love with Thierry. But I think he also knew that my nightwalker was in love with him. She'd made me turn my back on Thierry's wishes. She was the reason I was here, standing in front of Gideon in a cold, dark crypt at midnight, ready, willing, and able to turn him into a vampire and save his immortal soul.

"Sarah," Gideon said softly, bringing his hand to my face again. "I will miss you. But it has to be this way."

I swallowed and panic clutched my chest. "What are you—"

"Steven," he said louder. "Do it now."

I only had to wonder what he meant for a moment. The candles flickered out. Something came over me, creeping and crawling over my skin, but it wasn't anything tangible—it was magic. Steven's dark magic. And it touched me tentatively a moment before I felt it plunge inside.

I gasped. The darkness of my nightwalker grew more and more until it felt as if it oozed out and covered me from head to toe. I struggled to break free from this tight hold, but it held me frozen in place.

Then suddenly it was gone.

I blinked and looked around. The room had grown lighter, but there wasn't any more light in there than there was before. My eyesight had improved enough for me to literally see in the dark. My improved vision tracked over to where Gideon stood, now a few feet away. He cocked his head to the side.

"I had Steven push away your remaining inhibitions so you could fully embrace your nightwalker," he said tentatively. "How do you feel?"

Gideon. It was as if I couldn't really see him before. My thoughts had been so cloudy. I saw him now, past the black scarf, past the scars. I saw the hellfire steadily burning underneath his skin and his soul slowly being eaten away piece by torturous piece.

I walked slowly toward him and reached up to unwind his scarf. He flinched when I touched the scarred side of his face.

"How do I feel?" I repeated. "Much, much better."

I went up on my tiptoes and kissed him passionately on his lips.

Chapter 21

I looked up at Gideon after the kiss with eyes I knew were now pitch black. He looked surprised at me. I didn't know why he would be.

I felt calm and in complete control now. There was no dark thirst anymore. There was no guilt for what I was. Why should there be? The world felt a whole lot less scary now—only clear and wide open to anything I wanted to do.

Steven's magic had stripped away that whining part of me that angsted over every little thing. The part of me that wanted to get rid of this curse. What a strange word for something so completely *awesome*!

The old Sarah was gone. Totally and completely gone—her and her clinging need to stay with that ancient, humorless master vampire—

Thierry. No, I have to fight this.

—And I couldn't be happier.

Wait a minute. What was that? It didn't matter. I looked over at Steven.

"Powerful little freak, aren't you?" I asked.

"I'm sorry," he said.

Gideon touched my arm. "Are you ready?"

"I was born ready."

How could I ever have imagined myself with any man but him? He was perfect. No centuries of guilt to make him hide from the world. No fear of hurting those who trusted him.

I took his arm and left the unconscious body of Amy behind in the crypt. We emerged into a small cemetery. I could see everything around me as clearly as if it were day.

Something caught my eye. Veronique was waiting there.

I held back the annoyance as well as I could.

Did I have to deal with that bitch, no matter what man I chose?

So unfair.

Veronique frowned at me. "Sarah, my goodness, you look very strange."

"Great to see you, too, Vee."

She drew in a sharp breath. "You've lost the fight, haven't you? Your nightwalker has taken over."

"What the hell do you care? Aren't you a part of the big picture?"

She shook her head. "I've been having second thoughts. Gideon." She looked at him. "We need to discuss this. I need to plan my future, therefore I must know exactly what you mean to do after your siring. Where will you go? What will you do?"

He smiled at her. "I don't have time for this right now."

"Make time." Her voice became indignant. "Or I shall not help you any further. Perhaps I never should have to begin with. I thought if I intervened, I might be able to spare some bloodshed or unnecessary violence. But now, with Sarah not herself, I worry about what will happen next."

Survival instincts leading one to become entirely self-involved. *Check*.

I snaked my arm around Gideon's waist. "Gee, I guess you probably should have thought about that before sleeping with Gideon yesterday, huh?"

"I didn't sleep with him."

"What?"

Gideon laughed softly. "Like I told you, Sarah. I had a nap. You drew your own jealous conclusions. No, Veronique truly believes her intervening in my plans means she has some say in the outcome. I, however, disagree."

"Sarah," Veronique said softly. "What are you doing? I thought you were in love with my husband."

. . . Thierry . . .

"I swear, if you call him your husband one more time I'm going to punch you in the nose." A cold smile curled up the sides of my mouth. "What the hell are you doing here if you don't approve, then?"

She raised her chin. "Perhaps I am here to stop Gideon from going any further."

"Actually," Gideon said, "you're here for a much more important reason, Veronique."

Her eyebrows went up. "Oh, and what is that?"

His gaze shifted to that of a predator. "After the ritual, both Sarah and myself may need to eat something nutritious." A flick of his hand. "Steven."

I glanced at Steven in time to see a red flash of fire enter his eyes. The next moment Veronique was frozen in place, unable to move or talk.

"She does go on, doesn't she?" Gideon said.

I moved to stand in front of her with a hand on my hip. "Huh. I think this is the longest I've been in her presence without hearing her talk about herself. It's like a record, or something."

Then I turned my back on her. Rather a symbolic gesture, if I do say so myself.

There was a slight problem, though. Her mere presence reminded me of Thierry. And the image of him of ate away at the corners of my mind.

I love you, Thierry. I'm sorry I screwed up so bad.

"Oh, shut up," I snapped.

Gideon looked at me strangely. "Everything okay?"

I smiled at him. "Never better."

His jaw tightened. "We need to get started now."

It was so different to see through the eyes of a full nightwalker and still feel in control. It didn't matter to me who died tonight. Well, actually it did matter—*I* didn't want to die. I'd lived twenty-eight years trying to be a good person and what had it gotten me? Squat. But now I knew behind that heavy blanket of doubt and guilt, I could have so much more fun.

With Gideon.

Yeah, we could have a whole lot of immortal fun together.

I'd never sired any vampires before. Hell, I'd never bitten anybody on purpose when I'd been completely in control of myself. That was kind of odd, now that I thought about it. What kind of a vampire didn't bite people? It was like being a vegan mosquito.

"What will Steven do?" I asked.

"When I drink from you he will use his magic to help push your power into me. A mystical nudge."

"Works for me."

The light from the full moon shone on the small patch of cemetery Gideon had chosen for the ritual. Steven was so quiet that I glanced over at him just to make sure he was still there. He was. His eyes were red and glowing in the darkness.

"It's time," Gideon said, and there was a strain now to his voice. "Sire me, Sarah. Please."

I slid a finger down the line of his throat. "Well, since you asked so nicely."

I put my hands on either of his shoulders then, and with a little force he sank to his knees in front of me. Better position that way for someone as tall as him. Then I leaned over a little and without thinking any more about it, I sank my fangs into his skin.

No hesitation. No doubt. Just instinct.

He gasped.

Gideon's throat was warm and the blood flowed immediately. I felt him try to push me away for a moment—a subconscious survival instinct all on its own. But then he relaxed and let me do my thing. After all, he'd asked for this.

Be careful what you wish for.

Three minutes. That's how long I needed to feed shallowly from Gideon in order to transfer the right amount of virus to him to turn him. One hundred and eighty seconds. If it were possible for the change to happen any quicker than that, any casual little nibble might result in a new vampire. No, it had to be a conscious decision on the sire's part to create a fledgling. After all, there was no going back.

My eradication. I should have gone through with it no matter what the side effects were. Gideon can't become a vampire. He's too dangerous . . .

I ignored my guilt-ridden inner voice. Talk about a buzz kill.

So Gideon would be turned into a vampire by this act. His healing, however, would take place only when he drank from me. Thierry had been the first vampire I'd drunk from—although at the time his blood had been administered to me diluted in a glass of water. Gideon would be getting the full meal deal tonight.

Thierry . . .

No, I wouldn't think about him. I wouldn't think about anything except the man I currently had my fangs stuck in. Only seemed fair, really.

I tasted Gideon's fear as his human life slipped away and was transformed into something different. He might have wanted this, but he'd spent his entire life hunting vampires, both the good and the bad ones. There had to be something inside him that feared being on the victim side of a nasty monster like me. Even a monster that looked sexy as hell in a short black skirt.

Okay, somebody's vain, aren't they?

I frowned. *Shut up, annoying inner voice.*

Gideon clutched at me, digging his fingertips into my arms as if to push me away. But he didn't.

When the time was up, I released him and he fell weakly backward and hit the cold, snow-covered ground near a gravestone. His scarred face was pale, his breathing heavy. However, despite his weakened appearance, I hadn't even come close to draining him—he was dealing with the virus, was all.

The human body held six liters of blood. It would take a vamp with a serious appetite—or a whole lot of motivation—to come close to draining another in such a short amount of time. It wasn't impossible, but it sure wasn't recommended.

I licked the side of my mouth. Mmmm, that was tasty. Human blood was so different from vamp blood. Like comparing a filet mignon to a chocolate sundae.

"Here," Steven said from beside me. He held out a knife with a curved blade and I took it from him.

Then I stalked back over to where Gideon lay supine on the ground. I straddled his chest and sat down on top of him. He looked up at me with shock and sudden doubt as I traced the tip of the knife over his heart, cutting clean through his shirt so I could see his half-scarred chest beneath. He shivered from the cold, but it could have been Miami around me for as much as I could feel the winter chill.

I drew the sharp blade across my forearm and watched the line of red well up, much as it had the other night when I'd given Gideon enough blood to stop his pain for a short time. Much as it had for Thierry last night to heal his knife wound.

What are you doing? You can still stop this. He can't become a vampire. Please . . .

Damn conscience. The weak and needy bitch who had succeeded in nothing in life aside from getting herself into trouble poked at me, but she was far enough away that I could ignore her.

"Drink," I told Gideon and brought my arm to his mouth.

I stroked Gideon's hair as he drank and his scars began to disappear before my very eyes. A fleeting look at Steven confirmed his eyes were still red with magic. Somehow, he was helping in this strange ritual—helping me to heal Gideon and share the power of my blood with him. The power I'd gained from three master vampires.

One of whom currently watched us with wide eyes from a dozen feet away, still frozen in place on her Christian Louboutin stilettos. Suddenly, her gaze moved behind me.

The next moment I felt something grab my upper arm and pull me up and off Gideon's supine form. I spun around.

"Sarah—" Thierry's silver eyes were wide behind his red mask. "We need to go. Now."

My gaze shifted to the sharp wooden stake he held in his right hand. I pulled away from him. "Not so fast, cowboy."

"You shouldn't have come here alone." He drew in a breath as he continued to survey the scene in front of him. "Barry acted rashly in what he did, but I'm not angry."

"So glad to hear that," I said coolly.

He searched my eyes. "I found you. I used the connection we have to each other. It was difficult, but—"

"But here you are."

I'd known it was a possibility that he might be able to find me, no matter where Gideon had taken me in the city.

I guess I just thought we might have a little more time before we were so rudely interrupted.

A small piece of me, deep inside, filled with joy at seeing him.

I managed to douse that emotion very quickly.

He frowned deeply and touched my face. "Your nightwalker—"

I slapped his hand away. "Hands off."

Gideon slowly got to his feet to stand at my side. He placed a hand at the small of my back, but said nothing.

Thierry's eyes, which I once thought were the coldest and most guarded I'd ever seen—unable to convey any emotion—were now stormy. I saw anger and disappointment in them, and finally regret.

He knew.

The Sarah he claimed to love was gone. Forever.

Not quite. I'm still here, you heinous bitch.

"Please, Sarah," Thierry said. "We can fix this. There's still time."

I turned to Gideon and kissed him. He kissed me back and I felt his lips curve with amusement that I'd do this in front of the "Red Devil."

When I turned to look at Thierry again, his guard was back up. I couldn't read anything in his expression—or what little of it wasn't covered by that stupid mask.

"So are you cured now?" Thierry asked Gideon unpleasantly. "Did you get what you wanted?"

Gideon's hand moved down to squeeze my ass. "I got a great deal more than I wanted."

Thierry's eyes narrowed. "There's always more. The more blood you take from her, the more powerful you'll be." His eyes flicked to Steven. "And with help, you could hold the power of three master vampires inside you. That is, if Sarah is willing to continuing giving you what you want."

I smiled humorlessly. "I am a giver. Now, why don't you leave. Wouldn't want to outstay your welcome, *Red*."

Thierry cocked his head slightly to the side. "Red? You mean, even in your current state of disarray, you haven't told Gideon who I truly am?"

Gideon's grip on me increased. "She knows?"

"She does indeed."

Gideon moved me to face him. "Who is he? Tell me, Sarah."

I rubbed my lips together. I wanted to say it. I wanted to tell the world—it was on the tip of my tongue. But something stopped me.

I'll never tell. And neither will you, you stupid night-walking bitch!

I rolled my eyes with annoyance. *Shut up, already.*

Thierry's attention moved to Veronique. "Sarah knew when you did not. She knew without my having to tell her anything at all."

Veronique's expression grew confused, but she stayed quiet, since she currently had no other choice. Definitely the best spell on the evening's program as far as I was concerned.

"Don't—" I began, finding it impossible to stop the word that bubbled up in my throat.

Thierry looked at me. "Don't? Don't what?"

I shook my head.

"Tell me who you are," Gideon said evenly. "And maybe I'll let you live tonight."

Thierry said nothing for a long moment of silence.

I felt Gideon behind me then and the press of a knife's blade at my throat. I drew in an unneeded breath.

"Remove your mask," Gideon said.

"Gideon—" I gasped.

Thierry smiled thinly. "With pleasure."

And, without further delay, Thierry peeled off the heavy mask he wore to reveal who he was underneath. He let it fall to the ground.

My heart sank. How many years had this been a secret? And he'd give it up just to save my sorry ass?

Gideon removed the blade from my throat and brushed his lips against my cheek as if that was his quick version of an apology for using me as bait. I gave him a dirty look, and then glanced at Veronique.

Her eyes were so wide I swear they were about ready to drop out of her head and roll over by my feet.

Gideon laughed then, still a bit weakly, but with great amusement. "Thierry de Bennicoeur, the cowardly master vampire who has hidden himself away for all of these years, is actually the Red Devil himself?"

He's not a coward, my inner cheerleader growled. *He'll break your neck, you son of a bitch.*

"I'm sorry for what I had to do, Sarah." Gideon leaned into me.

"You mean pressing a knife against my throat?"

"Yes, that. And I forgive you for keeping this rather large secret from me."

I managed a tight smile. "We're even, then."

Gideon's gaze tracked up and down Thierry as if he was gauging the competition and finding him unworthy and vaguely disappointing. "So what are we going to do with you?"

"A very good question." Thierry hauled back and struck Gideon so hard across his now completely scar-free face that the hunter flew across the cemetery and hit his head against a marble gravestone, knocking him unconscious.

Damn showoff.

"I'll give you one more chance," Thierry said to me.

I glared at him. "No. It's over. One way or the other, it ends tonight, Thierry. I'm different now. And I like being like this."

"You're not a nightwalker."

"I am. I don't need the sunshine. I don't need to worry about who I might hurt. I don't need to be nice all the time." My eyes narrowed. "And I don't need *you*."

His chest moved in and out with labored breathing. "I don't want you to need me, Sarah. I want you to want me."

"No references to catchy seventies tunes, please. This is so not the time."

I grabbed his shirt and pulled him closer. I could use a quick drink of master vampire blood. Gideon hadn't taken more than a deep sip, but I did feel a bit parched now.

"Unhand me," Thierry growled.

"So bossy." I licked a line across his throat. "Never really cared for that much."

"That's too bad."

"It is, isn't it."

He pushed me roughly back from him. It would have knocked the breath out of me if I still needed to breathe.

I backhanded him hard across his face. It was strong enough to snap his head to the side. When he looked at me again his eyes were black and there was blood at the corner of his mouth.

"Manners, Sarah," he warned. "The fact that you've given in to your darkness doesn't mean you have to be a bitch about it."

My gaze moved back down to that stake he held. "Got something there for me, big boy?"

His knuckles whitened on the weapon. "Maybe."

"You know, I kept having this recurring dream about you staking me. But lately it's shifted so I'm the one staking you."

"Prophetic?"

I shrugged. "I guess we'll find out sooner or later, won't we?"

"Probably sooner than later."

"Right." I placed a hand on his chest and felt his heart beating beneath my touch. Faster than it should be for a master vampire, but much slower than a human. I held up my still-bleeding arm to him. "Sure you don't want a taste? I know how much you enjoy that."

His eyes moved to my arm. "Sorry, Sarah. But sloppy seconds aren't my style."

In a flash he grabbed both my wrists in one hand and pulled me closer to him. The stake came up to graze my chest.

"Are you truly lost to me?" he said, the strain now evident on his face.

I tried to pull away from him, but he was strong. I don't think I ever realized just how strong Thierry was before.

"Let go of me, you son of a bitch," I snarled through clenched teeth. "Or kill me. One or the other. Make your choice."

His expression darkened. "I'm deciding."

I managed a smile at that. "Right. Of course. Let me

think back to earlier today. I think I asked you to slap me and you couldn't. If you couldn't do that, then how could you stake me?"

"I can stake you if I have to," he growled. "And I will. I was instrumental in ending the last wave of nightwalkers that existed. I know very well the danger they represent."

"Blah blah blah. So, what happens after you stake me? Will the world go back to normal?"

"I won't know. You said to me once that if you couldn't live with me, you'd rather not live without me. Well, I feel exactly the same way about you."

"So sentimental." I said it snarkily, but my throat felt suddenly very thick. "Who knew?"

His black eyes narrowed. "Would you hesitate to stake me if you held this weapon in your hand right now?"

"Not for a moment."

All remaining hope left his eyes as I uttered that flat statement. "I see."

I gasped as I felt the sharp tip of the stake jab against my chest over my currently unbeating heart. He was going to do it.

"*Je t'aimerai toujours,*" he said. I'd never heard him speak French before.

"What?"

He pulled the stake away from me for a moment. I figured it was to get some velocity. After all, it takes a lot of upper body strength to properly pierce a rib cage.

I tried to prepare myself. I'd wanted this, I'd asked for this—hell I'd *begged* for it.

Be careful what you wish for: part two.

The very next moment, Thierry crushed his mouth

against mine. It was the last thing I'd expected. His tongue swept against mine in a kiss that nearly hurt.

Way different from being staked. And way, way better.

I blinked rapidly when he finally pulled away. My head swam.

"Was that a good-bye kiss?" I asked shakily.

He swallowed. "You were right. I can't stake you, Sarah. No matter the consequences."

"Wish I could say the same." I clutched the stake I'd snatched away from him during our impromptu make-out session and sliced it into his chest.

Chapter 22

Thierry clutched at the stake and staggered back from me a few steps before he fell to the ground. He looked very shocked.

Couldn't say I blamed him.

"Sarah," Gideon growled as he finally dragged himself back up next to me again. He looked down at Thierry. "You killed him."

Thierry continued to gasp for breath.

"No," I said. "I staked him, like I told him I would. There's a difference."

"You missed his heart?"

"If I hadn't, he'd be a sullen, moody puddle right now, wouldn't he?"

Gideon's jaw clenched. "Why didn't you finish him?"

I shrugged.

Gideon cast a dark look over at Steven. "What am I paying you for, boy? A little assistance or a warning might have been nice."

I tried to pay attention, but I was dealing with a rather

intense inner battle at the moment. I could have killed Thierry, but I didn't. Something stopped me.

When he kissed me it worked a bit like a slap, helping the other side of me gain much-needed strength.

He loves me. He wouldn't kill me.

Maybe he should have.

"Drink more, then," I heard Steven say. "If you want to."

"Give me everything," Gideon commanded. "I want her power. I want her strength. Everything."

"Understood."

"What are you—?" I began, but then felt Gideon's sharp fangs sink into my throat.

His fangs? He had fangs already? How was that even possible? Fledglings don't develop fangs for a long time after they're sired. I got mine quicker than normal only because I'd been on a fairly steady diet of master vampire blood from the beginning.

But Gideon wasn't a typical fledgling.

And he wanted more.

I tried to ignore the pain of his bite. I looked down at Thierry. He looked helplessly up at me. I wanted him to stay back. It was safer to have to deal with a stake in his chest at the moment than come any closer to this.

"Open yourself up to this, Sarah," Steven instructed. "Give Gideon everything."

"I can't," I said.

"You have to."

His voice was strange and different from before. Darker. Scarier. I tried to look at him and noticed that his eyes weren't just red anymore, they seemed to be blazing.

Hellfire.

It was the demon, wasn't it? Steven channeled demon

powers in order to work his wizard magic. Had Gideon known that? I didn't think so. It would have been too risky. Gideon was trying to avoid hell, not welcome it into his life and invite it out to a leisurely, candlelit dinner.

The demon wanted Gideon. And Gideon was trying to escape by having me sire him.

"Do it, Sarah," the demon possessing Steven again told me—only his lips didn't move. I heard his voice in my head. "Let it go. I can help you."

A helping hand from a demon to help transfer my power to Gideon Chase. Okay.

"No," the demon said as if it could read my mind. "Not just your power. Your curse as well. Everything."

My eyes widened. Then I slammed them shut and concentrated every ounce of energy I had on relaxing and opening up my mind. Gideon wasn't feeding only on blood then, but on everything behind it as well. My power—the energy that came from three separate master vampires. With the demon's help, I felt that strength slip away from me as it was channeled into Gideon.

A moment later he raised his eyes to mine. His were black with power. They looked exactly like death.

"More," he said. "I need more."

I hesitated. The part of me that cared for Gideon on some strange level tried to pull away in an attempt to save him from his own greed. But he held me firm and continued to drink.

"Give him everything," the demon instructed me in that voice as cold as the night around us.

I nodded, and I did as he said.

My nightwalker held on tight for a moment, kicking and screaming, as she was scraped away from my insides by the pull of the demon's magic. I felt the black poison of my curse curl into a ball from where it had settled deep inside me. She liked it there. It was comfortable. But, like rotten taffy, sticky and smelly, it finally pulled away and I felt it channel out of me and directly into Gideon.

His eyes widened and his lips peeled back from his long, sharp fangs. He looked around at the night as if seeing it for the first time.

"I never thought it would feel this good," he said. "You did it, Sarah. You gave me everything."

I swallowed hard. "You're welcome."

He smiled and it chilled my insides. He was a monster. He even looked like a monster now, black eyes, sharp teeth, and a strange maniacal look of too much power in too small a space.

I was afraid of him. And *for* him.

I wasn't sure if he knew just how much he'd taken from me. The demon inside Steven had transferred every last ounce of my extra master vampire strength to him. Plus, as an added bonus, he now had my nightwalker curse.

I'd leave the celebrating for a bit later, though.

Gideon cocked his head to the side and looked down at Thierry, who was now struggling to get back to his feet. "Why don't I finish him off for you, Sarah? I hate loose ends."

He took a step toward Thierry, but I moved to stand in his way.

"So now what?" I asked. "You got what you wanted. You're a vampire now."

"I'm more than just a vampire."

"True. But what's your next move?"

He smiled. "Anything I want. But I'm going to start

with killing the master vampire." He blinked those black eyes of his. "Both of them. I think I'll do it with my bare hands just for kicks."

"What about me?"

He studied me. "What do you want me to say?"

"Just tell me the truth."

His lips quirked. "For a moment I thought there was something there. But perhaps it was only the pain. I will be forever grateful for what you've done for me, Sarah. But I warn you not to stand in my way right now."

"Or what?"

"Or you'll be sorry you did."

I drew in a shaky breath. He noticed. He placed his hand over my chest to feel my heart beating and he raised an eyebrow. "Very interesting."

"You're the proud owner of a shiny black nightwalker curse."

"Lucky me."

"Probably sorry you burned the grimoire now, huh?"

"I'll get used to it. Like I said, it's an asset. It only gives me more power."

He flinched then and backed up a step from me. I realized that something invisible had slashed his chest. There was now a deep scratch on his flesh.

"What the hell was that?" he snarled.

I shook my head. "I don't know."

"I did that," the demon said.

I backed up until I felt Thierry behind me. Somehow, in the last couple of minutes he'd managed to soundlessly remove the stake from his chest. There was a sheen of perspiration on his forehead and his eyes were shadowed with pain.

"You're ours, Gideon," the demon said. He looked so harmless in the body of the teenaged wizard—Death Suck T-shirt under his black jacket. But he wasn't harmless. "Ever since the hellfire touched you, you've been ours. You can run, but you can't hide."

Gideon's black eyes went cold with fear. "But I'm healed. My scars are gone. The pain is gone."

"It doesn't matter," the demon said. "You think we give up that easy? You have no idea. You belong to us. Nothing you did would have made a bit of difference. You made your choices, now you must deal with the consequences."

Gideon touched the bleeding scratch on his chest. When he pulled his fingers away the blood caught fire. The hellfire was still inside him. And now the demon was coaxing it out.

"We're close to the end now. And if you don't step aside when the blood begins to flow it will devour you whole."

We were close to the end now. Gideon's end.

"I have money," Gideon said. "Lots of money. I can pay you whatever you want. Don't do this."

"Really?" the demon said. "How much are we talking about here?"

"Lots. Everything. I'll give you everything I have. Everything I am."

The demon smiled. "Yes, you will."

Gideon's expression twisted with fear and he looked at me. "Sarah—"

Thierry's arm curled around my waist as he pulled me farther away from Gideon, who now reached out to me.

"I'm sorry," I said as tears burned my eyes.

"So am I," Gideon said.

The hellfire inside Gideon leaked out through the cut

the demon had made. He looked down at his hands as they filled with flames. He blinked, and his eyes changed from black back to their normal emerald green.

"It doesn't hurt." He smiled at me. "I suppose I should count my blessings, right?"

A moment later the flames consumed him and he disappeared in a column of fire.

I choked out a sob and turned to Thierry, grabbing him into a tight hug. He gasped with pain.

"Sorry," I managed. "I'm sorry."

"For staking me?" he asked.

"For everything."

"Don't be." He took my face between his hands and stared down at me. "Are those tears for Gideon?"

"Some of them."

He kissed them away. "I understand."

"He's gone."

"I know."

He held me for a while until I calmed down a little. Then I pulled back from him and jabbed a finger in his direction. "I think I told you to stake me, mister. And you totally bailed on me like a chump."

"I did." He gingerly touched his chest. "And I think I paid the price for that."

"I did that to keep you safe."

"I'd hate to see what you'd do if you were very upset with me."

"But what if—"

"Enough talking." He pulled me—gently—against him and shut me up with a very deep kiss.

I felt a hand on my back after a moment. It was Steven.

He looked completely shaken, but at least his eyes were back to normal.

"Dude, what just happened?"

"You were possessed by a demon," I said.

He groaned. "Again? That so sucks."

"Do me a favor?" I asked. "Go let Amy out of the crypt?"

He nodded and ran off to two crypts nearby, letting out a now-conscious Amy from one and his mother from the other. Steven embraced his mom very hard, and she patted the top of his head.

"I'm sorry, Mom. I promise I won't do any more demon magic."

"It's fine," she said. "But we're still moving to Germany. And then you're grounded for six months. And I'm confiscating all of your CDs."

"Aww, Mom!"

Thierry stroked the hair back off my face. "How do you feel? Did he take too much blood?"

"I'm a bit woozy, but I'll survive." I looked up at him. "But he took everything. All of my extra strength. My curse. Everything. I've totally regressed." I ran the tip of my tongue over my teeth. "Still got the fangs, though."

"Perhaps if he'd continued to drain you, you might have become human again entirely."

"Let's not go overboard." I managed a smile. "Why would I want to give all of this excitement up?"

"An excellent point."

Veronique stood nearby with her arms crossed—the spell keeping her silent and still long over. She finally approached.

"I can't believe this," she said.

"Nor can I," Thierry replied. "You sided with Gideon?"

"In an attempt to help stave off any unnecessary bloodshed."

"Ah, I see. So it was entirely altruistic, was it?"

She sighed. "It did not turn out as I envisioned it."

"No, I don't suppose it did."

"I am sorry." She turned to me. "And to you as well."

I shook my head. "You know, I do question your methods, but if you weren't there yesterday letting me drink from you, things might have gone very badly."

She shook her head with stunned disbelief. "Thierry, you were the Red Devil . . . all this time? I can't believe it."

"I was," he said.

She tilted her head as she looked at him. "Although, now that you mention it, there is a striking similarity . . ." She swallowed. "How couldn't I have known? It all makes sense now. But you knew, Sarah. Just from seeing him with his mask. You saw who he was underneath."

I shrugged. "It took a couple of times, but yeah, I did."

"You truly love my husband, don't you?"

"Completely."

There was a strange look of wonder and disbelief on her face, as if she was only just now realizing that it could possibly be true.

She touched my hand. "I'm happy for you, then. Both of you."

I nodded. "Always glad to know my boyfriend's wife approves of our relationship."

Amy chose that moment to approach awkwardly. "Sarah?"

I moved toward her, but she took a step back from me. I held out my hands. "I'm so sorry about what happened before."

She touched her throat, by which I'd held her up against the wall like a rag doll. "Are you better now?"

"I'm better than better. I'm cured."

Her eyes widened. "No more curse?"

"It's history."

She made a little joyful noise and grabbed me in a huge hug, big enough to squeeze the breath out of me. It was so good to breathe again. Really, it's underrated, this breathing thing.

Ditto the heartbeat. I'd never take it for granted again.

My cell phone buzzed and I pulled it out of my purse to answer it.

"Sarah." George's weary voice was on the other end.

"Hey," I said.

"We have literally searched the entire city. Well, not literally, but you know what I mean. We can't find Amy anywhere and now it's after midnight." His voice quavered. "It's all my fault. Gideon's going to kill her and it's all my fault."

"Oh, well. You win some, you lose some."

"How can you sound so blasé? This is Amy! Little darling Amy, and she's dead! Barry is going to kill me."

"You're probably right. He's ornery, that one."

There was a long pause. "Did we miss something important?"

"Only a little. But Amy's okay, so don't worry. And Gideon . . . Gideon's gone." My throat felt thick as I said it.

George let out such a long sigh of relief I had to pull the

phone away from my ear. "I think I'm going to throw up. Like, seriously. Right here."

I handed off the phone to Amy so she could assure George of her current happy, healthy, still slightly buzzed status.

Thierry touched my arm. "You're upset."

"It's been a hell of a night." I swallowed. "Like, literally."

He nodded. "He's gone."

"I know."

He was quiet for a moment, then he led me away from everyone else so we could speak in private. "Were you in love with him?"

I licked my dry lips. "No. But, I cared for him. Parts of him."

Thierry raised an eyebrow. "Which parts?"

"You know what I mean. He was right about one thing he told me. Everyone has both good and bad in them. But actions speak louder than words. So, yeah, I did care for him despite who he was. But I love you."

He smiled. "I can accept that."

I frowned. "Aren't you in pain with that hole in your chest."

"I am a fast healer. But," he cringed, "it is unpleasant."

"Sorry."

"Don't be." He leaned over to brush his lips against mine. "We can work around it."

"That sounds very promising." I leaned back. "And what about the Red Devil?"

He looked down at the mask he'd discarded earlier. "I think I've hidden behind masks for far too long. If I'm going to try to make any changes in the world, from now on I'll do it without any secret identities."

"It's a deal." I hooked my arm through his. "But, seriously. The next time I ask you to kill me, I want you to do it, okay?"

"I promise. Next time I definitely will."

"You're still lying."

He looked down at me with those silver eyes. "You know me."

"A little. But I'm very willing to learn more."

"I think that can be arranged."

Chapter 23

Five Days Later

Do you, Janelle Parker, take Michael Quinn as your lawfully wedded husband, to love and cherish until death do you part?"

Janie, who was wearing a gorgeous white cocktail dress, smiled so widely I thought her face might actually split in half. "I do. And then some."

The justice of the peace turned to Quinn. "Do you, Michael Quinn, take Janelle Parker as your lawfully wedded wife, to love and cherish until death do you part?"

"Hell, yeah." He cleared his throat and grinned. "I mean, *I do.*"

"Then, with the power vested in me by the province of Ontario, I pronounce you husband and wife. Quinn, you may kiss your bride."

And he did. With gusto.

I didn't think tongue was appropriate for the occasion, but that was just my opinion.

Even with the porn-star kiss I couldn't keep the smile off my face. They looked so happy and glowing.

Two vampire hunters turned vampires about to begin eternity together.

I'd have thrown rice or confetti if that act didn't come with a fine. Instead, we blew bubbles as the bride and groom left City Hall.

Everyone was there . . . well, everyone who counted. Me and Thierry. Barry and Amy. George and his date, Jeremy the human resources guy, who had been my potential blind date hook-up only last week. I guess they did have chemistry after all, because George looked happier than I'd seen him in . . . well, *ever*, really. Even Janie's sister Angela and her boyfriend—one of my ex-bodyguards— Lenny had flown up from Florida for the ceremony and dinner at the 300 Restaurant at the top of the CN Tower.

It still looked like a stake to me.

Veronique had returned to Europe the day before yesterday. After everything that had happened, and despite some ill feelings toward her that still lingered for me, I'd decided to forgive her. She couldn't help who she was. At the end of the day, I do think there was more good than bad in her. Everybody's entitled to forgiveness for a few bad choices they make in their lives. Before she left, she made a point to find me, kiss me on both of my cheeks, and wish me and "her husband" well for the future.

"Hey." I ran my hand down Thierry's arm. "I was wondering if I could get my ring back now that we don't have to hide the fact that we're together anymore. Are you still carrying it in your pocket?"

He shook his head. "That won't be possible, I'm afraid."

He'd always promised that he'd give me back the eternity band—my promise ring from him—when everything was okay again. I opened my mouth to say something, to question him on what he meant, but before I could Quinn and Janie came over to us.

Thierry shook Quinn's hand firmly. "Congratulations to you. I mean that."

"Thanks." Quinn gave him a half-smile. "I know we've had our difficulties. I know I gave you a hard time in the beginning—"

"Hunters typically give vampires a hard time."

Quinn snorted at that. "That's an understatement if ever I've heard one. But . . . if it hadn't been for you," he looked at me, "for you both . . . I . . . I wouldn't be here. Like, at all. I would be dead and buried. I wouldn't have had the opportunity to embrace my second chance at life. And I wouldn't have connected with Janie."

"Fate," I said with a smile.

"You believe in that? Fate?"

I chewed my bottom lip. "Not always, but it sounds pretty good, doesn't it?"

"It does." Quinn gave me a very strong hug that actually lifted me off the ground. "Thank you, Sarah. For everything."

My throat felt thick with emotion. "You're very welcome. Janie's very lucky to have you. I hope she knows that."

When he released me, Janie eyed me, but it wasn't with jealousy anymore. "I *am* lucky, no question about it. Wow, I'd do the group hug thing but I'm *so* not into that."

"No problem."

She grinned. "Glad I didn't have to kill you, after all."

"You and me both."

Amy ran over to us. "Sarah, want me to order you any appetizers at the restaurant? We're heading over now."

"Can't eat," I said. "Solid food and me don't get along anymore, remember?"

She frowned. "Why do I always forget that? Sorry! I don't mean to rub it in."

"Not a problem. I've totally made my peace with it, really. But I'd love a Tequila Sunrise."

"Sure thing." She ran back over to join her husband, who nodded curtly at me. Ah, Barry. We'd never be buddies, but we'd definitely come to an understanding. Since Amy came away from the Gideon experience relatively unfazed, he didn't overtly hate me anymore. Baby steps.

"Weddings make me think about the future," George said.

Yeah, him and me both. "I know."

"Now that you're a business owner, do you think you might be paying me rent any time soon? Since I'm still unemployed, I'm kind of strapped for cash. Twenty bucks and a few dimes is enough of a wedding gift, right?"

Gideon hadn't been kidding. He'd really bought Darkside for me—the papers were in my name and everything was legal. I'd considered selling it, but changed my mind. I'd been a waitress and a bartender, so there was no reason I couldn't be an owner/operator/waitress/bartender.

Plus, it was a piece of Gideon. An odd thing to hold on to, I know, but thanks to Gideon Chase, there'd still be a place in the city vamps could go to have some fun until other clubs got back on their feet again. It was a strange tribute to the hard-to-forget leader of the vampire hunters.

I grimaced. "I'm sorry, George. I know I've been a mooch. But I appreciate your patience. And I thought you were going to work for me at the club?"

His eyebrows raised. "There has not yet been a formal offer of employment."

"Consider this formal. You can be my manager."

He gave me a big hug. "I totally accept. And when it comes to our current living arrangements . . . well, maybe it's finally time for you to shack up with tall, dark, and fangsome over there. As far as I'm concerned, it's way overdue."

I glanced over at Thierry. "We'll have to see about that."

The fact that Mr. Fangsome wasn't giving me back my promise ring was a sign any shacking up might not be in the cards. But I tried not to think about it for the moment. Today was all about Janie and Quinn and the eternity that had just begun for them.

Everyone began leaving for the restaurant in two separate cabs, but Thierry held me back. "I wanted a chance to speak with you privately first."

My stomach clenched. "That sounds very ominous."

He held his hand out to me. "Walk with me."

If I'd known we were going to be doing any power walking I would not have worn these heels, but I could handle it for a little while. I took his hand and walked with him over to Nathan Phillips Square near the outdoor skating rink.

Here it goes, I thought. He was going to break up with me. Officially. It was over. I'd kept telling him that I was trouble and a burden. After everything we'd been through over the last few months, he'd obviously decided I was right.

Maybe he wanted to see other people.

That was it.

Hell, if Veronique didn't care if he dated other women . . . vampire chicks or even humans . . . then why wouldn't he want to?

He obviously wanted to make up for lost time. About six hundred years' worth.

It was okay. Really. I could handle it. I wouldn't demean myself and cry when he ended things. I was an independent vampiress. I owned my own business now, even though I'd come by it in a very unusual way. I planned to throw all of my energy into keeping Darkside—to be renamed The Chase—open so vamps in the city would have a place to hang out and relax and enjoy themselves and maybe do a little dancing. I'd land on my feet. I was all about the girl power.

Men . . . *meh* . . . who needed them?

"So why can't I have the ring back?" I asked simply. Calm. Collected. Totally mature.

"Because I don't have it anymore," he said simply.

"Oh." I frowned.

"Besides, it was only a small piece of metal with some tiny diamonds on it—meaningless, really."

"Meaningless, huh?" I felt my cheeks heat with anger. Maybe I wasn't all that calm and collected after all.

A smile tugged at his lips. "You are upset over this. Why?"

I shook my head. "I'm not upset. I'm perfectly fine."

"I didn't think that something like a ring would mean

anything to you. After all, you agreed to be with me even knowing about Veronique, knowing that she has been my wife for a very long time. Even after she refused to agree to the annulment, you still wished to be with me. Has that changed?"

"Of course not." I blinked. "I love you. A stupid piece of paper doesn't change anything."

"It doesn't?"

"No."

He crossed his arms. "Then I guess it won't matter to you to learn that before she left Veronique did consent to sign the annulment papers after all. The fact that you were able to see past my mask when she was not made her realize how deep your feelings for me are, and in return how deep mine are for you."

I stared at him. "Uh . . . what did you just say?"

"Which part would you like me to repeat?"

"Veronique signed the annulment?"

"She did."

"Holy crap."

"Indeed." He looked amused by my reaction. "I was as surprised as you. But as self-involved as she might seem on the surface, Veronique is a romantic. She experienced true love herself a long time ago and that has stayed with her. She knows that I want to be with you, and since there is no chance at a reconciliation between us, she did what she knew was right and finally freed me from our vows."

This I didn't expect. I never would have thought, after everything that had happened, that Veronique would sign. But she did? She signed the annulment. She and Thierry were no longer married.

I was officially no longer the other woman!

I smiled at him and reached down to take his hand in mine. "Then I totally understand the ring thing."

"You do?"

"Yeah. After six hundred years, give or take, you're finally a bachelor again. Why would you want to get tied down so quickly? We can date, if you want to. Maybe even go to the movies some time. I haven't done that in ages."

He tilted his head to the side. "You want to *date* me?"

"Sure. I mean, it's not exactly the perfect fairy-tale ending I'd always dreamed of, but I'm totally okay with that. Honestly, Thierry, after everything we've been through, just to have you in my life is good enough. Hell, just not getting killed and being a normal, everyday vampire is happy ending enough for me. You're just a total bonus."

"Is that so?"

I nodded firmly. "Definitely. And no promise rings need apply. One day at a time is the way I like to think. I don't need any kind of ring to make me happy—"

"What about this ring?" he asked.

I looked down. He had opened a black velvet ring box and inside sat some serious bling. A three-carat, princess-cut solitaire diamond ring.

My mouth fell open. "What is that?"

He smiled. "What does it look like?"

I raised wide eyes to his. "About forty thousand bucks is what it looks like."

"Give or take." His lips twitched with amusement. "Now, it's not the ring I gave you before. I decided if I was going to replace that one then I should replace it with something worthy."

I was speechless. I didn't know what to say, which is

what speechless meant, of course. I opened my mouth but no sound came out.

"I love you." Thierry swallowed hard and squeezed my hand tightly in his. "You make every day special and worth living for me. Veronique has finally freed me. But I don't want to be alone. I don't want to be a bachelor. I want to be with you. I know it hasn't been very long at all since we met, and our road has not been an easy one, but I know you are the true love I've waited my entire existence to find—and I've waited damn well long enough. Will you spend eternity with me, Sarah?"

I licked my dry lips and my damp eyeballs shot up to his, my heart drumming wildly in my chest.

His smile widened at my stricken expression. "I'm asking you to marry me."

I still couldn't find enough air to breathe. I felt faint and woozy.

His expression flickered from happiness to one of doubt the longer he waited for me to say something. His smile faded and a deep frown creased his brow. "Perhaps I should have waited. I . . . I shouldn't have sprung this on you, today of all days. I will give you more time. I apologize for my enthusiasm. Let's go on to see Quinn and Janie at the restaurant."

"No, Thierry," I began.

"*No*," he repeated, the sound of the word heavy on his tongue. "Then I have my answer. I understand."

A smile burst free on my face. "I meant no, you weren't wrong."

He eyed me warily. "I wasn't?"

I shook my head. "You took me by surprise, that's all. I didn't expect this."

His Adam's apple shifted as he swallowed hard. "I went about this all wrong."

"Ask me again," I said.

"Ask you—" His frown deepened.

"Yes."

"Marry me," he said after a moment, raising his silver-eyed gaze to mine.

"Yes," I said quickly this time, my heart overflowing with happiness. "Yes, yes, yes!"

He smiled wide enough for me to see his fangs. "Yes?"

I nodded enthusiastically.

"That is the answer I was hoping for," he said.

The ring box fell to the ground and he slipped the most gorgeous ring I'd ever seen in my entire life on my finger. Then he took my face in his hands and pressed his mouth against mine in a knee-weakening kiss that made Janie and Quinn's nuptial one look chaste in comparison.

And you know what? I still meant it. A piece of paper didn't mean a damn thing, not when we're talking about eternity. I would have stayed with him with or without any promises of a future together. With or without a sparkly ring that fit perfectly and looked gorgeous on my hand. I loved Thierry without all of those things, there was no doubt in my mind.

But it sure didn't hurt.

Being a vampire would never be easy. I knew that. I couldn't eat solid food. I needed to drink blood, although from now on it would only come out of shiny silver kegs courtesy of well-paid donors. I didn't have a reflection unless I used an expensive shard mirror. Hunters would always be a problem; there would always be people who wanted to destroy what they didn't understand.

But there were a whole lot of good things, too.

I had great friends. The man I was crazy in love with loved me back—and hello? We were officially engaged. What more could a vampire gal like me ask for?

The future was as bright and sparkly as the ring I now wore. A long, happy future. Take away the wooden stakes, the vampire hunters, or even long walks off short bridges—and vampires *were* immortal.

Immortality might not bite, after all.

It was very good to know.

THE DISH

Where authors give you the inside scoop!

♥ ♥ ♥ ♥ ♥ ♥ ♥ ♥ ♥ ♥ ♥ ♥ ♥ ♥ ♥

From the desk of Susan Kearney

Dear Reader,

I came up with my idea for LUCAN (on sale now), the first book in the Pendragon Legacy Trilogy, in the usual way. A time machine landed in my backyard early one morning, and I forgot all about sleeping in—especially after a hunky alien sauntered right up to my back porch and knocked.

Scrambling from bed, I yanked on a cami and jeans, stashed a tape recorder in my back pocket and ran my fingers through my hair. Like any working writer worth her publisher's advance, I was willing to forego sleep for the sake of research.

I yanked open the back door.

Did I mention the guy was hot? No way would I have guessed he was an archeologist back from a mission to a planet named Pendragon. But I'm getting ahead of myself. From his squared jaw to the intelligent gleam in his eyes to his ripped chest, Lucan was all macho male.

And for the next few hours he was all mine.

"I understand you're interested in love stories written in the future," Lucan said, his lips widening into a charming grin.

"I am." Heart pounding with excitement, I joined him on the porch. We each took a chair.

Lucan steepled his hands under his chin. "In the future, global pollution will cause worldwide sterility."

Uh-oh. "Humanity is going to die?" I asked.

"Our best hope will be a star map I found in King Arthur's castle."

"A star map . . ." Oh, that sounded exciting. "You followed the map to the stars?"

"To find the Holy Grail."

"Because the Holy Grail will cure Earth's infertility problem?"

He nodded and I was pleased. I was a writer for a reason. I could put clues together. But I wanted more. "You mentioned a love story?"

Lucan's face softened. "Lady Cael, High Priestess of Avalon."

"She helped you?"

His full lips twisted into a handsome grin. "First, she almost killed me."

"But you're still alive," I prodded, settling back in my chair. There was nothing I liked better than a good adventure story about saving the world, especially when it involved romance and love.

If you'd like to read the story Lucan told me, the

book is in stores now. And if you'd like to contact me, you can do so at www.susankearney.com.

Enjoy!

Susan Kearney

♥ ♥ ♥ ♥ ♥ ♥ ♥ ♥ ♥ ♥ ♥ ♥ ♥ ♥ ♥

From the desk of Marliss Melton

Dear Readers,

"What inspires your stories?" my readers ask. I tell them *everything*—news stories, movies, dreams, but most especially personal experience. "Write what you know" is wise advice, especially when it comes to painting a vivid setting. Though I've never visited the jungles of Colombia the way my characters do in my latest book SHOW NO FEAR (on sale now), I did get to experience the jungle as a child living in Thailand. During my family's three-year tour there, we often vacationed at a game reserve called Kao Yai.

Children are wonderfully impressionable. I will

never forget the moist coolness of the jungle air or the ruckus of the gibbons, swinging in the canopy at dawn and again at sunset. And the birds! There was a great white hornbill named Sam, hand-raised by the park rangers, that liked to frighten unsuspecting tourists by dive-bombing them! One morning, I fed her Fruit Loops off my bungalow deck. By day, my parents would drag all five of us kids on mile-long hikes, an experience stamped indelibly into my mind, providing inspiration for Gus and Lucy's perilous hikes. Our labors were always rewarded by a swim in the basin of a thirty-foot waterfall. Behind the waterfall, I discovered a secret cave, just like Gus and Lucy's. On one hike in particular, we stumbled into a set of huge tiger tracks. Who knew how close a tiger was lurking? Luckily, it left us alone.

Without a doubt, my childhood adventures have provided me with tons of material for my writing. I hope you enjoyed Gus and Lucy's adventures in SHOW NO FEAR. To read more about my adventurous childhood and what inspires my writing, visit my Web site at www.marlissmelton.com.

Sincerely,

Marlis Melton

♥ ♥ ♥ ♥ ♥ ♥ ♥ ♥ ♥ ♥ ♥ ♥ ♥ ♥ ♥

From the desk of Michelle Rowen

Dear Reader,

In my *Immortality Bites* series, I've put fledgling vampire Sarah Dearly through a great many trials and tribulations, and she's weathered them all with her trademark sarcasm (her greatest weapon against nasty vampire hunters), grace, and charm (although this is usually mixed with a whole lot of anxiety and paranoia).

In TALL, DARK & FANGSOME (on sale now), the fifth and final book in the series, Sarah finds all of her vampire-related issues coming to a head. Her nightwalker curse seems likely to turn her permanently into an evil, bloodsucking vamp; she's being blackmailed into helping Gideon Chase, the leader of the vampire hunters, become the strongest vamp ever created; and her romance with master vamp Thierry seems destined to break both of their hearts.

Life sure ain't easy for a vamp.

How will it all work out? Will Sarah get the happily ever after she's been hoping for?

I wish I knew!

(Ha. I *do* know. I wrote it! But I can't just give away the ending so easily, can I?)

What I know for sure is that writing these crazy characters for the past five-plus years has been a pleasure and I'm going to miss them very much! I hope you've enjoyed the journey and that you're as pleased as I am with the ending to Sarah's story . . .

Happy Reading!

Michelle Rowen

www.michellerowen.com